STEINAR'S GIFT

VIRGINIE MARCONATO

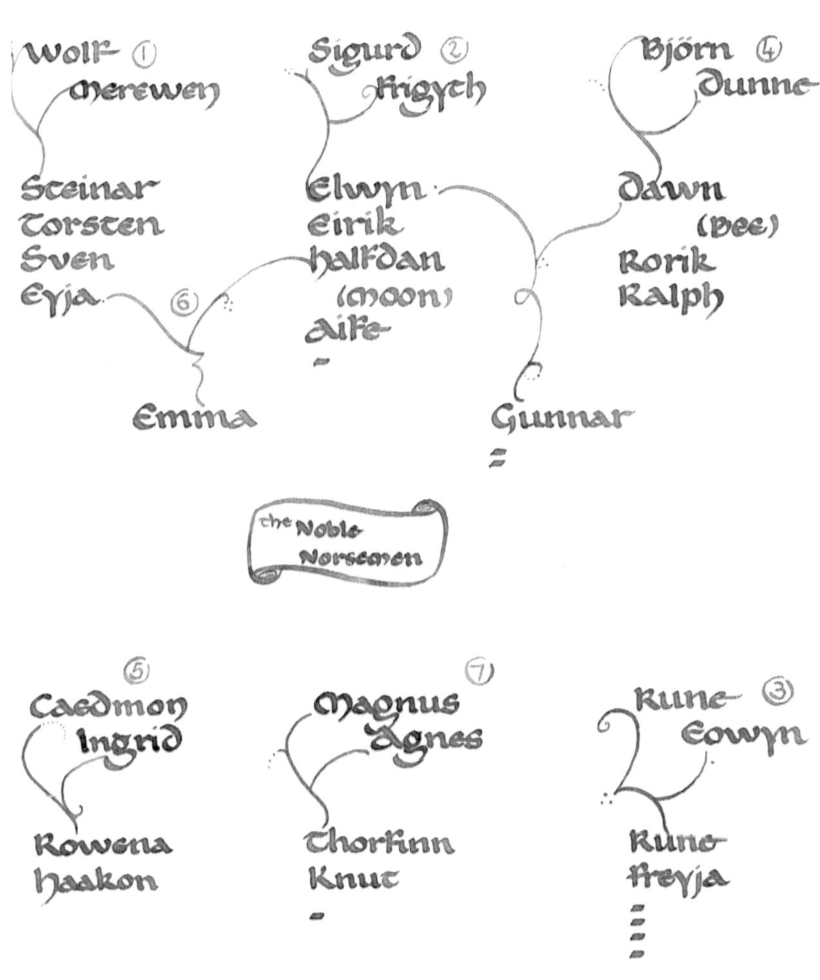

Wolf (1)
Merewen
Steinar
Torsten
Sven
Eyja
(6)
Emma
Sigurd (2)
Frigyth
Elwyn
Eirik
Halfdan
(Moon)
Aife
Gunnar
Björn (4)
Dunne
Dawn
(Bee)
Rorik
Ralph
the Noble Norsemen
(5)
Caedmon
Ingrid
Rowena
Haakon
(7)
Magnus
Agnes
Thorfinn
Knut
Rune (3)
Eowyn
Rune
Freyja

PROLOGUE

"I want *Moðir*."

Steinar sighed as he tightened his hold around his younger son. "I know, Rothgar, but *Moðir* is gone."

Gone. Yes. His wife had been dead for three days. The boy knew it and yet he kept asking for her with worrying frequency. He had spent the last two nights on his pallet with him, burrowing into his warmth, searching for comfort, comfort only a mother could offer.

Steinar stole a glance at his other son, Ulf, who was lying on his pallet to the right of the fire pit. Was he still awake, pondering the recent change in their lives, or had he finally fallen asleep? Being almost thirteen summers and fancying himself a man, he was trying to be braver than his six-year-old brother, but Astrid's death had hit him hard as well.

As for him, what did he feel? His wife's death at such a young age had come as a shock, admittedly, but was he devastated? Did he feel his life was over? No, and no. Their life had been too miserable for him to feel crippling grief. Whatever love he'd felt for her had long gone.

Still, there were uncomfortable questions to be asked. What

was he to do on his own with two little boys in need of a female presence? Would he tell his family the sad truth about his marriage to Astrid? How would he break the news to her parents? What would happen now? The next few weeks would be hard, undeniably, and he was not looking forward to it.

Eventually, Rothgar fell asleep in his arms. Relieved, Steinar allowed himself to relax. At least for now he could have some peace. He closed his eyes and let his body sink into oblivion.

Dawn had just broken when there was a knock on the door. Steinar jumped to his feet, shaken out of an agitated sleep in the most unpleasant manner. Who the hell thought it appropriate to come disturb him now? It was not particularly early, considering it was summer, but still, the day was ill chosen. Who could it be? Not his parents, or his brothers, who were aware of the difficulties he was having and would make sure the boys got the rest they needed, after the difficult three days they'd had.

He took a quick glance at his sons. Thankfully, the knock had been tentative and did not appear to have disturbed them. Small mercies. Before the foolish visitor grew impatient and started banging on the door in earnest, Steinar opened it as quietly as he could, exited the hut and planted himself in front of the intruder.

It was a woman, one he didn't know, a Saxon judging by her coloring. Well, obviously she was. If she had been a Norse-woman, chances were that he would have met her at least once. But he was certain he had never seen her before. She looked too distinctive for him to forget. Her eyes were huge, framed by long lashes, almost too big for her delicate face, and the brown in them so dark it was nearly black. The outer rim of her irises, however, was a rich amber that gave the jet a fascinating glow. Her hair, which was falling in thick waves over her shoulders, offered the same contrast. The color was that of a starless night, but the faintest trace of blue dancing through the strands prevented it from absorbing all the surrounding light, reflecting it instead. The effect was most fascinating.

For some reason, her unusual appeal only irritated him further. Someone from the village would have been bad enough, but after another night trying to soothe Rothgar, he was not in the mood to deal with strangers, especially if they happened to be female and beautiful.

"Yes?" he hissed. "What do you want?"

Steinar saw the effort it cost the woman not to flinch at his gruffness. Not that he was responsible for her distress, he didn't think. Her eyes were red-rimmed, and she looked very pale, proving she had cried even before she'd seen him standing in front of her in all his righteous fury.

"Forgive me for disturbing you so early," she started, her voice barely over a whisper. "Are you Steinar, Astrid's brother?"

He arched a brow. Brother? Why on earth would this woman think Astrid had been his sister? Because of his father, Wolf, everyone knew who he was around here. But then again, as he'd just remarked, it was obvious from her looks that the woman was a Saxon. Perhaps she had come a long way and had never heard of the Icelander. But then how did she know his wife?

"I am Steinar, but—"

"I'm Cwenthryth. I believe Astrid may have mentioned me?"

No. She had not, which was hardly surprising. The two of them had barely exchanged more than a dozen sentences a day in the last few months. Why would she have mentioned a Saxon woman he had no interest in?

He crossed his arms over his chest, feeling his patience about to snap. "Astrid was my wife, not my sister. And no, she never mentioned you."

What little color had been left in the woman's face drained at the words. "Wife?" she whispered, almost to herself. Then her eyes widened, as the meaning of what he'd said hit her. "Wait, what do you mean, *was*?"

"I mean that she's dead," he said harshly.

He didn't see any reason to impart the news more gently. He doubted she was a friend of Astrid's, considering she hadn't even known what her relationship to him was. And if she hadn't been close to his late wife, then she wouldn't care about her death.

Either way, she didn't have any reason to be here and he wanted her gone. He didn't have time for this, not now, not ever.

"Now, if you'll excuse me, I have to go. My sons are waiting for me."

It was a clear dismissal and the woman understood it. All the light left her eyes, leaving only darkness.

"I understand. I'm sorry. Forgive me."

She staggered away on legs that looked as if they would fold from under her at any moment. Perhaps the shock of finding out that Astrid was dead had stunned her, or perhaps she wasn't feeling well. Hadn't he thought a moment ago that she'd been crying and looked too pale?

Before he could turn around, she fell to the ground in one heap.

1

EAST ANGLIA, SUMMER 1070

The smell was different to the one Cwenthryth was used to. Dried herbs, smoked meat, metal. It was clean and earthy, nothing like the noxious fumes she had never gotten accustomed to in town. The furs under her were also nothing like the old ones she had on her pallet. These were soft and piled high, creating a cocoon around her. And the noise… Or rather, the lack of noise, was surprising. No merchant was shouting to passersby to encourage them to buy his wares, no carts were navigating the narrow, mud-splattered street, no children were screaming as they chased one another around the market square. The only thing she could hear were the creaking of a chain, as if someone was drawing water from a well, and the distant babble of a stream.

Where was she? Cwenthryth blinked a few times, fighting bone-deep fatigue, and opened her eyes, determined to find out. Her gaze landed on two well-worn leather boots, indicating that someone was standing by the fur pallet where she was lying. A man, judging from his attire. Her heart skipped a beat, an automatic reaction, but she quickly saw that it was not Godfrid. Who then?

She turned her head up to look at his face.

Oh, lord.

Towering above her was the tallest, most imposing man she had ever seen. No one she knew looked half as formidable. She had no idea who he might be. And yet she had the impression that she *had* seen him before. Where? He gave a grunt low in his throat and everything came back to her at the sound of his displeasure.

Yes. Of course. Steinar, the Norseman she had come to see. Astrid's brother, who was in need of someone to look after his sons. Except...except that she now knew he was not who she'd been told he was, and he clearly didn't wish to have anything to do with her. There would be no help coming from him, no refuge to be found in this hut that smelled so good.

No escape.

Cwenthryth started to cry. It was not a storm of tears, not a desperate attack of sobs, not a ploy meant to soften Steinar up or anything of the sort. She could tell it was useless and would likely not make her feel any better but it was inevitable. Tears simply started to fall down her cheeks, as unstoppable as if her body had been too full of them and they needed to get out. She made no move to wipe them away, knowing more would simply spill free if she did.

She was in a desperate situation. Thinking that Steinar would take her in had been a fragile hope, but at least it had given her the courage to leave a house where life had become unbearable.

But now she was told he was not who she'd thought he was, and he didn't need her. Worse, if what she had seen earlier was any indication, he wasn't prepared to offer his help. So where should she go? What should she do? There was no one else she could think of. She had taken the first step toward freedom, only to stumble on the second.

"Are you in pain?" he asked her, his voice as gruff as it had been earlier.

Cwenthryth almost smiled at the question. No doubt he meant physical pain. In which case the answer was *yes, a little*. It was to be expected after what she had gone through, she supposed. But it was nothing compared to the anguish twisting her guts.

"No," she lied.

"Well, then, if you're not in pain, I will ask you to leave."

Of course. Why would the man keep a stranger in his home when his wife had just died? Why would he want to help her, when she was not his responsibility? Still, the bluntness was a shock. She could have done with some compassion at this time, or even simple patience. But the man seemed immune to such feelings. He was staring at her through eyes as blue as ice, and he had not made the least effort to lower himself down while he talked, instead choosing to loom over her like one of those great Norse gods she had heard about. Which one was the one who considered humans like worms, barely worth his notice? Loki? Thor? She didn't remember, and perhaps all of them did that. In any case, she imagined that those fierce gods looked exactly like this tower of strength, crowned with golden hair braided into intricate plaits.

Awe-inspiring, unnaturally strong.

Remote.

"I'm sorry, it's just a bad moment for me," he added, taking her by surprise. Oh. Perhaps the man was capable of feeling compassion after all. But if he was not going to act on it, then it was of no use to her.

"I understand."

And she truly did.

If he had just lost his wife, it was indeed a bad moment for her to come knocking at his door. But the problem was, she couldn't think of any other option. Her friend Eahlswith would gladly have welcomed her in, but she lived in town, on the other side of the market square. In other words, far too close to her home and the man living in it for it to be safe. Cwenthryth had never been the kind to surround herself with dozens of people, and the years spent looking after her ailing father had ensured that the few friends she'd managed to retain from childhood had drifted away from her. And of course, living the life of a recluse, she didn't know anyone outside of town.

Seeking refuge at the Norsemen village had been her only recourse.

And it had failed.

Once Cwenthryth had managed to stand up, she felt her legs about to buckle from under her, which reminded her she hadn't eaten since the previous morning. Dare she ask Steinar for a drink and something to eat before she left? He had not offered her anything, and judging from his grim countenance, he was bound to balk at the request, but she felt so weak that she had no choice but to try. What was the worst that could happen? He was already throwing her out of his house so even if he got angry, she wouldn't have lost anything, and it was unlikely he would hit her for asking him to spare a sip of ale and a morsel of bread.

"Would you—"

Just then two little boys burst into the hut. Two little boys she knew very well and had not thought to see again. Ulf and Rothgar. They came to an abrupt halt when they saw her and stared in disbelief. She stared back. What were they doing here if Steinar was not Astrid's brother? Was she having visions brought on by hunger? Or… Had Steinar lied to her about being the father of the boys so that he could get rid of her?

There was no time to wonder more.

"Cwenthryth!" Rothgar said, throwing himself into her arms.

❧

W HAT THE *HELL*?

Steinar stared at his son nestled in the Saxon's arms, his head pillowed against her soft stomach. He was clinging to her as if… well, as if he'd found his mother again. Rothgar had not smiled in days, and here he was, ecstatic at being reunited with a stranger. What was happening?

Not thinking for a moment that they would know her, he had thought it best not to tell the boys about the woman lying on his pallet when they had woken up, shortly after he had brought her in the hut. He'd hidden her as best as he could while he'd sent them to break their fast with his parents. The idea had been to get rid of her before his sons could see her. They didn't need further disturbance in their lives.

And now this.

He drew Ulf to one side and asked in Norse. "Do you know this woman?" Cwenthryth, Rothgar had called her. The name was unfamiliar. How on earth could they know someone he didn't?

"Yes. She's a friend of *Moðir*'s. She's nice." A small smile stretched the boy's lips. "She makes the best flat cakes."

Flat cakes. Steinar could have asked him how he could possibly know such a thing, but he decided to ask her instead. He sensed this would be a discussion best held between adults. Besides, he could not deny being curious. Why was the woman convinced he'd been Astrid's brother? Why was she here at all? He placed a hand on his son's shoulder.

"Will you and Rothgar leave me and Cwenthryth alone a moment? I need a word with her."

"Of course." With those words, Ulf went to get his younger brother. "Come on, we were going to meet Gunnar, remember? He'll be waiting for us."

"Yes. Oh, but you're hurt!" As he drew away from the Saxon, Rothgar pointed to the bruise on her face Steinar had noticed earlier. While she'd been lying unconscious on his pallet, with her hair in disarray, he had seen a brownish shadow on her left temple. It was fading, as if it was already a few days old, but it was obvious the blow had been quite severe.

Cwenthryth placed a careful finger above her eye and shook her head. "This? 'Tis nothing. I bumped into a pillar at the market hall the other day. Too busy talking to my friend Eahlswith, I didn't see it in front of me."

"Oh. I do that all the time, walk into things because I don't look where I'm going." The little boy giggled, instantly reassured. "Ulf always get annoyed when I do."

"Well, it is annoying. You could at least—"

"Run along, now. You don't want to keep Gunnar waiting, do you?" Steinar's patience, already stretched beyond endurance, was in serious danger of snapping.

Rothgar gave the woman one last hug, then at last the boys disappeared through the door. Steinar was left alone with his mysterious visitor, Cwenthryth, who was wringing her hands together in the middle of the hut. Was she really that nervous? Should he try to appear less menacing? No, he decided, since he knew he would never actually hurt her. She had nothing to fear. He crossed his arms over his chest, a clear indication he was expecting her to explain who she was and what she was really doing here. She remained silent, however, so it was left up to him to start the conversation.

"Well. I don't know you but clearly, my sons do."

"Yes, they do."

"How?"

She wavered and placed a hand on the table to steady herself. "Please, I'm sorry, but could I have something to eat and drink before I explain how I know them? I'm afraid I feel rather faint."

She did look rather faint, he had to admit, just like she had before.

"Sit down then," he ordered gruffly, deciding that there had to be more to her lack of strength than the shock of being told Astrid was dead. The shadows under her eyes, which gave her a haunted look, had not been created in the last few moments. And of course, there was the bruise on her temple. Was she recovering from a serious injury? Her explanation about walking into a pillar had obviously been meant to placate Rothgar, and it did not satisfy him. Something had happened to her recently.

He shook his head, determined not to let it bother him. He had his own worries to deal with, his sons to look after, his life to rebuild. Whatever this woman had been through was nothing for him to worry about. If she really was in trouble, there would be other people she could turn to, family and friends.

While he busied himself pouring ale and slicing cheese, Cwenthryth cut herself a piece of bread from the loaf he'd placed in front of her. It was a very small piece, he noticed, as if she feared his reaction if she started eating too much. But he didn't care about that, he was more than able to provide for people. To show her he did not begrudge her the food, Steinar added a few strips of dried meat to her wooden plate. She thanked him with a nod, and took one with a shaky hand. He decided to give her time to eat before starting their conversation. It was clear she needed to eat and build her strength. In an effort to appear unconcerned by the delay, he poured himself a cup of ale also, and sipped it while he waited.

Who was this woman? Apparently, she knew both Astrid and his sons, and yet the two of them had never met, and she somehow thought him the boys' uncle. It was odd to say the least.

When he'd estimated she'd eaten enough to take the edge off her hunger, he spoke, unable to wait a moment longer. "Start from the beginning."

"I met your sister—forgive me, your wife—about a year ago."

"How? Where?"

Cwenthryth gave a little embarrassed cough. "She, er…visited my neighbor in town quite regularly."

Did she? As far as he was aware, Astrid didn't have any relatives in town, or know anyone.

"Why?" he growled, when it became obvious she was not going to offer any explanation of her own accord. Would he have to extract her every word from her mouth? It had better not be the case, as having his ignorance of his wife's whereabouts exposed in front of a stranger didn't help him hold on to his temper.

There was a silence, during which Cwenthryth went another shade paler, something he would have thought impossible a moment ago. But here she was, paler than whey. By the gods, perhaps he should try to scowl less. She would be no good to him if she could not speak from terror.

"I think you know why," she said when she found the courage to answer.

And suddenly, he did.

No wonder the Saxon looked about to faint from fright. She was telling him to his face that she had seen his wife go to her lover, not just once but repeatedly. She had every reason to fear his reaction. But he was not about to lash at her. He'd much rather try to make sense of the shocking declaration.

Steinar clenched his fists. If he were to believe the Saxon, Astrid had had a lover for an entire year, if not more. He'd known they had grown apart, but this was even worse than he had thought. But why should he believe the woman? She had not clearly said that Astrid had been her neighbor's lover, and she hadn't given any proof to support the claim. Yes, but what reason would she have to lie? Considering how strained things had been between him and his wife, she could well have decided to go to another man. And the boys did know the Saxon, that was irrefutable, so they *had* met at some point, without his knowing.

Why not in town, when their mother went on secret assignations with a man? That would explain how Ulf knew she made the best flat cakes. He had been inside her house.

"She sometimes came with the boys, who she told me were her nephews," Cwenthryth carried on, her tone more assured now that the worst of the revelation had been made. "We got to know one another quite well, as they often ended up coming into my house while they waited for their aunt—I mean mother."

"You mean she left them outside in the street while she…went to meet your neighbor?" He refused to be more explicit. There was no need anyway; Cwenthryth would have understood what he meant.

"Yes." The word was little more than a whisper. Evidently, she shared his dismay at Astrid's behavior. Then again, who would not? "I'm sorry. I can guess how you must feel. But you need not worry about them. I don't think they ever suspected anything. They would come in my house and have a bite to eat with me. We would play dice together. I loved having them around."

The smile playing on her lips told Steinar she was not lying just to appease him, she had loved the time spent with the boys. And they had loved it too, by the looks of things. He remembered how they had always seemed happy after going into town with their mother. Now he knew why. Because they had met with a kind friend who'd fed them cakes and played with them while their mother—

He rubbed a hand over his face, appalled by what he'd heard. They had been playing with a stranger while their mother was getting fucked without a care as to what might happen to them. Rain or wind, she would have left them to wait outside while she went to meet her lover. Ulf had not yet been twelve a year ago, Rothgar only five. Had the person living next door been less generous, they would have stayed in the cold and damp for hours. Had an ill-intentioned man walked past, they could have been hurt, or worse.

Steinar could barely breathe for anger, or say anything. So he just waited. More information had to be forthcoming; the Saxon couldn't leave it at that. He still had no idea why she had come to the village.

"About two weeks ago, Astrid told me that her brother, the boys' father, had been—"

"For the last time, I was not her brother! I was her husband, the one she was supposed to sleep with, the father of the little boys she abandoned so she could spend time with her lover!" Steinar exploded. After all he'd been through, he could not bear to be dismissed thus. He had counted in his wife's life, damn it all, or at least he should have!

Cwenthryth recoiled at his vehemence, dropping the piece of cheese she'd been holding. "I'm s-sorry, but that was what she told me. You asked me to describe what had happened. I-I'm only trying to—"

"Yes, of course. Forgive me. I did ask. Forgive me."

His anger vanished at the sight of the panic lighting in her eyes. He really was a bastard for making her fear he might hit her. What was he doing shouting at her when she already looked on the edge of collapse? It was not her fault Astrid had been such a deceitful creature and lied to her about the identity of her sons. He had indeed asked to be told how the two women knew one another, and Cwenthryth was only answering as honestly as she could. He should not be snapping at her thus.

"I'm sorry. All this has been rather hard on me. I've hardly slept since Astrid took to her bed with the flux last week, and the boys... Well, the death of their mother has hit them hard, as you can imagine."

As bad a wife as Astrid had been, she had done her best to look after her children—at least while in the village. She'd loved them and they'd loved her. Rothgar, in particular, had not suspected any of the tension between his parents, and thought himself living in a happy household. He hadn't had any inkling that he'd been about to lose his mother anyway.

Because the truth that no one in the village knew was, that had Astrid not died when she had, Steinar would have left her. Their life had become unbearable, and he would have done what he should have done years ago. Before the summer was over, he would have asked for a divorce. It would have been easy to obtain, on the grounds that she refused him another child. In reality, and though it was nothing but the truth, he didn't mind that; he even understood her thinking. What he minded were the consequences of their lack of intimacy in other aspects of their lives. They had grown apart, and increasingly dissatisfied with one another. They didn't have anything to talk about, so much so that Astrid had not thought it necessary to keep up the pretence anymore and gone to find elsewhere what she didn't have at home.

His wife had taken a lover…

He would have laughed if it had not been so pathetically commonplace. But how could he have imagined that the woman who claimed to be scared of falling with child would have gone to another man, at the risk of seeing that very thing happening? Or perhaps she wouldn't have minded having a child with her lover, perhaps it was really only *his* child she refused to carry? Perhaps she had, like him, reached the conclusion that a divorce was the only way forward? It certainly seemed so.

"Please carry on," he told Cwenthryth. "I promise I will keep a hold on my temper."

She nodded and took in a deep inhale. When she spoke, she

did so without looking at him, as if not trusting his promise. He noticed she had stopped eating, even though half the cheese was left on the plate.

"The last time I saw her, about two weeks ago, she told me her brother's wife had left him for another man and he was now alone with the two boys. She hinted that he was finding it hard to cope on his own, and might welcome the help of a woman who knew his sons already."

Bloody, bleeding hell.

Steinar could not delude himself any longer. Astrid had not only taken a lover, she had also planned to leave him, the village, and the boys. Her mind would have been made up, if she had all but arranged it for another woman to replace her in the life of her children. What about him? Had she arranged it for him to have what he needed also? Had she hinted at Cwenthryth that her "brother" would welcome a woman in his bed, that he was in dire need of a fuck because his wife had refused him for years? Was that why the Saxon was here? To offer herself to him in exchange for a home? Did she imagine she would stay only for a few days or was she after a more permanent position?

Disgust roiled in his stomach.

"So you decided to come offer your 'help,' for want of a better word," he said through gritted teeth. How could she use her body so cynically? And did she really think him so pathetic that he would bring a woman he didn't know anything about into his sons' lives in exchange for a tumble? Didn't she know that he could have anyone he wanted, only he had chosen to remain faithful to a wife who'd made a mockery of his efforts?

"I...well, it so happened that when she mentioned it, I had already elected to leave home," Cwenthryth replied, flushing slightly. "I thought perhaps I could..."

Her voice trailed when she stole a glance at him. The look on his face must have made it clear he was not going to be manipulated thus.

"You thought you would find a heartbroken man unable to cope with his wife's betrayal and unwilling to raise his children. You thought you would take advantage of the fact and settle in a new home. Well, I'm not heartbroken, or even remotely sorry to be on my own, and I don't need a stranger to help me look after my sons. I know how to take care of them, I love them, and I want what is best for them. Their mother just died. The last thing they need now is more disruption to their lives." He straightened to his full height, this time intent on impressing her. "And if you thought to use your charms to convince me to let you stay, you can forget it. I choose who I welcome to my bed, not the other way around."

Cwenthryth's insides withered when it became clear that all hope was lost. She would not find refuge here, with a man who didn't need or want her. She had been lied to, and made to think she could find shelter here at the village. In reality, she had found a man who did not really believe her story and thought her a schemer—and little better than a whore.

"And where is your bag?" Steinar carried on, crossing his arms over his massive chest. Was he doing so to intimidate her? If so, there was no need. She was already more than nervous. "You say you'd decided to leave home. Who sets off for a new life without taking their things with them?"

Desperate women, that was who, women who didn't want to alert their tormentors to the fact that they were about to flee, women who cared less about their meager possessions than they did about their freedom. "I-I don't—"

"No horse either? So did you find room in someone's cart, or did you walk here from town? And how come you arrived at dawn? Did you travel at night? Why? What do you have to hide?"

The questions came hard and fast, leaving her no time to think, confusing her further. "Where did you sleep?"

In a ditch. Last night she had decided to wait until the morning to go see Steinar, since she did not want to appear as if she had planned to force him to offer her shelter for the night. But, too frightened alone in the darkness, she had been unable to sleep and get the rest she desperately needed.

And now she felt drained of what little strength she'd had, and more dejected than ever, unable to think what to do next.

"I've never owned a horse," was all she said.

This was hopeless. Steinar would never listen to her now. He thought she was taking advantage of his wife's betrayal. He thought she was prepared to use her body to get what she wanted from him. She had to leave, before he got really angry and decided that if she was prepared to bed him anyway, he might as well make the most of her presence in his hut. If he pounced on her, there would be no fighting him; he was just too strong. She had to go while she still could. But the idea of walking back out without any money, protection, or even any idea of where to go was enough to make her retch.

"I'll go," she said, fighting the tears threatening to blur her vision. "I see that coming here was a mistake. An honest one, though. I truly thought you were Astrid's brother, and might welcome my help. I'm sorry… I can see it was not the case, so I'll go."

Using every ounce of determination she possessed, she stood up. Steinar was in front of her, blocking her way, before she could take a step. No! It seemed she had left it too late after all, and he was about to make her regret her weakness.

"Wait," he said with a sigh, looking at her from his great height. In that moment he didn't look like a madman about to assault her, rather a man overwhelmed by a series of events spinning out of his control.

It suddenly dawned on her that he was probably not consciously trying to intimidate her. His body was simply huge, something he could not do anything about, in the same way she had not decided to have dark hair or pale skin. And what she felt in front of him, she realized at the same time, was not really alarm, but rather a sort of delicious nervousness she had never felt at the contact of man, and had difficulty identifying. His very proximity made her skin prickle, she felt his presence deep in her bones. She could not explain it, but she was aware of every inch of him in ways she had not been with anyone else, noticing every detail of his anatomy.

How could she help it, though? She was only a woman, and the Norseman was, objectively, magnificent and full of intriguing surprises. Nothing was quite what it seemed with him, and she had the impression she could have spent years looking at him and yet still find something new to marvel at day after day.

His beard was a rich, deep amber, only a shade darker than the gold of his hair, but from her vantage point, she could see that a few darker hairs peppered his chin. His blue eyes, despite their frosty color, had the power to burn as surely as the hottest of fires. His mouth was full and tempting, and even his scowling could not make her forget the sensuality of his lips. His body, though strong as a warrior's, moved with the grace of a fawn's. The result was impossibly compelling.

"What is it?" she asked, her voice hoarse. Shouldn't she worry about her predicament instead of admiring him?

"Considering how long it will take you to walk back to town, and how weak you seem to be, you can sleep here tonight."

"H-here?" The last thing she had expected him to do was offer her shelter for the night. They were in the middle of an argument, and barely moments after she had woken up from her fainting fit, he had asked her to leave.

"Yes." He glanced at the table. "You cannot go now anyway, you haven't finished your food."

Everything within her relaxed. She was safe, at least for tonight. Here in the hut, she would be able to get the rest she needed, and with her mind free of worry, perhaps she would be able to think of a place to go. It was the best she could have hoped for, much better than a ditch, where she would be cold and afraid.

"Thank you. I don't know what to say."

A grunt was all the answer she got.

2

Steinar woke up alone in the gray predawn light.

For the first time since Astrid's death, Rothgar had not come to find him in bed. Dare he see this as an improvement? Did it mean the little boy had slept through the night, or that he had not wanted to be seen as weak and needy and chosen to battle his grief alone? Had he suffered on his own? The thought twisted at his guts.

Steinar sat up, intent on finding out, and stilled when he saw that the small pallet in the corner was empty. Alarm instantly spiked through him. Where had his son gone at this hour? Before he could rush out of the door, moved by instinct, he glanced over to the place where, the evening before, he had prepared a bed for their unexpected guest.

Of course. His son was lying next to Cwenthryth, as he should have predicted. His face buried in her tangled hair, he was holding her from behind, like he did with him, his arm wrapping around her slim waist more easily than it did around his much bigger body. She was asleep, and Steinar wondered if she was even aware of the little boy's embrace. Just when he stood up, she sighed and placed her hand over the little fingers, enfolding them in a gentle hold. Then she brought the hand to her mouth and kissed it. So she was awake, fully aware of who was pressed against her, and she didn't mind. Unsure of what to make of that notion, he shifted onto his feet—and she opened her eyes.

Their gazes met.

Her cheeks instantly flushed a deep pink, as if she'd been caught doing something forbidden. She had not, not precisely, but still, Steinar couldn't shake the feeling that this was wrong. Wrong that his son should cling to a woman he hardly knew as if she would become part of his life, because he would only end up being disappointed. It was even more wrong that he, who had only the day before been outraged at her sudden appearance and ready to send her away, should feel a stirring in his groin at the sight of her disheveled hair, or that he should notice how pale her skin was, how delicate her wrist, or how dark and soulful her eyes were. Or anything else.

He stormed out of the hut barefoot, angry at himself.

What a fool he was. There were things to be done today, he could not remain rooted to the spot, admiring a woman lying in his bed in a state of disarray. Not that she he had been in his bed, of course, or that he had admired her, exactly. She had not been in a state of disarray either, just deliciously mussed from sleeping on the furs he had—

Steinar yanked at the handle of the well with such force that it almost broke.

"Easy there, or you'll break it!" a voice called out from behind. Magnus, the blacksmith, was walking toward him, a mock scowl on his face. "And then, I'll have to make another one. I haven't the time, to be honest."

"Magnus. Good morning." Damn, it was just his luck that someone happened to walk past to witness his moment of anger. But the blacksmith was always first up in the village, so perhaps he should not be surprised to have been seen.

"Everything all right, Steinar?" the man asked once he had come to a stop in front of him.

"Of course. I'm only getting water," he growled, "like I do every morning."

"Mm." Magnus didn't appear convinced. "How is Rothgar?"

"He'll be fine."

Right now he was more than fine, snuggled up in bed close to a sweet-smelling Saxon woman who kissed his hands. Steinar started when he realized he sounded like a jealous suitor. He was nothing of the sort, and he cared not about having his hands kissed. And how did he know Cwenthryth smelled sweet anyway? For all he knew she smelled like boiled cabbage. Except… Except he knew that she did not; she smelled like liquorice root. Yes, that was what it was. He'd smelled the unusual, sensual scent when he had carried her to his pallet the day before and had tried to place it ever since. Damn Magnus for reminding him of it! Now it would be all he thought about when he saw her. How she smelled like some sweet delicacy.

"If you'll excuse me, I have water to bring inside," he told the blacksmith, before storming back to his hut.

Magnus looked at him oddly, but Steinar didn't let it worry him. His rudeness had become something people were used to. It was only when he reached the door that he noticed he was not carrying any bucket. That was why the blacksmith had appeared nonplussed. Oh well, he could think what he wanted. No doubt he would put the mistake down to lack of sleep, or grief, or worry over his children. Magnus was not to know his friend's son was actually getting distracted by the mysterious Saxon who had appeared on this doorstep the day before, since he had no idea she even existed.

Steinar stilled. How had he not thought of this before? Did anyone apart from his sons know Cwenthryth was here? Was anyone aware a woman had slept in his hut last night?

He dearly hoped not, or he would never hear the end of it. Some well-intentioned people might argue it was actually a sensible idea for him to let her stay a while, and help with the children, since she already knew them and they liked her. Others would tell him none too subtly that they hoped he would find happiness with the woman who had so pointedly arrived on his doorstep. A few lecherous men might even wink and congratulate him for not letting his wife's death get in the way of his pleasure.

None of it would do. She had to leave, and the sooner the better. At this time, he needed peace and a chance to heal, time alone with his children, not upheaval and worry.

He pushed the door open, wondering if he would find everyone awake. He did. All three of them were sitting around the table, sharing what was left of the loaf of rye bread in joyous companionship.

"Good morning," he called out to no one in particular.

"Good morning," Ulf replied, smiling as broadly as if he'd just been handed a new puppy. Inexplicably, the sight irritated Steinar further. His son wasn't supposed to look so happy mere days after his mother had died, was he? As soon as the thought crossed his mind, he berated himself for it. What was wrong with him? He should be glad his son was not crippled by grief, and in truth, he was. If only his joy had not been caused by the presence of the infuriating Saxon, it would be even better.

He directed his gaze to Cwenthryth, who was toying with her slice of bread as if worried about his reaction. As soon as he had entered, all mirth had been wiped off her face. Obviously, she agreed that she should not be laughing with the boys as if she had every right to be here. Well. At least she had some sense of what was appropriate or not.

"Look, Cwenthryth made me a kitten out of an old piece of rag I found," Rothgar exclaimed, waving a knotted piece of fabric in the air. Steinar recognized the shirt he'd torn on a nail the other day while out in the garden, which did not help him remain calm. He had planned to use the material to make a new shirt for Ulf, not to have it transformed into a cute but useless animal.

"So I see. Very clever," he said, his gaze still on the woman sitting at his table.

Very clever indeed. She was doing all she could to ingratiate herself toward his sons. Not that it would require a huge effort on her part. The two of them seemed already won over. Apparently an ability to make cakes and create animals out of nothing was all that was needed to coax one's way into his children's hearts.

That and giving them the tenderness they needed.

He clenched his jaw. Why had he asked her to sleep here last night? It would have been cruel to send her away when she could barely stand, but he didn't have to keep her under his roof. He should have sent her to one of his brothers for the night. They were both unattached and free to act on their desire for women. If, as he suspected, she was after a home in the village, she would have been welcome to try her wiles on them, and see what came of—

No.

The thought was ruthlessly crushed before it fully formed in his mind. Imagining Cwenthryth in Torsten's or, even worse, Sven's arms, moaning, writhing in pleasure, was enough to send his blood boiling. Why? What did he care what she did? Sending her to a man who wanted her in his bed would be the best way to rid himself of her, would it not? It should have been the perfect solution, but somehow it raised his hackles and he didn't understand why.

"A word with you," he clipped, already walking toward the door. She had better follow without complaint, for he would not be above throwing her over his shoulder if need be. "Boys, you stay here, finish your meal," he added in Norse, having no intention of seeing them intrude in their conversation.

He waited until he'd seen Cwenthryth exit the door before leading the way to the bench at the back of the hut. Exasperation washed through him when he gestured to her to sit down and she remained standing. So she wanted to be difficult? Very well. He could be difficult too. He would ask his questions, and to hell with any pretense at politeness.

"Now, tell me why you're really here. And do not even think of lying to me."

Something in his tone or in his face, or possibly both, must have made it very clear she had better obey, because she at last fell on the bench and said, "I'm trying to escape from someone. A man."

Mm. Why was he not surprised? That was precisely what a woman about to be thrown out of his house would have said to garner his sympathy. But perhaps it was the truth. His gaze flew to the faded bruise at her temple. Whatever he thought of her explanation she *had* been hurt. "You didn't walk into a pillar then?"

"No."

"Was the man in question the one who hit you?"

"Yes."

He did not even try to contain his annoyance. Why should he, when she was making no effort whatsoever? "Do you really intend to tell your story one word at a time? I'd better warn you now that I will not have the patience for it. Start talking."

Finally she did, tripping over her own words in her nervousness. "I live with a man who terrifies me. I left in a moment of panic, not sure where I could go. That is why I traveled at night and I don't have any bag. I cannot go back to my house while he is there. But perhaps if he thinks I've gone for good, he will leave. If I'm not there, he will have no reason to stay."

Steinar wasn't sure what to think. The story did make sense. The only problem was that it was drastically different to the one she had told him at first. It also seemed too convenient, an afterthought destined to shame him into helping her, something a woman might say to play on a man's protective instinct. He should know, as Astrid had once done the same and he had not taken the time to think about the implications of his decision to rescue her. Granted, this was different, and Cwenthryth was not asking for marriage, but he couldn't help but be wary. She'd had the whole night to think about her situation, and she'd realized she wouldn't be able to settle in the village, contrary to what Astrid told her, because Steinar didn't need or want her. What if, seeing her chances slip away, she was doing all she could to persuade him to let her stay anyway? He could not ignore it was a possibility.

She knew she would have to go sometime today, and she was trying what she could to be allowed to stay a bit longer.

"Are you married? Is that your husband we're talking about?" Regardless of her intentions, she *was* sporting a bruise. It was one thing pointing to her telling the truth. But it didn't necessarily mean that it had been inflicted by a tormentor. She could have walked into a pillar, as she'd said, or taken a tumble down the stairs, or fought with a cantankerous old woman wanting to sell her rotten meat, or whatever else people did to get injured. His sister Eyja had an impressive scar on the temple, the trace of an unlikely fall in a crevice. Anything was possible.

"I'm not married."

"Is that man your lover then?"

"N-no." She seemed to hesitate. Well, was he or was he not? She'd just said she lived with him. Why would he live with her if he was not her husband or lover? This was getting more and more suspicious.

"If this is the real reason you're here, why did not you say? Why pretend you came here because you wanted to look after

Astrid's supposed nephews? Why not tell the truth from the start?"

"I-I… I did not say I had come because I wanted to look after the boys, merely that my discussion with Astrid had made me think that perhaps I could come to the Norsemen village. Besides, I didn't think my story would move you to help me. It is far too common, unfortunately, and you don't know me."

"And now you think I will want to help you?"

"No. But you left me no choice. You made me tell you."

Yes, he had. That was the problem. She might well have come up with that story as a last resort, and he was done with believing women's lies. After years of struggle with Astrid, he yearned for peace of mind. This Saxon woman, with her eyes too big for her face and her convenient tales, was more trouble than he could bear at the moment. He should have sent her on her way as soon as he'd set eyes on her. He had, in fact, told her to go, twice. And yet, somehow she was still here. Why had he asked her why she was here instead of reminding her he had only agreed to let her spend the night under his roof? What difference would it make why she had come when she was to leave anyway? Why was he so confused?

Silence stretched between them. Cwenthryth was looking up from her place on the bench, waiting for him to talk, was probably already bracing herself for his request that she leave. He opened his mouth, then closed it when she licked her bottom lip in an innocent gesture.

"I need to go see my father," he said, turning away abruptly.

Apparently, he was a coward as well as a fool.

Heart still thudding from their conversation, Cwenthryth watched Steinar walk away and then collapsed against the wall at her back when he disappeared round the hut.

What had just happened?

In just a few moments, he had made her admit what she had

sworn to keep secret. But how could she have done otherwise? The man was far too commanding, his gaze far too intense for her to have a chance at ignoring his orders. Though it was nothing but the truth, he had not believed her story about having come to be with Astrid's brother and help look after his sons. Why? It didn't seem so far-fetched to her, and it was, if not the reason she had decided to leave her home, at least the reason why she had chosen to seek refuge here in preference to anywhere else. But because he'd not thought it a satisfactory explanation, she'd had to reveal what—who—had pushed her out of her home.

Godfrid.

The hated name sent shivers down her spine, and she did her best to chase the memory of his touch away. It had been hard, humiliating to reveal her ordeal to an unsympathetic stranger, and the worst of it was, it had been in vain. She could tell that Steinar didn't believe she was fleeing a man any more than he believed she had genuinely come to the village to help the boys' uncle.

Pensively, she touched the bruise on her temple. If he'd seen she'd been hurt, and yet still doubted her, how could she convince him she was telling the truth? She had no proof of what Astrid had told her, or even that she was fleeing a tormentor. Did it even matter what he thought? He was not who she'd thought to find, and in all probability, he would ask her to go as soon as he was back from seeing his father. It was already a miracle he had not done it as soon as he'd seen she was awake.

Slowly, she made her way back to the hut.

At least she could eat and drink something before she had to go into the unknown.

"YOU WILL HAVE to go see Astrid's parents," Wolf said, washing his hands in the basin of water. He'd been butterflying trout fillets ready for smoking, but had decided it could wait until after his conversation with his son. "They need to be told of Astrid's death, and it should come from you. It's been four days already."

"I know."

Steinar rubbed a hand at the back of his neck. His parents-in-law lived in one of the three villages of Norsemen spread along the coast. At the time of his birth, thirty-three years ago, there had been only one such settlement in the area, the majority of Norsemen having elected to live further north, around the town of Jorvik, in the heart of what was called Danelaw. But little by little, other villages had sprouted around the harbor, where merchants' ships regularly arrived from Denmark or Iceland. Drawn by the promise of abundant crops, many had decided to settle in this fertile land, and the community was growing fast.

Astrid had been raised in the village farthest away from here, and the two of them had only met as adults. To say that it had been love at first sight would be an exaggeration, but there had been an immediate physical attraction between them, attraction they had not tried to resist. After a night of feasting and drinking more than usual, Steinar had answered her unspoken invitation to follow her into the forest.

Still, he was not sure their night of passion would have ended up in marriage if Astrid had not come back a week later, saying she was afraid of what would happen to her. But she had come back, claiming that her father was going to make her pay for bedding a man who was not the one he'd intended for her to marry, and he had not shirked his responsibility. They had gotten married the following day, then gone together to announce the news to her family. In choosing him, a stranger from another village, she had gone against her father's wishes and neither he nor her mother had forgiven the slight. She had been sent away in disgrace and over the next thirteen years, had only seen her family a handful of times.

Her parents would not take the news of her sudden death well, and Steinar guessed they would somehow find a way to blame him for it, which was why he had put off the trip for as long as he had, using the excuse that his sons needed him at this difficult time to avoid going. Taking them with him to the village would have been the obvious solution but he didn't think Astrid's parents deserved to meet their grandsons when they had treated him and their daughter so appallingly. Even more to the point, he didn't want the boys to hear any unpleasant comments, as they were bound to do. No. As far as Ulf and Rothgar were concerned, they only had two grandparents, Wolf and Merewen, and it would remain that way.

Still, regardless of their past behavior, Astrid's parents had to be informed of her passing. Delaying any longer would be cruel. To say that the encounter would be unpleasant would be putting it mildly, but there was no other choice. As his father had just said, it had been four days already.

"Will you look after the boys for me?"

"Of course. Bring them when you're ready."

Nodding, Steinar made his way back to the hut. There was one more thing to do before he left, sending the Saxon on her way. He quickly crushed the flicker of unease the idea provoked inside him. If she was really fleeing a man, then there were other places she could go. He was not sending her back to her house, only out of his, where she could not stay. She would be fine, he reasoned. A beautiful, resourceful woman like her would soon find someone else to ensnare. If she truly wanted a man's protection, she could easily get it.

As he approached his hut, he heard a commotion.

The door was wide open and he could hear someone shouting inside, someone female—and Saxon. Damnation, what was happening now? Was Cwenthryth being attacked by one of the villagers intent on getting his pleasure? For all her arrival had upset him, she was undeniably appealing. He wouldn't be surprised if one of the men had decided to make the most of having a beautiful Saxon in the village for once.

Another scream, then a crash, as if his chair had fallen to the floor.

His feet picked up speed before he could order them to. What the hell was happening in that hut?

The spectacle meeting his eyes when he entered was not the one he'd expected to see. Cwenthryth was indeed inside the hut, she was indeed the one shouting and turning the interior inside out, but she was alone. Alone except for a huge crow flapping around the room, trying desperately to escape.

"Oh please," she was saying, trying to get out of its way. Or... He stilled. Was she actually trying to herd the bird to the open door? It was hard to tell from her frantic gestures. "Oh please, please, just go!"

She sounded afraid, almost panicked.

"The crow will not hurt you," Steinar told her, feeling stupid for having to point it out to her. Didn't she know it? It was only a bird. It had gotten itself trapped, getting in through the open door by mistake, but would eventually fly away. Right now, it was even more scared than she was.

"I know that," she rasped. "But it…"

Just then the crow shot out of the room, having finally found the opening. With one last indignant squawk, he disappeared into the distance, wings flapping hard. An eerie silence replaced the awful noise.

Cwenthryth fell on the only stool that hadn't been overturned, looking utterly out of breath. Steinar crossed his arms over his chest, brow arched, making it clear she had better offer an explanation for her extreme reaction. What had that been about?

"The bird was trapped," she finally said, refusing to meet his gaze.

"Yes." So what? "You would have known it would fly out eventually. It just did."

"I couldn't bear it, it was trapped," she repeated. Had she even heard him? "It was trapped."

"Cwenthryth, listen to me!" he snapped. The crow was gone but she was still as panicked as she had been a moment ago, perhaps even more so. He knelt at her feet and took her shoulders in his hands, resisting the urge to shake her. "You have to stop this. The bird is not trapped anymore, it's gone. It's over."

"Yes," she said slowly, lifting her eyes to him. The brown rim had returned to the black irises, lighting them up in the way the rising sun illuminated the horizon at dawn after a moonless night. "Yes. You're right. It's over. Thank the Lord, it's over."

With those words, she finally relaxed.

Steinar stayed in front of her, more puzzled than ever. Who got herself into such a state over a bird who'd been in no danger? An uncomfortable thought crossed his mind. Was she unhinged? Was that the reason she could not offer a satisfactory explanation for her presence here, because there was something wrong with her? He'd known a woman years ago whose mind had been unstable from birth. Her reactions had been unpredictable. Could Cwenthryth suffer from the same affliction?

No, apart from just now, she didn't behave like poor old Hilda had.

"I'm sorry," she said, lowering her gaze to the floor. "I don't know what came over me. I just panicked."

"It's all right. Just make sure it doesn't happen again."

Steinar started. Why was he saying that? It was not as if she could stop all birds from flying or even if he would be there to witness her next attack of nerves. Before the end of the day she would be gone.

"Yes. I'm sorry."

"Where are my sons?" he asked, standing back up. What was

he doing, kneeling at her feet like a puppy, talking calmly when he was inwardly furious?

In truth, he'd been in a bad mood since the moment he'd seen Cwenthryth and Rothgar entwined in bed together and met Magnus outside the well. Then, to make matters worse, he'd decided to go see Astrid's parents, something guaranteed to rouse his temper. The chaos with the bird hadn't helped, and having to ask a stranger where the boys were was threatening to push him over the edge.

By the gods, but he really needed to calm his nerves. He'd never been someone to spend his days in such a state of unrest, but as his marriage to Astrid had become more and more strained, he'd started to become bitter and impatient, snapping at people for little or no reason. It was exhausting, and he longed to revert back to the carefree man he had once been.

"They went to see their friend Gunnar, or so they told me," Cwenthryth answered, looking more settled at last.

Ah, yes. He should have known. The three of them were inseparable, spending almost all their time together. He left the hut without a word. It was rude, but if she wanted to be here, she would just have to live with his moods. This was his home, his village, he could come and go as he pleased, damn it, he didn't owe her any explanation.

"Good morning, Bee."

Steinar greeted Gunnar's mother, Dawn, with the affectionate nickname everyone used when she opened the door. At the back of the hut her husband, Elwyn, was sharpening his axe. He lifted his head briefly, nodding his greeting.

Bee wiped her hands on her apron and smiled at him. "Good

morning. The boys are out the back, helping Gunnar and the girls build a new raft, if you're looking for them."

"Thanks."

Steinar made his way around the hut in a pensive mood. He knew everyone in the village inside out and they knew him just as well. Bee had guessed why he had come, he in turn knew exactly where to find the children, and why they needed to build a new raft—the previous one had sailed right into a tree, which had proved to be more durable than the fragile construction. He didn't mind living in such a tight-knit community, but it could get quite stifling at times to know what everyone was doing and have them know what you were going through. There simply was no hiding.

That was one of the reasons he'd agreed to marry Astrid. It had not been all about the lust she'd stirred in him or the protection she'd said she needed. The women of marriageable age who lived in the village had held no mystery for him. He'd grown up alongside them, knew their weaknesses, and could even remember them as children. As a consequence, he found it hard to see them as conquests he could bed, much less potential wives. But Astrid had been a complete stranger, he'd had to learn everything about her. It had been exciting to discover her mind at the same time as he'd learned to pleasure her body. Of course, not having known her before their hasty wedding had also meant that there had been some unpleasant surprises along the way, but that was another matter.

At the time, she had been a welcome breath of fresh air.

Cwenthryth's arrival, whether he wanted to accept it or not, had been another breath of fresh air. And at any other time, it would have been just as welcome. But right now, having to deal with her was the last thing he needed. By the gods, she knew him so little that, up until he had told her the truth, she had thought he was the boys' uncle! He, in turn, didn't know anything about her.

Yes, and that was the problem, he told himself sternly, *not* the appeal. He didn't know her, so he didn't know if he could trust or even believe her. There were too many problems with her story, too many questions unanswered. After Astrid's betrayal, he was wary of making another mistake. The woman he had married had turned out to be so ill-suited to his needs that she had forced him to live a life he didn't want and made him utterly miserable. As if that were not enough, she had ended up betraying him and choosing another man over him. He wasn't sure he wanted to give a stranger, who would soon be gone anyway, the benefit of the doubt. It was not worth the risk.

Well, enough about the Saxon, he decided, as the children appeared from behind a bush. She would be gone before the day was over, anyway.

"Ulf, Rothgar," he called out to the boys, "I need a moment with you."

While their friends carried on weaving ropes around well-trimmed branches to secure the base of the raft, he brought his sons to one side and sat them down on a fallen log.

"I will leave for your mother's village in the morning. Her parents need to be told what happened."

They nodded gravely, and did not ask if they could come with him. Though this was their grandparents they were talking about, they knew their presence would not be welcome. It broke Steinar's heart a little to see it, but it could not be helped.

"Will you be gone long?" Rothgar asked, throwing himself into his arms.

"No." He placed a kiss on top of the head that still had the faint smell of the baby he had once been. "Three or four days at most, I should think."

"What about Cwenthryth?" Ulf tilted his head, looking uncharacteristically serious. "You know she cannot go back home."

Where had his son received this information? Cwenthryth had

admittedly claimed she was fleeing a man earlier that day, but it had been in confidence. Had the boy listened in on their conversation or did he know something he didn't? Ulf was talking as if he knew for a fact she needed a place to stay, but Steinar was still not convinced her story could be trusted.

Well, perhaps he should take the opportunity of this trip to the coast to go and see for himself what the situation was. He could easily stop in town on the way back from Astrid's parents' village. Half a day's delay would make little difference and would put his mind at rest once and for all. He would finally be able to tell if Cwenthryth was in any danger or if she was lying in order to manipulate him into offering her a home. Instead of claims, he would get facts.

Yes, it was the best thing to do. And when he'd gathered all the information he needed, he would make a decision as to what to do with her. Assuming there was something to do with her, of course. Even if she were fleeing a man, she wasn't his responsibility, was she? She might be looking for shelter, but the problem was, he'd already been there once, giving a woman in need a home, and it had ended up in disaster. He was done with beautiful women running to him in search of protection, using the feelings they provoked inside him to sway him.

If she was really in trouble, then he would find someone to help her and appease his conscience that way. If she wasn't, then he would be able to send her away without any scruples.

"Very well. She can stay at the hut while I'm gone," he told his sons. Since he wouldn't be here anyway, he could afford to be generous. Whatever else the Saxon was lying about, one thing was certain, she looked too frail to be healthy. Let him give her a few days to build up her strength and think of another place to go. It would cost him nothing to allow her to remain in the hut while he was out. "She can leave when I come back."

"So then she can look after us. We don't need to go to someone else while you're gone."

Ulf appeared delighted at the idea but that had not been the plan. Steinar had imagined he would leave them with his parents, as he'd just told his father.

"I would prefer if you went to stay with—"

"Yes, good idea!" Rothgar piped before he could even finish the sentence. "We haven't had any flat cakes yet."

Steinar sighed. It seemed there would be no convincing the boys they would be better off with their grandparents.

3

———

Later that afternoon his sister came to visit. Steinar was slicing strips of smoked meat in preparation for his journey to Astrid's parents when Eyja walked in through the open door, one hand on the small of her back in the familiar attitude of women heavy with child.

"Sit down," he immediately ordered, bringing a stool up to her.

Having only one sister, he'd always felt very protective of her, never more so than now she was carrying her second child. She was fast approaching her term and it hurt just to look at her, even if she seemed quite oblivious to the weight or the size of the bulge distending her stomach. Not for the first time, Steinar reflected that men, for all their supposed superior physical strength, didn't have to endure half of what women endured throughout their lifetime, and this without a word of complaint. It didn't seem fair.

"Thank you." Eyja smiled as she sat down, then winced slightly. Perhaps she was not as oblivious to the weight of the babe as it appeared. He poured her a cup of ale, then picked up his knife again.

"What brings you here?"

She took a sip of the ale he had placed in front of her before answering. "I've come to ask a favor, actually. Moon was wondering if you could lend him Fáfnir for a few days. He needs to go to the harbor to see about a ship of Dane merchants he's heard about, and Grendel is lame."

Steinar paused his cutting. "Sorry, but I need my horse. I was just telling the boys that I am leaving in the morning to go see Astrid's parents. I'd rather not delay any longer."

"Oh, of course. I'm sorry. I hope it goes well, even if I don't expect it will." His sister placed a hand over his forearm in sympathy. She knew what an ordeal it would be for him to see his estranged parents-in-law.

"Perhaps Moon can ask Torsten or Sven to lend him his horse?" he asked, popping a strip of meat into his mouth. Mm. Not bad. Rubbing crushed juniper berries over the lamb before drying it had definitely been a good idea, something he would do again.

"Yes, don't worry, we'll find a solution." Eyja pushed herself back to a standing position and sighed. "Not long to go now. Well, I'd better go. Good luck for tomorrow."

Just then Cwenthryth walked in through the door, carrying a bucket of water. Eyja stilled, as if surprised to see an unknown woman acting so at ease in his hut, and no wonder. So soon after his wife's death, he should be alone with the boys, not entertaining lovers. Not that he was doing that, he chided himself, even if it looked like it. Bloody hell, was the woman destined to create problems for him at every turn? Now that she'd seen her, he would never convince his imp of a sister that there was nothing between them.

For an uncomfortably long moment the three of them looked at one another, unsure what to say. Steinar struggled to swallow the last mouthful of meat. On second thought, perhaps the juniper flavor was a bit too strong.

"Well, are you not going to introduce me to your friend?"

"We are not friends, exactly," he replied, once he'd regained the ability to talk. It was hard to blame Eyja for assuming the two of them shared intimacy. In that moment the Saxon looked as if she had a place in his home, bringing in water from the well, entering the hut without knocking, behaving for all intents and purposes like a lover, or even a wife would.

We are not friends, much less lovers, so get this idea right out of your head. The Saxon and I are nothing to one another.

Eyja arched a brow at the blatant rudeness. "Well, you can still introduce us, can't you? Maybe she can become my friend."

Wonderful. His sister was taking the woman's side against her own brother. Steinar scowled. This was the last thing he needed, for Cwenthryth to carve her hole into his life a little bit deeper by meeting members of his family.

Instead of scurrying back outside, as he would have preferred her to, she placed the bucket on the table and gave a tentative smile. "I'm Cwenthryth," she said, wiping her hands on the front of her dress. The gesture forced Steinar's gaze to land on her hips, and he noticed that, frail as she may be, she had all the curves a man could want. Not that it mattered in any way, of course, he reminded himself sternly.

"Nice to meet you, Cwenthryth. I'm Eyja, Steinar's sister. I'm sure he hasn't told you he had a sister, or that she was—"

"Weren't you leaving? Come, we'll go see Torsten about this horse together," he said, taking his meddlesome little sister by the elbow. Another moment and she would tell the stranger she was glad her brother was not alone anymore, he could feel it. It would be a disaster. "Isn't that while you came?"

"WHAT ARE YOU DOING HERE? Didn't I tell you last time not to bother coming back?"

"Good morning." Steinar forced himself to behave with calm. The news he was about to impart was bad enough. No need to antagonize Astrid's father any more than necessary, even if the man was not making it easy for him to remain cordial.

"Get out."

Another deep breath. "I'm sorry, but I came to tell you that your daughter died last week. A bloody flux," he added, when neither Astrid's father nor her mother asked what had caused her death. "There was nothing the healer could do."

Silence met his declaration. Well, what had he expected? That they would dissolve into tears? Ask him how he felt?

"I never understood why Astrid chose to go with you when she could have stayed in our village with the man we'd found for her to marry," her father said eventually, a completely pointless comment. What did her decision to marry him have to do with her death? It was not as if he had killed her, was it?

"No, I know," Steinar said through gritted teeth. "You have told me enough times."

He had often wondered himself how his life would have turned out if he'd met Astrid in a moment when he'd been able to think clearly. If he had not bedded her before getting to know her. Given how things had ended between them, it was hard not to think that they should never have married. Not that he would confide any of this to her parents, of course. It would serve nothing to tell them that their marriage had been dead for years and their daughter had been about to leave him for another man. At best, they would think he was being petty, trying to make her appear like the guilty party; at worst, they would rejoice in his misfortune and claim he'd only gotten what he deserved. It was not worth it.

"I could never tell you enough times how unsuitable you were to marry Astrid, and it seems I was proven right. If she had married Leif instead of you, she would still be alive. *His* wife is still thriving, I'll have you know. I saw her only this morning, carrying her seventh child."

Seven children in twelve years. Steinar winced inwardly. Poor woman. Astrid, who'd had a hard time bearing children, would definitely not have lasted long as the blacksmith's wife.

"Well, perhaps your daughter didn't want to be married to an old lecher who only cares about his pleasure and doesn't think of giving his wife some respite between births. She was not—"

"What she, or even worse, *you* wanted was of no importance. I was her father! Who she married was my choice to make. Had you asked for my permission beforehand, like an honorable man, I would never have accepted, and I'm sure no one could blame me," he hissed. "For what man would entrust his daughter to a savage whose father killed his own wife?"

Steinar recoiled at the accusation he had not seen coming. *This* was what the man had held against him all this time? That he was the son of a wife killer? It was such an old story he was amazed this man who lived in another village even knew about it, never mind use it to justify his aversion of him. Two years before he'd met his second wife, Merewen, Wolf had been sent into exile from his native Iceland for the supposed murder of his first wife. But he'd been innocent, and his name had been cleared shortly after his wedding to the Saxon. No one had even dared allude to it in more than thirty years.

Until Astrid's father. Would there be no end to the man's vindictiveness?

"My father was proven innocent of the crime, as everyone knows," Steinar said, his voice low and menacing. "His wife was killed by a neighbor who coveted his land, a man called Jón Sölvasson. He is no more a wife killer than I am."

"Well. That's what you say."

"It is what happened."

The man made a face, clearly unconvinced. "All I know is that you both ended up being widowed well before your time." Was that a note of jealousy in his voice? Did he wish he could be rid of his own wife? It would not surprise Steinar. As bitter as dandelion leaves, incapable of a kind word or a smile, the woman was not exactly one anyone would like to be shackled to. Still, that was no reason for the man to go about accusing innocent people.

"Neither my father nor I had anything to do with the poor women's deaths."

"So you say," Astrid's father repeated.

"Yes, so I say. If you want to challenge me on that, I'd be happy to oblige you." Steinar tightened his hand on the blade at his belt. His fingers were itching to draw it out and finish this once and for all. "But I would be very careful if I were you. I will give no quarter, not even for an older man, not even for my father-in-law, not when my honor is at stake."

The two men glared at each other. Then Steinar decided he'd had enough. He'd done what he had come to accomplish, there was no need to prolong the moment. It was not worth staying at the risk of hearing any more ludicrous and painful accusations, or worse, ending up killing a man in a fit of rage too longer contained. Astrid's parents now knew that their only daughter, the daughter they had never loved, was dead. It was all that mattered.

"Well. I'd better go. Both your grandsons are fine, by the way."

Not that the old man or his wife had asked. Not that either of them cared.

There was no answer.

Steinar slammed the door behind him and strode over to the clearing where he'd tethered Fáfnir earlier. He sat down a moment before setting off. The poor beast did not deserve to have an irate rider on his back, urging him into a reckless gallop that would do little to ease his frustration. Before he climbed into the saddle he needed to calm down. This visit had been even worse than he'd expected it to be.

He'd all but been accused of killing his wife.

How could he have ended up in such a situation? How could his life have become such a nightmare?

The answer was simple: by allowing Astrid to appeal to his sense of honor, and play on his sensibilities. When she had explained that her parents had never cared about her, and had chosen for her a husband she feared, he had taken pity on her. Having been raised in a loving family, Steinar had been horrified to hear that anyone could treat their child thus. Was she not exaggerating? But after a visit to her aggressive father and greedy mother, he had seen that she was absolutely right. Her parents felt nothing for her. They only wanted to marry her off to the black-smith because he was the richest man in the village, which meant he would provide for them in their old age, nothing more. They did not care about her happiness or wonder if that was what she wanted.

The only problem was, this generous instinct had proven to be the mistake of his life. Because of it, he'd denied his sons the love of half their grandparents, and he'd endured years of misery and humiliation. He should have enquired about the kind of person she was before welcoming her into his life and into his heart. There would have been other ways to help her escape the fate her parents had in store for her; he didn't have to marry her himself. Well, it had been a lesson hard learned, and he would not make the same mistake a second time.

But fate seemed determined to make him her pawn.

Mere days after Astrid's death, Cwenthryth had burst into his life, asking for help, dazzling him with her beauty just like his late wife had done all those years ago. History was repeating itself, but things had changed. He was not the same man, no longer a gullible, inexperienced youth but an older, wiser man. Besides, it was not just about him anymore. He now had his children to worry about, he owed it to them to be sensible.

He would not be trapped again, especially not by black-haired Saxons who smelled of liquorice.

While he was steeling his resolve, footsteps in the under-growth made him turn his head. Who had followed him? He hardly knew anyone in that village, but it was possible someone recognized him for Astrid's husband and wanted news of her.

The tall, slightly mannish figure appearing though the bushes was Astrid's mother. Steinar barely repressed a sigh. The woman hadn't said a word during the confrontation with her husband, but it seemed she had something to tell him before he left. He braced himself for more insults, because he knew how unpleasant she could get. The day he and Astrid had come to tell them of their wedding, her father had been too stunned to do much more than glare. Her mother had been the one asking if they'd already slept together and getting herself in a state when her daughter had confirmed that they had, and that was the reason they had gotten married. She had seemed to take it as a personal slight.

"What do you want?"

Taking him by surprise, she sat next to him like a friend would. He waited, unsure what to do or say. He'd been expecting a tongue-lashing and she seemed poised on the edge of a confidence.

"You know, Steinar..." She shuffled closer to him, so close that he realized that she, unlike Cwenthryth, smelled of boiled cabbage. His stomach started to churn. Please let her just say what she had come here to say and leave. "My husband is a fool. But I'm not. I never wondered what had possessed my daughter to leave her village and abandon everyone, go against her father's wishes to marry Leif."

"Oh?"

This was not the impression she'd given him at the time, but he did not comment further. He didn't actually care about what she thought. Now that his mission had been accomplished, he just wanted to leave and return home as soon as possible, His sons who would be waiting for him.

"Yes. What woman in her right mind wouldn't want a man like you? So strong, so virile, so…" Instead of finishing her sentence, she groaned, a sound of feminine desire that sent ice down his spine. This was not a sound any man wanted to hear in his mother-in-law's mouth. "I have spent years wondering what Astrid was getting in your bed, dreaming about it. But perhaps now that she is gone, I don't have to wonder. Perhaps you could just show me."

A hand landed on his thigh. Gave a squeeze. Started to creep higher.

Bile flooded Steinar's throat. Was this really happening? Was the woman who had given birth to his late wife really suggesting what he thought she was? To think he'd dreaded the confrontation because he'd thought to have to deal with insults.

This was far, far worse.

"Take your hand off me," he rasped, fighting the urge to push her away, "before I snap your wrist off when I do it myself." She liked virile men, did she? He would get positively feral if she didn't run away right this instant. But she might not like it as much as she thought.

The hand retreated. The woman stood up, her face purple with rage—or was it mortification?

"No need to react in that way. As if you didn't know what effect you have on women. One look at you and they want you. Why should I feel any different? I'm a woman, aren't I? Astrid was lucky to get you, but now she's dead. There will be no harm in you and I—"

He stood up so fast he nearly sent her tumbling to the ground. "I'm leaving."

With those words, he vaulted onto Fáfnir's back, determined to escape this nightmare. Why had he come? He should have sent a message to Astrid's parents with Magnus, who regularly traveled between the Norse villages. It would have been enough, and more courtesy than they deserved.

"Go back to your husband, or whoever else you want to bed," he told the woman, not looking at her. "You and I will never meet again."

As he galloped away, her words kept playing in his mind. She'd claimed women wanted him as soon as they saw him. Was this really true? He had no idea. Married very young, in love with his wife, at least at first, then wholly set on making his marriage work and being a good father in spite of less than ideal circumstances, he had not worried himself about what women thought when they saw him, or even noticed.

Out of nowhere, an image of Cwenthryth flashed through his mind. Had he had the same effect on her? Was that why she had decided to convince him to let her stay? Did she want him in her bed, or rather, to be welcomed in his?

The thought sat ill with him, because he wanted to be more than a strong, virile body women lusted after.

And why was he constantly thinking about Cwenthryth anyway? He'd barely known her three days.

He still had to go to town to enquire about the man she was supposedly fleeing from, that had to be why. Until he had put this to rest, he would likely obsess about her. Gritting his teeth, he urged his horse toward the walls crowning the hill in the distance.

It was high time he found out who the Saxon really was.

4

———————

As she straightened her back from sweeping the ashes from the firepit, Cwenthryth found herself face-to face with Steinar's sister Eyja, whom she had met the other day. The woman was smiling at her from the doorway, one hand resting on her swollen stomach.

"Good morning. Cwenthryth, is it not? We never had the chance to talk the other day," she said, coming forward.

"No." And no wonder. A glowering Steinar in the background was not conducive to any kind of conversation. He had almost tripped over his own feet whisking his sister away, as if he feared her pervading influence.

"Well, we could do it now, could we not? No one is going to object this time." Eyja offered, her smile widening. "Would you accompany me to the lake beyond the forest? It's such a hot day, I feel like a swim. You might enjoy a dip in the water too."

Could she refuse? Did she even have a reason to? No. It was hot today, and she'd just spent the best part of the morning cleaning the hut. A swim would do her good.

"Of course. Just let me wash my hands first."

A moment later the two of them were on the road to the lake. The day was not only hot, but gorgeous as well. The land around them was bursting with life. Birds were chirping in the trees, and small white butterflies fluttered amongst the swaying wild carrots' umbrellas. As she inhaled their sharp smell, combined with that of the wild mint she was crushing underfoot, Cwenthryth understood that she wouldn't be able to live in a town anymore. This was just perfect. As a child, she and a group of girls from her street had spent as much time as they could running in the fields outside the town walls, chasing dragonflies, gathering sweet berries, rolling in the grass, bathing in rivers, and imagining a cleaner, simpler life.

As an adult, the responsibility of looking after an ailing father had prevented her from leaving the house much, and she had become increasingly cut away from nature. Up until now, she had not realized how much she had missed it. Being out in the forest and fields again was wonderful. Soothing.

As soon as she left the Norsemen village, she would find another such place to live. It seemed the only option to finally start to heal.

She and her companion kept a steady stream of conversation going as they walked, their pace slower than it would normally have been, in consideration for Eyja's great belly. With her ready wit and unusual boldness, the woman reminded Cwenthryth of her friend, Eahlswith, and as a result, she could easily fool herself that the two of them had known each other their whole lives.

When they eventually reached the lake, instead of heading to the shore, they sat down in the shade of a mighty oak.

"Forgive me, I think I need to rest for a while before I get into the water," Eyja said, giving her a tight smile. "Perhaps the walk was a bit too much for me at this time."

Yes. It was a wonder she had wanted to attempt it at all with her stomach. It was even bigger than Cwenthryth remembered from the other day. But then again, at that point, she had been too nervous to notice the size of the woman's stomach. "When are you due?"

"Very soon, I should think. This is my second child." Eyja stroked her stomach tenderly. "I had a difficult birth with my daughter, Emma, who was breached. My husband was so scared it would happen again he made me take herbs to prevent conception for a whole year after I had weaned her. He can be rather over-protective, I'm afraid." The smile she gave indicated she didn't resent it—on the contrary. "In any case, I stopped taking the herbs eventually but it was more than two years before I fell with child again, despite…well, despite our very active love life. I was starting to wonder whether Emma's difficult birth had made me barren. You hear about these things happening, you know." A cloud went over the woman's blue eyes as she remembered the dark times. "Moon never said a word, but I know he was thinking the same."

Yes, understandably they would have worried. Cwenthryth could only sympathize. She had wondered more than once if her own ordeal would affect her ability to carry children in the future.

"Your husband is called Moon?" she asked, careful to keep her tone light. This seemed a far safer conversation topic than the possibility of a woman having her body damaged for future children. "How unusual. Is that a typical Norse name?"

"Oh no!" Eyja giggled. "His name is really Halfdan, but everyone calls him Moon, on account of the birthmark he has on his wrist, shaped just like a moon crescent."

"I see."

"Our fathers being such close friends, we practically grew up together. He was like a fourth brother to me. And then one day I saw that he was in fact the most alluring man I'd ever seen. To this day, I have no idea how I did not see it before. Oh well, better late than never, I suppose. But the change wasn't easy to accept at first, even for us." She leaned in to whisper in her ear. "My father wanted to be sure he was serious in his intentions and my brothers tried to beat him to a pulp for touching me. Torsten, who's always been his best friend, and Steinar, by virtue of being the eldest brother, in particular. Sven has always been more measured."

Yes, Cwenthryth could well imagine there had been nothing measured in Steinar's reaction. If he'd almost bitten her head off for doing nothing more than repeat wrong information, she preferred not to think what he had done to a man he thought was dallying with his only sister.

"How do you know my brother, then?" Eyja asked, leaning back against the tree once more.

"I don't really. He didn't lie when he told you as much the other day," Cwenthryth said, remembering how Steinar had denied being friends with her. His vehemence had stung, but ultimately, he was right. They weren't anything to each other. "I knew his wife a little, and the boys."

There was a silence while Eyja seemed to wonder what to make of that. "Well, don't let him frighten you with his gruffness. He's not usually like this, but in the last few years... He's not been happy, and as a consequence, he's started to live up to his name. Steinar means 'stone' in our father's language," she specified, when Cwenthryth shook her head in incomprehension.

Stone.

She barely repressed a snort. How apt. She couldn't have chosen a better name for him if she'd tried. Or perhaps "steel" would have done just as well. Or "ice."

"I suppose it does fit. But I cannot blame him for not welcoming me in when he heard that Astrid had lied about his identity. It will have hurt." It would have felt as if his wife were ashamed to admit she was married to him.

Eyja frowned. "What do you mean, she lied about his identity?"

Keeping to herself the fact that Steinar's late wife had had a lover, Cwenthryth explained how she'd been told he was only the boys' uncle.

"Oh, the wretched woman! Unfortunately, this sounds just like something she would do." Eyja was incensed.

"I came to the village because Astrid told me the three of them might need my help. And I wanted to escape, so I thought…"

As soon as the word passed her lips, Cwenthryth regretted them. Why had she added that detail? Obviously, it was too much to hope that Eyja's curiosity had not been pricked. She was looking at her with glimmering eyes.

"You needed to escape? From what?"

"I…" Damn, why hadn't she kept her mouth shut? She resisted the urge to touch the side of her head. Was her bruise still showing? She hoped not. "A man."

That would have to suffice. She didn't need to say that the man in question was living in her house, or that she had just lost his baby, did she? Eahlswith was the only one who knew about her loss and she meant to keep it that way. No one else needed to know.

"A man who hurt you?" Eyja insisted nonetheless.

"Yes."

No point in ignoring the question, Steinar's sister would only ask it again. She really was as opinionated as Eahlswith. She proved it by asking. "Who would hurt you again if he saw you?"

"Yes."

"Have you told Steinar about it?"

Here, Cwenthryth hesitated, because it was not that simple. She had told him, but it had been obvious that he had not believed her. She wasn't even sure he believed the story about how she had met Astrid. Of course it was hard to blame him for being suspicious. She had given him two different versions of why she had come to the village and to him in particular, and at first, she had mistaken him for the boys' uncle. Even though it wasn't her fault, it did look bad, as if she were making things up as she went along.

"I did tell him," she said eventually.

The tension left Eyja's shoulders. "Well then, you don't have anything to worry about. My brother is a good man, for all his newfound gruffness. He'll keep you safe until you find a solution."

Dare she tell her he had already asked her to leave, and had only agreed to have her stay for a few days because he had gone away himself? No, it would not be fair, because Steinar had indeed given her a respite, short as it was, and he had given her a shelter while she thought of some more permanent solution. It was time she gave it some serious thought, because he had been gone three days already and she was no closer to knowing what to do. So far, all she had established was that she needed to ensure she didn't see Godfrid again, and that she wanted to live in nature rather than in town. As plans went, it was rather a weak one, but that was something for her to worry about, no one else.

She forced a smile. "Godfrid won't find me here. I'll be fine, don't worry."

Eyja's gaze flicked to her temple. Apparently, the bruise was still visible enough to make the other woman doubt her word. The two of them looked at one another, feminine solidarity shining in their eyes. It was then that Cwenthryth understood that her new friend had probably also suffered at a man's hand. She seemed to know how it felt to fear meeting with a tormentor.

Mercifully, she didn't press on, as if sensing Cwenthryth's fragile composure was about to shatter.

"Now. Shall we go for that swim? It will do me good, I think."

"Yes, me too."

With her help, Eyja stood back up. As soon as she was on her feet, however, her face underwent a transformation.

"What's wrong?" Cwenthryth was instantly on alert. Had she seen something in the distance? Was someone coming? Godfrid? Had he somehow found her whereabouts? Ice replaced blood in her veins. Please, *no*. She could not face him now. Or ever. "Eyja, what is it? What's wrong?"

"The babe." Her new friend lifted the hem of her gown with careful, wary gestures, revealing her right leg, which was completely wet. "I think it's coming."

It QUICKLY BECAME clear that Eyja was not mistaken. The babe had indeed chosen this moment to be born.

Dear God.

After an initial moment of panic, faced with the inevitability of what was happening, Cwenthryth had no choice but to calm down and do what needed to be done. There was no point wishing herself well away from the mess; she had to stay with Eyja and deliver the baby on her own. Going to the village to get someone to help would take far too long. By the time they were back, the babe might well be born. She simply could not take that risk and leave poor Eyja to face the ordeal alone.

Doing her best to keep fear at bay, she followed Eyja's instructions to the best of her abilities, and made sure to soothe the panting woman with reassuring words. Her friend was no midwife, but she had already given birth once, and could draw on the experience to remember what had to be done. By contrast, all Cwenthryth knew about having a babe was…

Was best forgotten, and useless in this instance.

She took in a deep breath and focused on doing whatever she could to help the other woman through the different phases of labor. It was hard not to be awed by Eyja's courage. It was clear the mother was doing all she could to give her babe the best chance at survival, not worrying about her own comfort and pushing through the excruciating pain. After what seemed like an eternity, Cwenthryth found herself holding a perfectly healthy little girl. The relief was overwhelming, so much so that she started crying. Considering how the birth of Emma had gone, she had been very worried indeed. Dealing with a normal birth was stressful enough; anything more challenging would have been a nightmare. But thankfully, the baby had been positioned as it should, and the whole thing had gone as easily as it could go, or so she imagined. Now all she could do was hope Eyja was not carrying twins. She wasn't sure her nerves would survive it.

Cwenthryth handed the little girl to her mother, who was crying in relief herself, slumped against the oak tree.

"There you are. A beautiful daughter."

"All is well, then?"

"Yes. As far as I can tell, all is well. She's perfect."

Eyja made a grimace. "There is still the afterbirth to come," she said, preparing herself.

Thankfully, this part of the operation was dealt with quickly and easily. Once it was over, Cwenthryth used her own shawl to cover the babe, who had snuggled against her mother's chest in search of warmth and comfort.

The two—three—women stayed silent a moment, enjoying the relief of knowing the hard part was over. Then Cwenthryth busied herself with cleaning Eyja as best as she could. Once she was reassured mother and daughter could be left alone, she stood up, and went to wash her hands in the lake.

"Stay here," she instructed when she came back. The babe had already started nursing and everything appeared safe. "I'll go back to the village, find someone to get you both."

Eyja would not be able to walk the distance, not after what she had gone through, so she needed someone with a horse or even better, a cart, to come get her.

"Thank you. Oh, if only Moon were here! But he's gone to the coast."

"Don't worry, I'll find someone."

The first man she saw was, inevitably, tall and blond. He also seemed friendly and ready to help, nothing like a certain scowling Norseman she could think of. Deciding he could be trusted, she approached him. When she said she had come on behalf of Eyja, he introduced himself as Rorik, and explained that he was Moon's cousin. Even better. Certain now that he would help her, Cwenthryth told him why she needed him.

"Eyja's had the babe then?" He sounded utterly bewildered, which was no wonder. "Already? But how? When? I saw her only this morning. She looked the same as usual."

"I'll explain everything while we ride." The explanation could wait, but she didn't want to leave the mother and child alone longer than absolutely necessary. "Do you have a horse, or a cart? Or could you borrow one? We need to go get her and her baby. They're by the lake, and night will soon fall."

"Yes. Moon has gone away for a few days, but he's due to come back tonight. We had better get his wife and child home before he does, so he can see for himself all is well. Otherwise there will be hell to pay, even if obviously, neither of us is responsible for the birth happening out in the open."

Oh no. Cwenthryth's stomach fell. Not another gruff, forbidding Norseman who would throw unfair accusations at her... She'd had enough of that with Steinar. Would this Moon bark at her for not taking his wife to safety before she delivered the babe? For leaving her alone so soon after the birth? For allowing her to walk as far as the lake in the first place? Would he listen to her explanations and believe her when she told him there had been no other choice? Eyja had said he could be over-protective. And now his cousin was saying they had better not let him find his wife and child outside. This could be a disaster, one she was not ready for.

"Let's go," she agreed.

The sooner the better.

5

There it was. The market hall with its wooden pillars.

Before leaving the hut, Steinar had not dared ask Ulf too many details about where Cwenthryth lived, for fear of raising his suspicions, and Rothgar had been as vague as a six-year-old could be. Nevertheless, there could not be many market halls in the small town, and it was what she had used to explain the bruise at her temple. She might not have thought of it so readily if she didn't live in its proximity. The house he was looking for could not be too far. But where?

An old man was sitting on a bench in the shade of the timber structure, watching people go past. He looked like the kind of man who made it his business to know about everything that was going on in town, and old enough to have met everyone at some point or another. Perfect. Steinar made his way to him.

"Good morning. I'm hoping you might be able to help me. I'm looking for a woman called Cwenthryth. She is friends with another woman called Eahlswith," he said, making sure to give as much information as possible to identify her. "She's slender, with dark hair and black eyes, rather pale. I was told she lived around here. Do you know her?"

The man didn't even blink. "Aye, of course, I've known her all my life." Just as Steinar had suspected, then. "Sweet girl. She lives on the road over there, in the house opposite the cooper, the one with the smallish door."

Yes, he could see the door from here. Excellent. "Does she live alone or with a man?"

Steinar clenched his jaw when the old man arched a brow at the admittedly odd question. He should have perhaps tried to appear less keen but the words had just shot out of him. Whether she lived with a dangerous man was all he wanted to know. He didn't need to be told she was a sweet girl. He could decide that on his own.

"I see. Maybe I don't need to ask why you're looking for Cwenthryth... And why not? I might be tempted to woo her myself, were I forty years younger. Alas, even if my mind is still as sharp as ever, my body is not what it once was." He chuckled, looking at the gnarled hands resting on the pommel of his walking stick. "Well, you're in luck, because no, she doesn't live with a man, only with her brother. The father died a few weeks ago, poor man."

Brother. Father.

This was not what he had wanted to hear. Steinar nodded as the inescapable truth hit him. Cwenthryth had said that the man who'd hurt her lived with her and might leave when he saw she was not coming back. But there was no man. The only person living in the house at present with her was her brother, who would have no reason to leave, whether she disappeared or not. As to the father, even if had mistreated her, as Astrid's father once had mistreated her, he was now dead. She had nothing to fear from him.

There was only one conclusion to draw from this. She had lied.

Why was he even surprised? Hadn't he guessed she had only told him what she needed to say to ensure his help?

"But I have to warn you, young man, you might not find it as easy as you think to seduce the girl, despite your advantageous physique," the old man carried on, oblivious to his dismay. "I've never seen her with a sweetheart, or even heard that she favored anyone with her advances. As far as I can tell, she lives a life as chaste as any nun's. Pity. A girl like her should know a man's touch."

Well, that was pretty clear. Not only did she not live with an abusive lover, but she had never even been in contact with a man. What else had she lied about? Had she fabricated the story of his wife having a lover as well? He doubted it, since he knew Astrid had gone to town on numerous occasions, and the boys had confirmed that she'd left them with Cwenthryth while she went into the same house each time. No, everything pointed to her having indeed come to see a man.

Well, since he was here, with a man disposed to talking, and knowledgeable, he might as well ask a few more questions.

"And what about her neighbor? Do you know him? I was told he was skilled at carpentry and could advise me on my crumbling roof," he improvised.

"Aldred?" The man chuckled again. "I'd be surprised if he were skilled at carpentry or indeed anything else. Not only is he too lazy to learn a trade, but he's also too busy bedding all the women he can find. There are only so many hours in the day. A man cannot be both hammering nails and hammering…well, you get my meaning."

Steinar gritted his teeth while the man cackled to himself, proud of his jest. Astrid had intended to leave him and their children for a man who'd seduced half the women in town and didn't seem ready to settle down. How much more pathetic could this get? Had she known about this Aldred's other conquests? Or had she honestly thought that what they had was special? As he asked himself the questions, he found that he didn't really care. Something in his chest expanded.

He didn't care.

It was a welcome revelation. Finally, after years of misery, his late wife had lost the power to hurt him. Finally, he might be able to resume his life in the way he wanted. Finally, he was free.

"If you really need help with your roof I can recommend my nephew. Now there's a skilled carpenter. But he lives a few miles outside town, on the south road."

It took Steinar a moment to understand what the old man was talking about and then he remembered that he'd pretended to need this Aldred's help. "No, thank you, you're very kind, but I'm sure I can find someone closer to my village to see to it. I wish you good day."

"You as well."

Unable to resist the temptation of seeing where Cwenthryth lived while he was here, even if he suspected he wouldn't gain anything from it, he walked over to the house opposite the cooper. The door was indeed rather small, Steinar suspected he would have to duck quite significantly to be able to enter it. It looked almost abandoned. There was no sign of the brother Cwenthryth had inexplicably failed to mention when she'd claimed not to be able to return home. Next to it, there was a bigger house. Aldred's. Just as he was wondering whether it was worth knocking on the door to see who Astrid had chosen to replace him, a woman did just that. Checking left and right first to ensure herself no one was looking, she rapped what sounded like a signal. The kind old man hadn't lied. This was clearly a well-rehearsed ritual and she was likely not the first one to use it.

A moment later, the door swung open and Steinar was afforded a glimpse of his wife's lover. Of medium height, with limp brown hair and a small face, the Saxon was rather unremarkable. Well, what had he expected? A giant of a man, with a flowing red mane of hair and blazing eyes? Perhaps. At least someone you couldn't fail to notice. Aldred's unprepossessing physique had come as a surprise. Why on earth had Astrid thought him more attractive than him, the man she had married?

Their gazes met. Something shifted in the man's clear eyes. Alarm? Had he identified him as a Norseman, and therefore guessed who he might be? Or was he wondering whether the stranger staring at him so intently was the husband of the woman who was even now entering the house and he feared a confrontation?

Steinar turned on his heel, not interested in frightening him. He'd seen what he had come here to see. Two things had been established.

His wife had been a fool—and Cwenthryth's story could not be trusted.

CWENTHRYTH WAS CLOSING the gate to the pig enclosure when she felt a presence behind her. A huge, looming presence. Her heartbeat instantly picked up. Was Steinar back? He had been gone four days now, more than she had expected. Surely it would not be long before he came back to see his children. But was she ready for the confrontation? She wasn't certain.

Slowly, she turned around.

Standing behind her was not the giant she was expecting, but one with a baby tucked in the crook of his arm. He was blond, strong and handsome, however, almost as much as Steinar. Despite having never seen him before, she knew he would be Eyja's husband, Halfdan—Moon. Who else would be holding the newborn little girl she had helped birth the day before?

What was he doing here? Was he about to snap at her for

allowing Eyja to walk all the way to the lake when she was so near her term, thereby forcing her to give birth out in the open? Rorik had told her his cousin was rather formidable, and warned her he would not be happy to find out what had happened to his wife. Well, he certainly looked formidable, even if he didn't seem irate at the moment. Or perhaps he wanted to ascertain who she was before he unleashed his fury. It would be the sensible thing to do.

"Cwenthryth?" he asked, stopping in front of her. Ah, there it was, the preliminary question. She nodded cautiously and returned the bucket to its place. "I'm Moon, Eyja's husband."

Yes, that much she had already guessed. "Good morning."

"I came here to… Well, I came to thank you for what you did for my wife and daughter, but now I'm here, I'm afraid I don't know how to do it. How do you thank someone for saving people you love?"

And just like that, her alarm melted away. The man was not formidable, he was simply in love with his wife, and worried for her. Now that she'd had the chance to talk to him, she saw that he was in fact nothing like Steinar. He was just as blond, strong, and handsome, admittedly, but she could never have mistaken one for the other. Comparing the two Norsemen would have been like comparing summer clouds to thunder, sunlight to lightening. Moon was everything Steinar was not, approachable and unsure how to talk to her. Relief spread through her. She had nothing to fear from this man. He would never bark at her or look at her as if he wanted her out of his sight. On the contrary, he seemed struck dumb by gratitude toward her. Gratitude she wasn't even sure she deserved.

"Please. There is no need to thank me. I did not exactly save anyone. I only—"

"You were there for Eyja in one of the most important moments of her life. You reassured her, you helped her keep panic at bay, you made sure both she and our baby were safe. It means everything. I would not have had her alone in such a moment. So, thank you."

She gave a smile. "I am relieved. If you must know, I thought you'd be angry for not dissuading her from going as far as the lake."

Head thrown back, Moon let out a throaty laugh, and in that moment Cwenthryth understood why Eyja had stopped seeing him as a friend. It would be all too easy to fall under the man's spell. He truly was dazzling.

"Believe me, I would have been amazed if you had dissuaded the imp from doing anything," he told her, his lips stretching in a wide grin. "I've never been able to do so. To my delight, she is the most stubborn, determined woman I've ever seen, and utterly unstoppable when her mind is made up."

Something in his blue eyes glimmered and Cwenthryth found herself blushing. Without knowing quite why, she had the impression he had just admitted to something very private.

"She was very brave," she murmured, remembering the woman's unwavering resolve to do what needed to be done for her child.

Moon sobered in the blink of an eye. "Yes," he said, his voice gruff. "I'm not surprised. She is the toughest warrior I know. The birth of our first daughter was so long, so hard on her, that for a frightful moment I thought she would not make it. She never gave up, finally bringing Emma into the world despite the difficulty. It was the most awe-inspiring thing I'd ever seen. After that, we never thought we would..."

He shook his head, and placed a kiss on the little girl's forehead. There was such love in that gesture that Cwenthryth's chest constricted. Would she one day see a man kissing a child she had given him with half as much emotion? It seemed unlikely, for who would want her now?

"Well, I'm glad to have been there for her," she said, pushing the maudlin thought away. "I trust she's doing well?"

"Yes. She and Emma are napping together." He didn't need to add what he thought of the idea of the two of them entwined on the pallet. She saw it in his eyes. Yes, Moon was definitely a man in love and proud of his family.

The sunlight behind her suddenly dimmed and Cwenthryth's body stiffened of its own accord. The very air seemed to still around her. This time she knew Steinar would be the man looming over her when she turned around.

He appeared in the corner of her eye, his hair tangled by the ride, his beard longer than when he'd left. Her heart skipped a beat. Heavens, but he had never looked better than he did now.

"Moon," he greeted, completely ignoring her.

"Steinar. You're back just in time to meet Frida, your new niece. Here." He nodded at the little girl, who was yawning. "She's just woken up. Would you like to hold her?"

"Of course," Steinar answered, already holding out his arms.

Cwenthryth had not expected him to agree so readily. Nor had she been prepared for the sight of him with the fragile babe cradled in his arms. It was already hard not to melt when he hugged little Rothgar, but this... This was an even more challenging proposition. He looked so full of awe, so relaxed, nothing like his usual self. And then, to her shock, he smiled at the little girl.

She had never seen him smile before, and unsurprisingly, he was transformed by it. In that moment she saw the man he could be if he were happy—and she understood she would never see him in the same way ever again.

"I'll be honest, I didn't expect to be greeted with such a lovely surprise. How did it go?" he asked his brother-in-law, his gaze still on the little girl. He seemed utterly fascinated by her. "Better than Emma's birth, I hope?"

Moon rubbed the back of his neck like a man plagued with worries. Evidently, despite the assurance that all was well with his wife, his mind was still not at rest and he was still imagining what could have happened. "Yes, by all accounts, it went well, and much faster, thanks be to the gods. I wasn't there with Eyja, though. Cwenthryth was the one who delivered Frida."

"Was she?"

The tone was frigid, and when he finally looked at her, all traces of tenderness and awe had vanished. His blue eyes seemed to have gone two shades darker. The babe in his arms started to fuss, perhaps responding to the tension in his body.

"Yes. I don't know what we would have done without her," Moon carried on, oblivious to the change in him.

The little girl's writhing became a moan, then a cry. Yes, definitely tension here.

"Take her back to her mother," Steinar said, handing Frida to her father. "I think she's hungry."

Moon didn't need to be told twice. Placing his daughter's well-being before anything else, he nodded his goodbyes and strode away. Cwenthryth found herself alone with a glowering Steinar. Dear Lord, what had happened to him during the last few days? He'd not been best pleased to see her irrupt into his life the other day, and she could understand that, given the circumstances, but he was now looking at her as he would to an enemy.

She didn't know what to make of it, or how to respond. Perhaps fleeing would be the best option, if the most cowardly. She turned her face to the chicken coop.

"I still have to feed the chickens, so I'd better—"

A hand closed around her wrist, stopping her retreat. "The chickens can wait. I can't."

Oh. Cwenthryth was sure she should panic at the way he was restraining her, not melt. She was sure she should tremble at the growl in his voice, not go all warm inside. But the problem was, the hold on her wrist felt sensual rather than menacing, and his words were rather suggestive. He'd made it sound as if he couldn't wait to take her to bed after his prologued absence. So she did melt, and she did go all warm inside.

"What is it?" she asked, heart thumping hard.

Silence met her question. He was still holding her, his fingers warm against her skin. Then finally, he spoke.

"My, you didn't waste your time while I was away, have you? You've already started to make yourself indispensable to my sons, now you helped my sister give birth to my niece and earned my brother-in-law's eternal gratitude… What else?" He sounded angry and bitter all at once. Dangerous. "Whom will you try to ensnare next? My mother? My brothers? I should warn you before you start, it will be in vain. I will not let you stay here permanently, no matter how hard you try to sway me."

"I'm not trying to sway you, I haven't tried to ensnare anyone!" Cwenthryth cried out, snatching her wrist from his hold. From the way she easily managed it, she understood he'd not really wanted to keep her captive. She would never have freed herself if he had, he was just too strong. "I just happened to be with Eyja when her waters broke. And I have no intention of staying here permanently. I only came here because I had to hide, as I told you. I never meant to—"

"Hide. Oh yes. Let me see. You had to hide from the man you live with, did you not? Remind me, which one is it? The father who is already dead or the brother? Certainly not the lover you've never had."

Cwenthryth recoiled. He knew her father was dead? He knew about Godfrid? He knew she'd never been with a man of her choosing? But how? And why did it make him so angry?

"How… You…" She was too shocked to formulate her question.

"On my way back from Astrid's parents I stopped in town. I learned some interesting things about you there."

"Such as?" Lord, but there were so many horrid things he could have been told. Cwenthryth was now really worried. Who had he spoken to?

"The only man living in your house is your brother, and people who've known you all your life are convinced that you've never even been with a man. Not quite the story you've given me, as I'm sure you will agree." Blue eyes glittered. "So I think you can understand my displeasure at being made a fool out of."

Well, yes, if that was what he'd been told, she did indeed understand. He would think her the worst liar and manipulator. His attitude made sense now. He'd gone to town with the express purpose of finding out more about her and he'd been told a different story to the one she'd given him. This was why he was looking at her like an enemy.

He'd made some enquiries about her because he didn't believe her. And, unfortunately, what he'd heard had only confirmed his opinion of her. He was convinced she was lying to carve herself a place in his home, in his life. To add to the problem, the first thing he'd been told upon coming back to the village was that she had been of assistance to his sister. Had he been in a more accommodating mood, he would have seen that there was no way she could have planned it that way, but Steinar had already made up his mind about her being intent on taking advantage of him. He would not change his opinion about her now.

Tears sprang to her eyes.

"You don't need to be displeased because I am telling you the truth. You just don't want to hear it."

"I have heard it, thank you, from someone who, unlike you, had no reason to lie to me. Or do you deny that your father is dead?"

"No. He is dead." Her chest tightened when she remembered

his last moments, the awful emptiness crushing her when she'd understood he really was gone and she was on her own. At least the poor man had not suffered, slipping away peacefully in his sleep. The only one to suffer was her, who was left behind.

"And isn't the only other person living in your house your brother? Where is the dangerous lover you told me about, I might wonder?"

"It's… It's not that simple. Will you let me explain?"

"I think I've heard all I needed to hear, thank you."

How had she hoped he would say yes? Steinar just stared at her, stony eyed. He didn't care about her explanations, she was no one to him. He had already dismissed her from his life.

"I'm going to see Magnus, the blacksmith, about a commission. When I come back, I want you to be gone."

6

———————

Cwenthryth stared at the dying fire in the middle of the hut. This was it. The temporary refuge she'd found had been denied to her.

Maybe it was not as bad as it could have been. In the end, though Steinar had made it clear he didn't need her moments after she had arrived on his doorstep, she had been able to spend some time in the Norsemen village. It had now been almost a week ago since she had disappeared. With luck, Godfrid would think her gone for good and he would have left himself. With her father dead and her gone, why would he stay in town? He would move on, find his next victims to torment. It was a possibility she had to hold on to for fear of going mad with terror.

A quick look around the hut reminded her she had nothing to take with her, not even food. Nothing here belonged to her. She could leave right now, as she was wearing what little she owned anyway.

Before she could gather the courage to move, the door opened behind her. Not Steinar already? He'd said he was going to the blacksmith to discuss a commission. Surely he would need more time than that? She braced herself for another confrontation but when she turned around, she found herself face-to-face with his sons. Everything within her relaxed. She was not going to be glared or shouted at.

"Cwenthryth, there you are. Ulf and I are hungry. Will you make some flat cakes for us? Uncle Torsten's just given us some honey, look."

Little Rothgar, so adorable, was looking at her with big, imploring eyes. Even Ulf, who, at twelve, would not dare admit he wanted a sweet treat, seemed interested at the prospect. Could she agree to their request?

If Steinar came back before she had finished frying the cakes, he would be angry, there was no denying it. He had ordered her to leave, and no doubt expected her to comply without delay. But perhaps she had a little time. It would not surprise her if he lingered at the forge to ensure she was well and truly gone by the time he came back home. Besides, if he yelled at her, it would make no difference. He had already told her to leave, what else would he do? He would roar and rant as he was wont, but he would not hurt her.

Besides, how could she refuse the two boys when they were looking at her with such a hopeful expression on their faces?

"I will make them if you go and get more kindling for the fire," she told the brothers. More than likely, it would be the last time she saw them, she didn't want to leave without having given them this last treat. "I doubt the fire we have at the moment will last long enough for me to bake more than one cake each."

"Oh, we definitely want more than one each!" Rothgar piped.

She couldn't help a smile. He was so different from his brooding father. Had Steinar once been a joyous, carefree little boy? It was hard to imagine him as a child when he was all masculine presence.

"Well, then, go while I get the dough ready."

"WHAT THE HELL is going on here?"

Cwenthryth dropped the spoon she was holding when the voice sliced through the air. Damn! She had hoped Steinar would linger with the blacksmith and never find out about the cakes.

Slowly, she turned around. Six-foot-three of irate male was glowering at her. The sight had become so familiar that somehow it did not impress her as much as it should have. She knew she had nothing to fear, as he would never actually hit her.

"I'm making flat cakes, as you can see."

As soon as the words were out, she knew she had made a mistake. Steinar's jaw clenched, betraying barely controlled fury.

"You're making *cakes*? Didn't I tell you to get the hell out of here?"

What was it with him and his obsession with hell? How did the Norseman he was even know about it? Well, she'd had enough of it. She had done nothing wrong, she had only tried to please the two sweetest little boys she had ever seen before leaving them for good. Was that such a crime? Why couldn't he see that she posed no threat to him, that she was not trying to "ensnare" anyone?

"You did tell me to leave. But then the boys asked me to make the cakes and I didn't think it would be such a—"

"The boys, again!" he erupted. "Who is master here?"

She bristled at this show of dominance she had not seen coming. So far, he had not struck her as one of those men who thought their opinion was the only one that mattered and who expected everyone to obey their orders blindly. Perhaps she should have, considering how he had acted with her.

"You," she answered frigidly, disappointment giving her courage. "Or at least you like to think you are. With such an overbearing, unreasonable husband, it is no wonder Astrid went to another man."

Thunder falling on the roof of the hut at this moment would have stunned them less. Cwenthryth was horrified at her daring. Had she really told this man she sympathized with his dead wife, and that she would have taken a lover too, had she been in her place? If he'd been angry at her before, by rights he would now be ready to rip her to shreds.

"Get. The. H—"

"Yes. I know," she cut in. "Don't worry. I'll get the hell out of here."

Ulf appeared in the door frame, a stack of branches cradled in his arms. "What's happening here?" he asked, uncertainty making his voice waver.

"Nothing," his father snapped. "Cwenthryth was leaving. You can tell her goodbye now that you're here."

Rothgar appeared from behind him, carrying a bundle almost as big as he was. "But what about the flat—"

Steinar placed a hand on his son's shoulder, stopping the protest on his lips. "We will make the cakes ourselves. We don't need anyone's help."

Well, that was clear enough, and the boys had the good sense not to protest. The little family didn't need anyone, least of all her. Cwenthryth swallowed her frustration, her hurt, and her tears. How could it all end this way when she had done nothing wrong?

"Goodbye," she told the children with as much dignity as she could muster.

She didn't tell them she would miss them, she didn't draw them into a last hug. Instead, she just walked out the door, doing her best not to betray how weak her legs felt in that moment.

It was only when she entered the forest that Cwenthryth grasped the enormity of the situation. This was really it. She was on her own. What was she to do? Where was she to go? Night was falling fast, wrapping the landscape in darkness and a distinctively chilly mist. It was too late to go back to town now, even supposing that was what she wanted to do. But where could she hide? The people in the village were not an option, as Steinar was sure to find out who had welcomed her, and the last thing she wanted was to face any more of his accusations or create problems for someone else.

But the idea of lying in a ditch again had her shiver in dread and cold combined. She screwed her eyes shut, causing a tear to fall down her cheeks. Steinar had told her to go to hell, and in that moment, she certainly felt as if she were heading that way.

Just then, footsteps were heard from behind her, too light to be those of a great big, hulking Norseman. She knew whom she would see even before she turned around.

"Ulf. You shouldn't be here," she said, wiping at her cheeks as discreetly as she could.

He ignored her protest, but the look on his face showed he knew she was right. "Don't worry about *Faðir*," he told her, glancing back as if worried he'd been followed.

"Worry about what?"

"Our father. *Faðir*, that's what we call him," Ulf explained. "He's not normally like this. But he's not been himself lately because…well, you know why."

Yes, she did know why. But unfortunately, it didn't excuse everything. She hadn't done anything wrong, and shouldn't be treated as if she were the worst of schemers, and a liar trying to take advantage of him and manipulate innocent children.

"Of course," she told the boy nonetheless. He shouldn't have to pay for Steinar's stubbornness. He had done nothing wrong either.

"Where will you go now?"

He was looking at her with those intense eyes that were so like Steinar's, blue as a pure summer sky, and she understood he knew she had cried. Her chest squeezed. How she would miss him and his brother! And if she were honest, she would admit that she would miss his bear of a father also, albeit for different reasons. She would have liked a chance to see the man hidden under the snarling beast. Everyone kept telling her that he existed, somewhere. She believed it, since she'd had a glimpse of him with little Frida this afternoon. For a brief moment, with the baby in his arms, Steinar had appeared like a different man. And that man was possibly the most compelling one she had ever seen. What would it take to coax him out? It seemed she would never find out.

"Don't worry about me," she told Ulf. The boy was only twelve, he shouldn't have to worry about such things. "I'll be fine."

More footsteps were heard, short, hurried ones this time, and then it was Rothgar's turn to appear between the bushes. When he spoke, it was clear that he'd heard the last part of the conversation.

"She could go sleep in the tree house," he told his brother, his own blue eyes huge with excitement. "No one but us ever goes there. *Faðir* would never know."

"I don't want to create problems for—"

"Rothgar is right. *Faðir* would never know," Ulf interrupted. "At least for tonight, while we think of another, better solution. 'Twill be dark and cold soon. You cannot stay outside on your own or walk all the way to town now."

Cwenthryth couldn't help a smile. The boy would grow into a wonderful man one day, caring and generous. And perhaps she could take advantage of the suggestion. It did seem like the safest option at the moment, the one she'd desperately needed.

"Thank you."

"The house is just between here and the river, in a big ash tree. You can't miss it. We will bring you some food and ale in the morning. And there are already blankets there, and old furs. You could make a pallet out of—"

"Yes, thank you," she repeated. "I'm sure I will be fine. Now go, or your father will worry."

It would not do for Steinar to see them all together, or to know that his sons had found her a hiding place in the village; he would only fly into one of his rages. She waited until the children were gone, making sure they were safe, then she went in search of the tree house. It was not hard to find, even in the fading light, and she ascended the rope ladder quickly, before she could be spotted.

Once inside, she breathed a sigh of relief. Thank God for the boys' generosity. She would be safe, for another night at least.

In the corner next to two little stools were the blankets and furs Ulf had told her about. They looked soft and inviting, making her realize how tired she was. Though she had been able to relax these last few days, it was clear she had not completely recovered from her ordeal.

Nestled on the soft pallet, Cwenthryth fell into a deep slumber.

7

"Where's your brother?" Steinar asked his eldest son, a frown creasing his brow.

Upon waking up, he had found the little boy's pallet empty. But as, thankfully, Rothgar had gone back to sleeping as well as he always did, he should be in his bed at this hour. So where had he gone?

Though worry had spiked through him, Steinar fought to remain calm. He'd been irritable those last two days. He had no idea why that might be. but it didn't help him react sensibly when he saw that his son was missing.

"Where is Rothgar?" he repeated, eyes narrowing. It seemed obvious from the way Ulf was avoiding his gaze that he was hiding something from him.

"I… I think he might have gone to the tree house."

Steinar relaxed. So what if he had? Going to play wasn't forbidden, even if it was early to have left the hut. But he'd dreaded to hear much worse.

"The tree house," he said in a breath, relief washing through him. He'd been getting himself agitated for nothing. He really had to calm down, understand what was bothering him and start behaving in a manner he could be proud of. Hadn't he thought only the other day that, now that he was free from his late wife's hold over his life, he could start being himself again? It was time to start.

"He's only little," Ulf carried on. "It's not his fault he misses *Moðir* so much."

"Of course, it's normal. I never said it wasn't."

Why did the boy think he would be angry at Rothgar for missing his mother—or going to the tree house, for that matter? Steinar knew all too well that his son missed Astrid. Had he not gone to nestle in Cwenthryth's arms the other night for that very reason, because he'd needed to cuddle in a woman's warmth? As much as he would have liked to comfort the boy, feminine softness was not something he, his father, could offer him.

Realization hit.

Suddenly he had a very good idea why Rothgar might have gone to the tree house in the middle of the night—and why Ulf might be reluctant to admit to it. He also saw with clarity why he had not felt himself these last few days. Because his mind was full of Cwenthryth. Full of images of her lying on the pallet like a Saxon goddess of sensuality trying to lure weak mortals like him into her arms.

It was time to put an end to it.

"Stay here," he instructed his son.

Determined to see if his gut feeling was correct, Steinar stormed out the door. Just as he reached the oak at the edge of the forest, he saw Rothgar place his foot on the top rung of the ladder hanging from the tree house. In his fist was a scrap of cloth tied in knots so as to resemble an animal—a rabbit, if the long ears were to be trusted.

Cwenthryth.

It made no doubt that she was the one who'd created the animal, just like it made no doubt she was sleeping in the hut, despite him having sent her away two days ago. Would he never be rid of the woman? No matter how many times he'd asked her to go, it seemed she was still here in the village. Steinar gritted his teeth as he watched his son descend the ladder. When he saw who was waiting for him at the bottom, the little boy's eyes went wide as cartwheels, betraying both guilt and alarm.

"*Faðir?*"

"Go inside the hut and stay with Ulf. We'll talk later."

"Please, don't be angry at me."

"I'm not," Steinar replied curtly.

And he wasn't. Rothgar had not done anything wrong. He missed his mother, that was all. No, his anger was directed at another person, one who shamelessly exploited this weakness for her own benefit.

He grabbed the rope ladder and hoisted himself up.

"I KNEW you'd want another anim—"

Cwenthryth froze, the knotted fox in her hand. Appearing in the doorway, blocking all the light was not Rothgar, back for another rag pet, but his father. His formidable, even more furious than usual father.

"I don't want any of your damned animals," he snarled, coming forward with all the deadly intent of a predator. "Or anything else from you."

"Steinar."

His name escaped her lips with what little breath had not yet been stolen by dread. But really, it would have been a miracle not to be impressed. No man had ever looked more menacing than he did in that moment.

"Yes, Steinar. Why do you look so surprised? Had you forgotten I existed? Had you forgotten I asked you to leave?"

"No." How could she, when she knew she had nowhere safe to go? "But I—"

"You thought to use my sons against me, is that it? You forced them to choose a camp, no doubt with the promise of those bloody flat cakes or more of your pathetic, limp animals!" He gestured at the rags Rothgar had found for her with as much distaste as if they had been soaked in pig's urine. "You thought that if they begged me to let you stay, I'd not be able to resist and would eventually agree."

Her hold on the little fox tightened, as if in search of support. "No, I swear, I didn't do any of that. They were the ones who suggested—"

"Well, let me tell you, it's not going to work."

She'd never thought it would, because she'd never thought to take advantage of the sweet little boys' good nature. She had been desperate, and they had offered her a solution she had gratefully taken. But she had known it could only be temporary. In fact, she had made up her mind to leave today, before she was found out.

Well, too late for that.

Cwenthryth placed the rag fox on one of the stools hoping Rothgar would find once she was gone. "Please, Steinar, don't be angry at the boys, don't punish them. They only thought to help me."

"Help you. So you're sticking to your story, even after all I've found out about you?"

Anger flashed through her, giving her the strength to stand up to him. "It's not a story! It's the truth!"

What was wrong with him? Why could he not believe her? She did need to flee from a man, and she had thought to find refuge in the Norsemen village. This was not such an implausible story. She had not claimed to have been sent to his door by a soothsayer who'd predicted she would marry a blond man whose name matched his stony personality, or to have stumbled in the village while running away from King William, the new Norman king. No, what was happening to her was unfortunately far too common.

Something changed in Steinar's eyes and he took a step forward. "You want to stay with me, then?"

"Yes." The word escaped her lips before she could think because it was the truth. A few days ago she might have said she *needed* to stay with him, but now she knew she *wanted* to stay with him and the boys.

Another step. He was now dangerously close. "You want the protection I can offer?"

"Yes." But not only that. Strangely enough, considering his behavior toward her, she felt at home here, in the village, in his hut that smelled so good. It was inexplicable, given his attitude toward her, but she did feel as if the two of them had been meant to meet.

"Is that the only thing you want from me, I wonder?"

With those words he caged her in against the wall, turning her away first so that her back was to him. Her heart started to beat a wild rhythm that had nothing to do with alarm. How odd. Had anyone else trapped her thus, she would have panicked. Every time Godfrid had come within touching distance of her, she had died inside. Yet now she felt alive, vibrant.

"What else could I want from you?" she said, her voice hoarse.

"This."

When he brought his body in contact with hers, Cwenthryth felt something hot and hard press against the small of her back. She was not an innocent, she knew exactly what it was. It was the proof that, despite his anger, he desired her. Her throat went dry. *Did* she want this?

Yes. If she were honest with herself, she would admit that she had wanted this from the moment she had met the tall, striking

Norseman, only she had not dared to acknowledge it. How could she not have been attracted to him? He was so different from the man she was trying to flee, so obviously protective, despite the apparent gruffness. The way he held his sons and talked to them betrayed a caring, loving nature, one she wanted aimed at her for once.

"Answer me, Cwenthryth, and do not think of lying, because as you can see, I've almost lost the ability to think straight," Steinar rasped. He did sound like a man about to lose control, but she still wasn't afraid. "I will stop if you tell me to, but it will have to be now. So. Answer me. Do you want this?"

Another nudge made his meaning clear. And suddenly there was only one answer she could have given him, because her whole body was on fire.

"Yes."

"You're not afraid of me, despite the way I talk to you," he growled in her ear. It was not a question, he seemed to have seen that for himself. "You don't push me away, despite the way I act." Two hands landed on her breasts, the gesture possessive. She bit her lips to repress a moan. "Why is that?"

Easy, Cwenthryth thought. She wasn't afraid because there was another man who scared her, a Saxon far more dangerous than he would ever be. The Norseman might be fearsome in appearance and growl more than he spoke, but he would never raise a hand to her, he would never cause her any bodily harm. The woman in her knew the difference between the two men, and *that* was why she didn't push him away.

"Because I know you would never hurt me," she found herself answering.

There was a silence. Steinar was still pressed tight against her, his hardness digging into the small of her back, his body caging hers, engulfing hers. So domineering, yet so careful. So hot. "No, I would never hurt a woman. Are you a virgin?"

"No." He grunted, and she wondered if he distrusted her word, as he usually did.

"Mm. So you are not afraid and you are not untouched. You want me." His mouth was still at her ear, his voice had gone smooth as silk. Cwenthryth closed her eyes in delight. She could get used to this new, sensual side of Steinar. "Answer me this then. Do you want me to fuck you? Here? Now?"

Oh, why was he being so crude? Why did it arouse her so? And why did she give her answer with such eagerness? "Yes."

"Very well." The growl in her ear caused all the hairs at the back of her neck to stand up on end. "I'll fuck you then."

Yes. Preferably before she expired from need. Feeling him hard against her, ready to take her, had made her chest flare up and her bones sizzle. Or something equally bewildering. There was only one thing she needed to tell him.

"Please, don't be rough."

Not like him.

"Rough." The word was said in what sounded like a bark. Gone was the silky smoothness that had captured her senses earlier. Steinar's whole body had tensed up, as if in protest. "I'm a Norseman, a Barbarian, therefore I must be rough with women, take them like a brute, is that what you mean?"

"No, it's not," she breathed, horrified to have sounded as if she thought him capable of hurting his lovers. She did not. This was her issue entirely, it had nothing to do with him being a Norseman. Godfrid had been rough, and yet he was a Saxon.

What she'd meant was that she needed Steinar to not do anything that would frighten her and cause her arousal to change into dread. As much as she wanted him, she knew that if he did anything that reminded her of her tormentor, she would freeze. And she didn't want that. She wanted to enjoy his touch to the full, melt into his arms. She was a woman like any other. Didn't she deserve to know how it felt to be taken by a man she'd chosen? It was the first time it had happened, and it had happened when she had lost all hope she would ever feel desire for anyone. It was a miracle, and she didn't want anything to ruin the moment. She sensed Steinar would be a good lover, and she owed it to herself to know the joy men and women were supposed to experience together. Eahlswith had told her that it was glorious. Thus far, Cwenthryth had only known painful and frightening. She wanted glorious.

She was ready for it.

"No, I don't think that," she repeated. "But you're angry with me, and—"

"I am angry, and yet I'm desperate for you." Another nudge against her proved it. He was hard as…well, as stone. "I cannot explain it and I hate it. Which is why I'm going to punish you for thinking you can take advantage of my weakness, for thinking you can just have me when it pleases you, for making me want you more than I want my next breath."

Punish her? She stiffened. That sounded exactly like what she didn't want to happen. "Please, no, I won't—"

He cut her off by wrapping his body around her once more. "Not in the way you think. I swear I won't hurt you." His mouth at her ear, his voice reduced to a purr, he delivered his threat. "On the contrary. I'll be so gentle that it won't be long before you beg me to fuck you harder. But I'll deny you for as long as I want, for as long as it is good for me. I'll keep sliding in and out of you too slowly for you to get what you need. Only when I'm satisfied you've understood who is in charge will I start pounding into you. And I will make myself come, regardless of whether you've achieved your release or not. Do you understand? This will be for me, not for you."

Oh, Lord.

Cwenthryth had never heard anything half as scandalous in her life—and it aroused her like nothing else ever had. Her body had gone liquid, so much so that she barely registered it when Steinar took a step back, releasing her. Hands at her hips, he made her take a step backward, then he pressed on the place between her shoulder blades to signify she should lower her chest. A moment later, she was bent over at the waist, with both her hands braced against the wall and her legs spread wide, in a shocking position of submission. Everything within her melted, when it perhaps should have rebelled. But there was no "should" about this whole situation. It was what it was.

Inevitable.

She only understood he had lifted the hem of her gown when she felt cool air brush against her intimate folds. This was it. She closed her eyes, readying herself for the assault she'd unwittingly provoked. In a moment Steinar would tear at his braies and slam deep inside—

"Ah!"

What was that? She'd been expecting a hard, pulsing shaft to push past her entrance and instead she got a soft, wet...*tongue*? Surely that wasn't right? Surely men didn't put their tongues in women's—

Another lick, another jolt.

Dear God, what was that?

Then Steinar's earlier words came back to her and she understood what was happening. He meant to torture her. He'd said he would be so gentle that she would beg him to fuck her hard. This would be his way of doing it. He would deny her the part of him she craved the most, and watch as she suffered. But Cwenthryth didn't think she would beg him to do anything different. She didn't want hard, she'd endured it too many times. She wanted gentle. His tongue was just perfect, hot and soft, and impossibly smooth; she wanted nothing else. He'd thought to torment her, instead he was gifting her with the most intimate, selfless pleasure anyone could offer.

She risked a glance back and whimpered at the sight meeting her gaze. The most forbidding, masculine, authoritative man she knew was on his knees with the sole intent of making her melt. It seemed too good to be true.

"Yes, Steinar," she moaned, arching her back to bring her folds closer to his mouth. "Lick me."

Her eyes flew open in shock. Was she really encouraging a man to lick her, rubbing herself over his face, demanding more? It seemed that she was, because he groaned and started to flick his tongue over a place she had discovered during her tentative nightly explorations. He was more skilled at bringing it to life than she was. Under his ministrations, she was soon panting with delight. Yes, she needed more of this gentle suckling, this sensual torture. Slow and assured, a finger pushed into her, teasing her a moment, before a second one joined it, adding yet another dimension to the wonderful sensation of his tongue swirling between her legs. Heat gathered momentum, blood raced to the point Steinar was still licking and Cwenthryth took fright.

She was going to collapse, she was going to die, she was going to—

The keening noise she made when pleasure crashed over her would have shocked her had all her attention not been on staying upright and breathing. So *this* was pleasure!

Complete, unadulterated pleasure. It had been, just as Eahlswith had promised, glorious.

And, held as she was by two strong hands, there was nothing she could do but take it.

Steinar jumped back to his feet and ripped at his braies, almost tearing the laces in his haste to feel Cwenthryth against him. Here it was at last, the moment she would beg him to take her, hard, fast, and deep, the moment he would sink into her scalding softness. He rubbed his impossibly hard shaft against her swollen folds. She was so wet, he could easily glide up and down along the intimate seam in a delicate caress.

She'd said she was not a virgin, despite the man in town hinting at the contrary, and for once he didn't think to doubt her because it meant he could have her with scruples, and without causing her pain. Hadn't she come to the village on the understanding that "Astrid's brother" might want to bed her, as a reward for welcoming her in?

Well, Astrid's widower wanted to fuck her, as a way of easing the need boiling in his loins. He wanted it badly.

"Yes," Cwenthryth moaned again, sounding ready for another release. "Just like that."

No, not like that, stroking her was not enough, damn it all, he needed to be inside her. The taste of her lingering on his tongue was sending him mad with need, the wet flesh massaging his shaft was bringing him closer and closer to release with each move. He was hard enough to hammer nails and desperate to push into the entrance so daringly offered to him. But he would not take her before she begged. This was supposed to be a punishment, he was supposed to be in charge, she was supposed to crave his touch. When would she beg him to fuck her? He'd thought to torment her, but he was the one suffering, the one desperate for more, the one about to beg.

And no wonder.

It had been too long—years—since he'd bedded a woman properly, the way he wanted. As soon as Rothgar had been weaned, Astrid had refused him access to her bed. Of course, at that point they had already stopped having marital relations. From the moment she'd known she was with child, she'd been too uncomfortable to allow him to touch her, then later on she'd had to recover from the birth. All in all, they had not shared any intimacy in over a year when she announced her decision.

"I refuse to bear another child, do you hear?" she'd snapped.

"It was hard enough giving birth twice, but losing a third child was even worse. I can't bear to have such a thing happen ever again."

Steinar could only agree. She'd had a hard time of it all, but going back to her bed didn't mean he wanted more children, only that he wanted a real marriage, and to recapture some of the happiness they had enjoyed in the months after their wedding.

"I understand, but there are ways to prevent conception," he soothed. "I can always withdraw, like I did for years, between the two births. You could also take plants to—"

"No, I don't want to risk it. I've given you two sons. It will have to be enough."

None of his entreaties had worked. Incapable of forcing a woman, be she his wife, to do anything she was not comfortable with, Steinar had had no other choice but to respect her wishes. For long months, he'd seen to his needs himself. Eventually, starved of pleasure, Astrid had relented, but not completely. She'd let him caress and lick her and had even offered him relief with her hand and mouth on occasion. But the only way she had allowed him to possess her had been anally. It had not been the same. Steinar didn't want to rut like an animal to reach his release. He'd wanted what he was missing, her womanly softness and the connection of two people getting lost in the pleasure they gave one another. Each encounter made him feel worse than the last, used, unwanted, and soiled.

In the end, he had been the one putting an end to these couplings which offered him little satisfaction.

He could have gone to another woman, of course, and tell his wife why he was doing it, but fool that he was, he had not thought it an option. What he craved was not physical release, but intimacy, a happy family, and a wife who was eager to bed him. Perhaps in time he would get it back, so it was worth the wait.

Astrid, he now knew, had had no such scruples in breaking her vows. Had the Saxon in town been her only lover? Had she allowed him to possess her in every way he wanted, despite the risks? Had she ended up falling with Aldred's child? Was that why she had decided to abandon her family? It was not impossible.

Well, none of this mattered now, not when he was moments away from getting what he'd not had for years—a hot, responsive woman in his arms.

He carried on rubbing Cwenthryth's sweet folds, relishing the idea that soon, he would get to plunge inside the softness he'd missed so much. To his surprise, though, this was almost as satisfactory. The anticipation of the release to come was delicious, almost as pleasurable as the possession itself. He could feel that Cwenthryth's body was ready to welcome him in, the wetness coating his hardness proved it. He also could hear her desperation. Her moans were getting louder and louder, more and more scandalous, encouraging him to carry on. Unable to resist, he reached around to stroke her intimately, intent on breaking through her last vestige of reserve, on making her beg at last. She arched her back and whimpered—but still she didn't ask for more. And then she spasmed again, the ripples he could feel against the taut, sensitive skin of his shaft pushing him over the edge in turn.

Steinar erupted, panting in shock and pleasure combined, his seed coating Cwenthryth's buttocks, the color a perfect match for her creamy skin. What the hell? This release had been nothing like what he'd expected, nothing like what he'd thought he wanted. It had happened with a woman he'd only touched to teach her a lesson, and yet inexplicable as it was, he was thoroughly satisfied. Because there had been intimacy, he had felt how much she wanted him. She had relished every stroke, every caress, and he'd not felt sullied.

As soon as he removed his hands from Cwenthryth's waist she dropped to the floor. For a long moment she lay on her side, hugging her knees, muttering to herself, screwing her eyes shut.

"I never knew… I thought all men—rough… I never knew…"

What was she saying? He could barely understand her through the sobs. Well, one thing was for sure. He could not go now, leave her like this, alone, huddled in a ball, crying her heart out, and demand she leave, as she should have done two days ago.

He was not such a bastard.

Hastily, Steinar tucked himself back into his braies and scooped her up in his arms. Sitting on the floor with his back against the wall, he cradled her in his lap as he would Rothgar when the little boy was prey to a nightmare. Well, not quite. The hold around her was sensual rather than comforting, and the sensations bubbling in his groin right now were absent when he held his son.

"It's all right. I never knew either," he found himself telling her.

After so long wishing he could get back inside a woman, he'd not known he could find so much satisfaction without actually doing it. Having never bedded anyone in anger before, he'd not known fury could transform into a blaze of lust such as could burn everything in its path. With Cwenthryth, everything had been different, new. He'd not been the dominant partner he usually enjoyed being. Licking her and tasting her pleasure had brought him to the brink of release. Feeling her spasming against his cock had been enough to push him over the edge.

"I had no idea I could feel so much pleasure with someone who makes me so mad. And I'm not sure what to think either. This was all too—"

It was only when Cwenthryth lifted her head to him, confusion etched on her face, that he realized he had spoken in Norse.

What the hell was happening?

Only a moment ago, he'd been beside himself with anger, intent on making her pay for manipulating him, for lying about the situation she was facing, for taking advantage of the people he loved, and here he was, recovering from the most shocking release of his life, cradling the woman he'd considered his enemy, and whispering words in her ear she couldn't even understand.

He was really a fool.

"*Faðir?*"

Everything within Steinar lurched. No! Not now!

He deposited Cwenthryth next to him and shot to his feet before Ulf could enter. Young as he was, he would understand why his father had spent so long in the tree house if he saw him and Cwenthryth in each other's arms. The last thing he needed was for other people to know what had just happened.

His son's blond head appeared in the door frame. "Everything all right?"

He sounded nervous, as if worried Steinar would have strangled Cwenthryth. No, he had not strangled her, he'd not even hurt her. Quite the opposite. But she'd been crying, which would look bad. What would Ulf think when he noticed? What could they offer as an explanation for her tears? The truth, namely that she'd been overwhelmed by the strength of the pleasure he'd given her, was out of the question.

Mercifully, Cwenthryth had started to tidy up her makeshift pallet, a good way of hiding her red eyes and wet cheeks from the boy. He was grateful to her for the effort.

"Yes, everything is fine. Cwenthryth and I were having a discussion that's all," he told his son rather gruffly.

He was finding it hard to behave normally with his body feeling so languid. Even his mind seemed to have difficulty functioning. It was as if everything had melted inside him, every knot, every tension, every stiffness had dissolved, leaving only a sense of peace he hadn't known for years.

"Come. Let us go back to the hut and break our fast." He glanced back to the corner of the tree house and his decision was made in a heartbeat. "Cwenthryth, please join us."

8

———

As she finished the last spoonful of gruel sweetened with honey, Cwenthryth wondered the same thing she had wondered all week. What would happen next?

Steinar had invited her to eat something in the hut because he'd not wanted to give his sons cause to worry, but she could tell his wishes had not changed despite the intimacy they'd just shared. If anything, things had gone even more awkward between them. The look in his eyes when he finally dared to look at her was telling.

He wasn't sure how to handle what had happened, but he still didn't trust her, and he still wanted her gone—the sooner, the better.

She cleared her throat. This time, there would be no hiding anywhere in the village. She wouldn't put it past him to escort her back into town himself to make sure she was gone for good.

This time it was really over.

She stood up and placed her empty bowl on top of the other three. Should she offer to wash them? Would it not be seen as an attempt to prolong the moment and ease her way into Steinar's good graces? Well, what if it was, she thought with a sudden burst of anger? It hardly mattered. He already thought she was trying to take advantage of him and his sons' good nature. Nothing she did now would change that, so she might as well be polite and act as she would in normal circumstances, stay true to her principles.

Without a word, Cwenthryth took the bowls and spoons and headed toward the river. No one tried to stop her.

While she washed the bowls with quick, efficient gestures, she observed the view offered to her. The trees were vibrant with different shades of green, the sun was high in the sky and warm on her back. Summer was still in full bloom, but soon the days would start to shorten, the food would become scarce, the cold would settle over the land for months on end. It made it more imperative than ever for her to find a permanent refuge. Sleeping in ditches would not be an option in winter. Perhaps she could go south and not stop until she'd reached the sea, leave her old life behind, and start in a place where no one knew her.

Where no one would doubt her story.

Gritting her teeth against a fresh onset of tears, she stood up. She was done feeling sorry for herself, since no one cared anyway.

When she came back to the hut, she found herself walking alongside a young woman who arched a brow when she saw that she was headed toward Steinar's hut with clean bowls and spoons in her hand. Her surprise was understandable, as it looked like a very domestic arrangement. The girl, obviously someone from the village, would be wondering who was this Saxon woman who appeared to live with Steinar and washed his dirty dishes.

When it became obvious the two of them were going the same way, the Norsewoman smiled and Cwenthryth ended up telling her her name. It seemed silly to ignore one another until they reached the hut, where introductions would become inevitable.

"I'm Rowena," the girl answered, "Caedmon and Ingrid's daughter. The goldsmith and his wife?" she added, when Cwenthryth's expression made it clear she had no idea who those people might be.

"I'm sorry, but I'm afraid I don't really know anyone in the village. I... Apart from Steinar, that is."

Oh, yes, she definitely knew who *he* was. She knew him so well that she could still feel the tremors he'd created in her body earlier that morning. His caresses had been as scandalous as could be, and yet she'd not been embarrassed, as if they had shared such intimacies a hundred times before, as if men as virile as him were supposed to go down on their knees to pleasure women in such a selfless manner, plunge their tongue inside them and make them—

"And I know his sons, of course," she added, pushing the lewd thoughts away. What was she doing, thinking of such things while talking to another person? "And his sister, Eyja, and Moon, and little Frida. I have met Rorik as well, but only very briefly."

She was rambling now, but it was no wonder. She had just spotted Steinar standing in the doorframe. No doubt the sound of voices coming his way had drawn him out of the hut. He was glowering, as he was wont to do every time someone talked to her. No doubt he would be thinking that she was trying to get Rowena to side with her before leaving, which she was not.

Unfortunately, at that moment, they came to a stop in front of the hut and the girl said the one thing guaranteed to raise his hackles.

"Never mind. You'll be able to meet everyone tomorrow."

"What's tomorrow?" Cwenthryth asked, doing her best to avoid looking at Steinar. Not that it mattered what was planned for the following day, as she would be long gone by then.

"My wedding. I'm marrying Thorfinn, the blacksmith's son." Rowena's cheeks went a beautiful pink color, betraying her joy at the prospect. "Our fathers have been working together for years, and we practically grew up together. It was only a question of time before we fell in love, I suppose."

It was an interesting way of seeing things. Eyja had told her more or less the same thing the day she'd given birth to her daughter, that she had married an old childhood friend who'd suddenly become more. Cwenthryth had never thought such a man would ever tempt her into matrimony. All the boys she had grown up with seemed somehow immature. Or perhaps they were not, and the issue was with her; but she still saw them as the children they had once been. That made it impossible, in her mind, to see them as men who could rouse irresistible desire inside her. In bed with them, she would feel too self-conscious, as if they were doing something wrong. She would much rather fall under the spell of a handsome stranger, be struck by his masculine presence the first time she laid eyes on him.

That idea was so much more exciting.

Well, on principle, it was. Because in reality, of course, handsome strangers were more prone to glower at her and send her to hell than fall under her spell. She should know. Such a man was standing in front of her right now, and it was clear he didn't see her as the answer to his life's questions.

"I'm sorry, but I won't be here tomorrow. I was actually about to leave the village," Cwenthryth hurried to tell Rowena, not wanting to give Steinar any more reasons to think her a schemer.

The girl looked horrified, as if her departure had been intended as a personal slight. "Oh no, you can't leave now! You absolutely have to stay another day at least, and celebrate with us. The more, the merrier. My brother, Haakon, will be glad to have someone new to meet, especially a woman as lovely as you."

Cwenthryth thought she heard Steinar growl, and the sound sent shivers all down her spine. Dear Lord. Eyja had told her that his name meant stone, and she'd agreed that it was a fitting name. Then she'd found out the previous day that his father's name was

Wolf, and here he was, all-out growling like the wild beast. What else would she find out about him? Was the cloak he wore in winter made from the pelt of some fearsome animal, an animal he shared his gruff temper with?

"Please. Say you'll come," Rowena pressed, taking her hand in hers.

Cwenthryth had no idea why her presence mattered so much to the girl. They didn't know one another, they had only just met. Had she promised her brother she would find him a bride from outside the village and she'd finally seen a chance to make good on that promise? Was that what this was about? Was this Haakon looking to settle and his sister thought she could help?

She was about to refuse, but then she realized that she was done with having a man who had no right over her decide what she could or could not do. For a whole year she'd endured that precise same thing and hated it. But it was over now. There was no reason she couldn't accept Rowena's kind invitation. Steinar did not own her. If he didn't want to have her sleep under his roof tonight, then he didn't have to. She could go to the tree house for one last night, or even to Moon and Eyja's. She was certain they would welcome her in, even if she preferred to be on her own. Or she could sleep in a ditch, if she had to. She'd done it once, she could do it again.

In any case, she would be there tomorrow to celebrate the new couple's union.

She smiled at Rowena, feeling happier than she had in weeks.

"I will be delighted to come, thank you."

THAT NIGHT, without asking for permission, Cwenthryth went to sleep in the tree house. Though Steinar had to have suspected her intention, he did nothing to stop her. It was not quite an agreement, but as close to one as she would ever get from him.

As soon as she entered the small space, she was assaulted by memories of their fiery encounter of the morning. What he had done to her had taken her by complete surprise. Considering how formidable he was in life, she had imagined he would be a demanding, if not downright dominating lover. Instead he'd been tender, generous, patient.

Perfect, exactly what she'd needed.

Without even taking her, he had shown her what lovemaking was all about. When Eahlswith had told her that being with a man was one of the most pleasurable things a woman could experience, Cwenthryth had not believed her. Based on what she had gone through with Godfrid, she'd deemed it both degrading and painful.

In one masterful demonstration, Steinar had changed her opinion forever.

Averting her gaze from the wall where she'd braced herself while he'd devoured her like the wolf he was, she settled on the furs in the corner. Steinar was a beast, yes, in some ways, but one who could be tamed, not a frightening, wild one, nothing like Godfrid, who had been a real monster.

Out of nowhere, another memory assailed her.

Once, a few years ago, Cwenthryth had found herself out of the city walls later than usual—and face-to-face with a lone wolf in search of prey. It was obvious that the animal had been driven out of the protection of the woods by hunger, and yet he had not harmed her, defenceless as she'd been. He'd looked at her a long moment, as if considering what to do, and then trotted away on silent paws.

To this day, she had no idea what had made the animal leave her alone, but she still remembered the dread mingled with fascination she'd felt upon staring into his glowing amber eyes. It was the same fascination she felt when she looked into Steinar's intense blue gaze.

Son of the wolf, indeed.

Despite the turmoil agitating her soul, it wasn't long before she fell into a dreamless sleep, the same restorative sleep she'd slept since the moment she'd arrived in the village.

In the morning, Cwenthryth was awakened by the sound of music. The preparations for the wedding were already under way, it seemed. Smiling in anticipation of the happy day, she scrambled back to her feet. The sight that met her eyes when she walked out of the tree house had her mouth fall open in awe. The whole village had been transformed while she slept. It was like waking up in an enchanted, distant land. The trees were adorned with woven garlands, long tables covered with linen drapings had been positioned around the well, and everyone was wearing their best, most colorful clothes. Even the sky had made an effort. It was stretching over the scene in one gorgeous blue canvas. Cwenthryth could not imagine a more suitable day for celebrating two young people's love. Moved by a fresh burst of optimism, she descended the rope ladder.

"What can I do to help?" she asked Rorik, the first person she recognized in the crowd milling around. He was carrying a stack of stools to the nearest table, displaying impressive strength.

"Cwenthryth, good morning." He didn't seem surprised to see her, as if she belonged in the village. "Perhaps you could go to the hut over there and see what needs to be done? I know it is where the food is being prepared, so they might welcome the help."

"Of course."

A moment later she was chopping onions and herbs to add to an enormous pot of stew. A woman who'd introduced herself as Moon's sister was making dough for rye bread, while her mother, a Saxon woman called Frigyth, was frying oatcakes over the fire. Two other women were cutting legs of smoked lamb into thin slices, and a boy was roasting what looked like a boar on a spit over a second fire. Everyone worked in happy companionship, and Cwenthryth felt as if she had always been part of the community. It was a wonderful feeling.

Finally, everything was ready.

"Let's go," Frigyth said, cleaning her hands in a bowl of water. "I can hear everyone making their way to the river."

"Yes."

Cwenthryth had heard that the ceremony was to be held at the round boulder, like all important moments in the village.

As she took her place alongside everyone, she congratulated herself on having agreed to stay for the wedding. The celebration promised to be joyous, nothing like the ones she was used to. The few weddings she had been to had all been held in the cold town church, and the couples hadn't seemed particularly happy to be there. Rowena and Thorfinn, by contrast, looked as if they were bursting with joy, and their happiness was infectious.

Witnessing such a moment would be the perfect way to steer her mind away from the formidable Norseman dominating her thoughts, and give her courage for what was to come. This glimpse into a simple, carefree life gave her hope for the future. Somehow in the misery and solitude of the last year she had forgotten that there could be happiness and beauty in the world. The reminder was a welcome one.

Cwenthryth watched as Rowena and Thorfinn kissed, the love between them obvious. Her eyes started to burn and she noticed that she was not the only one who had gone emotional, which was little wonder. Having a man look at her thus was every woman's dream. Moon's sister, Aife, whom she'd met in the tent earlier, seemed particularly affected. Did a man from the village make her heartbeat go faster, Cwenthryth wondered? Was she hoping to be the next bride?

Once the ceremony was over, everyone started to make their

way back to the well and the feast waiting for them. Before Cwenthryth could decide where to sit—nowhere near Steinar, obviously—a man with intricately braided hair and a neatly trimmed beard came to stand in front of her.

"Good afternoon. I'm guessing you must be Cwenthryth?" Like most people in the village, he spoke her language without any accent.

"Yes."

The man smiled at her obvious surprise. "I'm Haakon, Rowena's twin brother. I believe she may have mentioned me?"

"She has."

The girl had done more than mention her brother; she'd said he would be delighted to meet someone new. And it seemed she'd been right. The man was smiling at her as if she were the best thing to have happened to him in years. Not quite how Thorfinn had looked at his new bride when their vows had been exchanged, but close enough.

Cwenthryth's heart skipped a beat. Could this be it? Could *he* be the handsome stranger of her dreams? The one who would fall under her spell upon meeting her? He certainly seemed delighted to see her and he was attractive enough. Were all the men in this village as alluring, she wondered? It appeared so. All the ones she had seen so far had been tall, blond, and strong. Haakon was no exception, and he was also in possession of twinkling eyes, a winning smile, and a deep, rich voice. A perfect combination.

And yet… And yet looking at him did not cause her heart to skip any beats.

He was just too tame, too young, too polished, nothing like…

Before she knew what she was doing, she looked to the place where Steinar stood, talking to two other men. Her heart sank. Did she really have to compare everyone to him and find the others lacking? Yes, apparently she did.

She turned her attention back to Haakon, who was waiting for her to resume the conversation.

"Rowena didn't tell me anything about you, though, I'm afraid," she said, deciding all was not lost. Attraction was not always instantaneous. Perhaps tonight she could find out something about Rowena's twin brother that would capture her interest.

The laugh that answered her was honest and deliciously hoarse, yet another point in his favor.

"My sister was being very wise, as always, keeping the less flattering aspects of me to herself." Haakon offered her his arm. "Come on, let's go eat. By the time night has fallen, I'm confident we'll have unwrapped each other's every secret."

9

——————

"I can't."

"Of course you can," Haakon coaxed, his voice going even deeper than usual. "It's easy. Just open your mouth, and put it in. Then swallow. Please. For me. I promise you'll like it."

Cwenthryth warily eyed up the pastry he was handing her. After the longest and most delicious meal of her life, she could not possibly have eaten another thing. She was as full as she had ever been and still Haakon was trying to tempt her. The treat looked delicious, she had to admit, but she knew she could not eat another bite, never mind a whole tart bursting with berries.

"I can't," she repeated.

"It's only a small—"

"Have you suddenly gone deaf, man? She told you she was not hungry."

The growl accompanying the rude declaration could only have been uttered by one person. Cwenthryth was therefore not surprised when she turned to see Steinar standing behind her with eyes like thunder. How did he know the man was trying to entice her into eating one last pastry? Had he been watching them during the meal? Perhaps, and the way he was glaring at Haakon seemed to indicate he hadn't liked anything that had happened that evening.

Well, she'd been watching him as well, and she hadn't liked seeing women throwing themselves at him either. That he had appeared oblivious to their seduction ploys had been small consolation. It had made her feel inadequate and unwanted.

"I think I will go and offer my congratulations to Rowena and Thorfinn," she announced, standing up. She was not going to stay while the two men ripped one another over her. What was Steinar doing anyway? It was not as if he wanted her for himself, was it? He had no right to be upset, any more than she had the right to be jealous of the women vying for his attention. Tomorrow they would go their separate ways.

She left before anyone could point out she had already congratulated the happy couple earlier.

Instead of going to see the newlyweds, however, she took refuge behind the smithy, eager for some privacy. With the bonfires hidden from view, cooling darkness wrapped over her. Only the faint blue light coming from the moon crescent suspended above the thatched roofs prevented her from being swallowed in obscurity.

Cwenthryth sagged against the wall of the forge, feeling utterly dejected. Her plan for finding the man of her dreams hadn't worked. Haakon had been perfectly amiable, but nothing he'd said during the feast had caused her interest to spark, and every time their hands had brushed against one another—more often than necessary, she was sure—his touch had left her cold. The fault for her unresponsiveness no doubt lay with the Norseman currently having words with him. The man she had come to have feelings about.

Yes, that was the obvious explanation behind her misery.

She was developing feelings for Steinar, feelings as far

removed from annoyance and resentment as could be, which was a problem. What had happened in the tree house this morning only made her feel the hopelessness of her situation more keenly. With any other man, she might have been able to build on the connection they had shared, however brief, however purely carnal, but with a man who wanted her out of his life, what could she do? Nothing.

Waiting for him to change his mind about her would lead nowhere, except to more heartache.

The painful irony of it twisted her guts. In the end, Steinar would not have to ask her to leave again; she would do that of her own volition. She had come to him to make sure her body was not abused again, she would now leave to protect her heart. Staying so close to Steinar would only hurt it. Yes, but the problem was, going back to town might prove dangerous. Still, she had to go, make sure Godfrid was gone. Before moving on, she had to see for herself she was really free from him.

Would she find the courage to go tomorrow?

She closed her eyes. A moment later, she felt a presence behind her. Without turning she knew Steinar would be standing by the wrought-iron gate. Her body had recognized him, as it did every time. How had he known where she would be? *Did* he spend his time watching her? She was really starting to wonder.

"Why didn't you tell the man to go to hell?" he growled, when it became obvious she was not going to acknowledge his presence. She couldn't help smiling to herself. Had she not guessed who had come, the mention of hell would have been enough to confirm the man's identity.

"Because I would never do such a thing," she said, finally turning to face him. "That's something you would do, not me." Something he did do on a regular basis, in fact, at least to her. "And anyway, Haakon didn't deserve being sent to hell or being snapped at the way you snapped at him. He was only being nice."

"Nice?" A scoff. "By forcing you to put things you don't want into your mouth and telling you you would like it?"

Cwenthryth shuffled to her feet, suddenly uncomfortable. "That's not what he was—"

"Come," he cut in. "You do know he made it sound like the lewdest possible proposition? Like he was trying to convince you you'd like nothing more than to pleasure him with your mouth?"

Well, no, she had not thought that at the time, but now that Steinar had pointed it out to her, she couldn't help but wonder at Haakon's choice of words and the glint in his eyes when he'd looked at her. Both had been very suggestive, undeniably.

Just open your mouth, and put it in. Then swallow.

Lord. How had she been so naïve? It *had* been a lewd proposition, he *had* imagined her on her knees, offering him her mouth to use for his pleasure. Still, if anyone should take offence at the liberty Haakon had taken, it was her, not Steinar.

Embarrassment and annoyance flashed through her, making her snap. In that moment she did want to send Steinar to hell, and see how he liked the place.

"So what if he made it sound that way? What if he propositioned me?" Steinar shouldn't care, since he did not care anything about her. "What is it to you?"

"You mean you had been about to agree?" he snarled, ignoring her question. "Had I not intervened you would have led him into the woods and sucked him off just for the asking? Is that what you're saying? That you like it when men ram their cocks down your throat, regardless of what you want?"

Cwenthryth's shock was such that for a long while she could not move, or utter a sound, or even breathe. Had he really asked her that question? Had he really talked in such offensive terms to her? When she finally recovered, two things happened, one straight after the other. First heat exploded in her chest—and then she slapped him.

Hard. So hard her hand hurt.

Steinar didn't react, didn't retaliate, didn't say anything, he just stared at her, his eyes glittering in the moonlight. It was impossible to know what he was thinking. The heat in Cwenthryth's chest receded slightly, allowing her to talk.

"How dare you! I do not… I do not…"

The unbearably crude questions had brought her back to what she had endured at Godfrid's hands. And, unfortunately, she knew all too well that she did *not* like it when men used her mouth in that way, regardless of what she wanted.

It was too dark for her to be sure but it seemed to her that Steinar's shoulders had sagged, in defeat or in shame, she wasn't sure. She didn't care either way. The slap hadn't felt like a victory, more like a desperate attempt to hide her hurt, and if he felt guilty for what he'd said, then it was too late anyway. The damage had been done.

He had split her heart in two.

"Cwenthryth, I—"

"Whatever it is, I don't want to hear it. Just stay away from me, do you hear?"

Oh, but her life was decidedly a cursed one. How had she had the misfortune to fall in love with a man who could be so horrible? She'd heard Eyja and Ulf tell her he'd not always been like that, that his new gruffness had been brought on by unhappiness and it might well be true. But this assurance was no good to her, because he certainly was horrible now, incapable of trust and compassion. She had better stay well away from him and preserve what little dignity she had left.

Cwenthryth ran in the direction of the forest, tears blurring her vision. Not that she could see where she was going anyway. Under the cover of the trees, it was so dark that she soon had to come to a halt for her own safety. Anything could be hiding ahead of her. A hole, a low branch, an animal ready to pounce. It was better to stop moving now that she was alone. No sense in hurting herself because of an impossibly overbearing Norseman. He was probably not interested in coming after her, since he thought so lowly of her.

His harsh words rang in her ears in an incessant chant. His silky voice didn't make them any less unbearable.

You like it when men ram their cocks down your throat, regardless of what you want.

She had been shocked to hear that was what he thought, but perhaps it was inevitable that he should think her the most debauched wanton. Hadn't she admitted to not being a virgin this morning? Hadn't she agreed to being, in his own words, "fucked" against a wall? Hadn't she rubbed herself against his mouth in encouragement when he'd devoured her? He had every reason to think she would have followed Haakon into the woods and let him use her in any way he wanted.

All the blood drained from her veins, along with her hopes and dreams. Was that how Steinar would remember her? As a schemer, lying her way into people's homes, using her wiles on the men she could find as a way to trick them into offering her a life of idleness? And this while she remembered him as the first man she had ever had fallen in love with.

Cwenthryth fell to her knees, allowing the tears she had fought to finally spill down her cheeks. It would seem she wasn't done feeling for herself after all.

WHERE WAS CWENTHRYTH? Damn it all to hell, she should have been back by now.

Steinar stared into the darkness to the place where he'd last seen her, willing her to come back, getting increasingly worried. Had she gotten lost in the forest? Fallen into a hole? Hit her head on a low branch? Been attacked by a beast? It was all too possible, but if anything had happed to her, it would be his fault. He had been the one driving her away. He'd been too harsh, he knew it, asked her an unforgivably coarse question. What had possessed him to ask her if she enjoyed having men ramming their—

Bloody hell, he could not even think back to what he'd said without wincing. No matter how riled he'd been at seeing her laugh with another man, he should never have allowed himself to speak to her thus. No wonder she had run away. But she should be back by now. It would not have taken her long to see that he had not launched himself in hot pursuit.

Or…

Or perhaps there was a good reason for her absence, and she was not in any danger whatsoever.

Steinar looked back to the banquet table, wondering. Haakon had disappeared as well. Had he gone in search of Cwenthryth? Had the two of them agreed to go for a tryst in the woods earlier, while they were dancing? Was that where she actually was? With her young suitor, offering him her body? And if she was, why should he care?

He stood up.

Because, damn it all, he did care. Haakon would not get under her skirts, or offer her something other than pastry to put into her mouth, not if Steinar had anything to do with it. Bunching his fists, he headed toward the forest.

Under the trees the obscurity was almost complete, but he pushed on. He could not sit idly by the fire with the others, he had to know where Cwenthryth was—and with whom. Either she was in trouble and she needed help, or she was with that accursed Haakon and she needed… Well, she needed to not be. His sanity depended on it.

He walked a while, making sure to look all around, then stopped dead when he heard a feminine voice on the other side of a clump of bushes. Though it was probably too dark for anyone to see him, he automatically crouched down, because he fully intended to ascertain the identity of the woman before moving on. Only once he was certain that this was not Cwenthryth could he resume his search.

"Not here!" the woman was saying in an urgent whisper. "Someone could see us."

"Here. Now." The man with her sounded equally urgent. "No one will see a thing, 'tis far too dark. I've watched you dance all evening in your new dress. I can't take it anymore. I need you naked and under me. Now."

There was a series of crude Norse words, followed by the unmistakable sound of clothes being discarded in haste.

Everything within Steinar stilled. The two lovers had spoken too low for him to recognize their voices, but he had an awful suspicion he knew who the Norseman might be, and the woman he was trying to entice could all too easily be Cwenthryth.

"Fuck, how is it that every time I touch you, I feel like the sixteen-year-old who fell in love with you?"

Before Steinar could wonder how on earth Haakon could have met Cwenthryth as a youth, the woman answered, her voice little more than a moan.

"I don't know, but it is the same for me. Touch me, Björn, please, kiss me."

Oh, what an unreasonable, ridiculous idiot he really was. The adventurous couple was not the one he'd dreaded to find, it was none other than Björn and his wife Dunne, who had indeed met when he was just a youth.

Thanking his lucky stars he had not pounced on the two lovers before ascertaining who they were, Steinar made to stand up.

Just then someone walked straight into him, compromising his fragile balance—and sent him sprawling to the ground.

Cwenthryth.

This time he did not hesitate. He would have recognized her delicious, liquorice scent anywhere. She fell on top of him, her soft breasts cushioned against his chest, her face buried in the crook of his neck. They remained in this way along moment, not talking, adjusting to the sudden intimacy, trying to contain the wild beating of their hearts.

"Take me now! Hard."

Even though Cwenthryth had not been the one uttering the lewd order, Steinar's whole body surged. It was exactly what he'd hoped she would ask him to do the previous morning in the tree house, and his blood reacted accordingly.

"I thought you didn't want to be taken here?" Björn purred, oblivious to the fact that someone could hear them.

"Will you stop teasing me and just take me!" Dunne exploded.

The noises coming from behind the bushes soon made it clear that her husband was obeying the order with all the passion he was capable of. Steinar closed his eyes, fighting the desire raging in his own body. Cwenthryth still had not slid to the ground and he'd made no move to lift her off him. They were still as close as only lovers could be. She was lying on top of him, her weight delicious, her warmth spreading through his clothes all the way to his skin. He wanted to roll over and do to her what Björn was doing to his wife. He could not; they had to go, now. Having to listen to another man getting his pleasure was more than he could bear at the moment.

"Please, can we leave?" Cwenthryth murmured, her breath hot on the skin of his neck. "This is embarrassing."

Yes. *Embarrassing* was not quite the word he would have used, but they certainly had better leave, before he surrendered to the desire burning his loins. Before long there would be only cinders left. And then he would not be answerable for his actions. But he could not touch her, not after what he'd told her earlier.

"Let's go."

He could not help placing his hands on Cwenthryth's waist before she could scramble back up, to keep her against him a heartbeat longer. By the gods, but she felt so good, so lush and womanly, so pliable and warm. So—

A raw cry split the night, telling them Dunne's body had just gone up in flames.

"Please. Let's leave."

Once they were up, Steinar took Cwenthryth's hand to lead her back to the village. Unlike her, he'd been wandering in these woods since he'd been a child, so despite the lack of light, there was no chance he would ever get lost. He guessed that was what had happened to her. It would explain why she had stayed away so long. It was clear at least that, unlike what he had feared, she had not been waylaid by any young Norsemen looking to use her for their pleasure.

Small mercies.

Not ready to be parted from her yet, he stopped as soon as they got a glimpse of the three fires burning around the long banquet table. To his relief, Cwenthryth did not protest, did not disentangle her fingers from his. Instead, she lifted her head to him. Her eyes were two bottomless pools mirroring the starry night sky above. Steinar could not take his gaze from her. So beautiful. And so... The word that popped in his head was, oddly enough, *innocent*. Odd, considering that not so long ago he'd been certain she was trying to manipulate him.

"Thank you for coming to get me. I was starting to think I would have to wait until morning to find my way back," she murmured.

He nodded. Perhaps his fit of jealousy had had one benefit. Without it, she would still be wandering in the dark woods alone and afraid. It was something, he supposed.

"Listen, I'm sorry," he said, eager to address the issue before it poisoned the air between them. She didn't seem angry any longer, but he knew he'd acted like a fool and he wasn't above admitting it, not when he felt so bad about it. "About what I told you before, about suggesting you liked—"

"It's all right." He guessed from the hoarseness in her tone that she had gone bright red. "It's forgotten. As long as you know I don't—"

"No, I don't. I'm sorry. You should have slapped me harder. It was all I deserved for being so crude." That was why he had not reacted when she'd hit him. Even moments after having uttered the words, he'd know he'd gone too far.

"I don't think I could have done that if my life depended on it. I almost broke my arm in half as it was. Have you ever tried slapping stone?" She gave a tentative smile.

"No, I cannot say I have." He returned the smile.

"I don't recommend it."

Before he knew what he was doing, Steinar raised the hand he was still holding to his lips. It was the right one, the one she had used to slap him. "Here. Let me kiss it better." Gaze planted into hers, he repeated, speaking against the fragrant skin of her palm, "I truly am sorry."

"I know. But, please, I don't want to talk about this ever again."

"Of course." But before he laid the topic to rest, there was still one question he needed to ask her. "You are not seriously considering letting the pup woo you, though, are you?" Steinar asked, unable to let it go.

He had to know if she was interested in Rowena's brother, because the man was indeed looking to settle down, and he'd often jested that he would like to find a Saxon bride, like so many men in the village had done before him. Would Cwenthryth be interested in the prospect of a Norse husband? It was not impossible. And yet it was…well, impossible. He would never bear to see her settled in the village as another man's bride.

Not that he wanted to marry her himself, of course. He wanted her gone. Now more than ever, because he could not ignore any longer that she was not good for his peace of mind. Or for keeping control over his body's urges. Or for helping him to think straight.

"Haakon is not so young," she defended, sidestepping the question.

Perhaps not, and admittedly, he was a grown man, able to provide for a family, but he was still a good decade younger than Steinar was. Perhaps that was the source of his annoyance. He felt inadequate when compared to a young, attractive, more personable man. He was already three-and-thirty, not three-and-twenty anymore, and he had two children, something some women might find hard to accept. Haakon was much closer to Cwenthryth in age, he didn't live with anyone, and his winning smile would be a stark—and no doubt welcome—contrast to his own scowling countenance. Why would she not want to give him a chance, now that she knew he was interested? She was free to do so, was she not?

"He's younger than me," he said, rather needlessly.

"Yes. Too young, really. I've always preferred older, more mature men."

Steinar blinked. Had she really said that? Had she meant for him to hear the confession? And what was she saying? *He* was older, more mature. Was she saying that she preferred him? Something in his chest leaped at the thought.

Before he could wonder any further, she took a step back, eased her hand from his, and spoke again.

"I wanted to stay for the wedding because Rowena was kind enough to ask me and I'm glad I did. But I will leave in the morning, don't worry."

"I'm not worried." If he were honest, her presence here was no longer a concern. He'd once been eager to see her go, but he was now wondering if he wouldn't have preferred her to stay. Which was the real worrying thing.

Since their fiery encounter in the tree house, his mind was full of her, so much so that he was barking at his friends for no reason and getting jealous, something that had never happened before. His body was consumed with the need to possess her, so much so that he'd spent the day in an almost constant state of arousal.

In short, he was losing control, and this when he had to focus on sorting out a new chapter of his life, adjust to being a widower, and ensure his sons' happiness.

So yes, he could only agree that she had better leave.

"Yes," he said, taking a step back himself. "I think it's for the best."

10

"Cwenthryth! What are you doing here?" Eahlswith exclaimed as soon as she'd opened the door. "Where have you been? Are you back for good? Are you all right? Actually, never mind the rest, answer me this one question first, are you all right?"

Cwenthryth fell into her friend's arms, sobbing. "Yes. I'm all right."

Or at least, she would be, eventually. Right now, she was not quite sure. There had been a weight pressing down her chest since she had left the Norsemen village—and the man she had come to love—and she didn't know how long it would take for it to go away.

"I've been so worried over you! You disappeared without a word, and after what happened, I thought perhaps you had decided to—"

"No, I didn't kill myself," Cwenthryth murmured, understanding what Eahlswith had not dared say. "I went to see a friend in another village, thinking that time away from home would help."

There was no need to tell her more about the "friend" in question, say that he was in fact the most compelling man she had ever met, and that he had shown her pleasure beyond her wildest imaginings—or that he wanted nothing to do with her, even though that was the painful truth.

Foolishly, she had hoped Steinar would try to stop her when she'd announced she would leave in the morning. He had not. Despite what they had shared in the tree house, he had let her go, and she knew they would never meet again. They had no reason to.

Eahlswith nodded, reassured. "Well, I'm proud of you for doing what you needed to do. How are you?"

Her friend was the only person who knew about what she had gone through in the last year. Cwenthryth was not sure she would have found the courage to tell her about her ordeal if left to her own device but in the end, there had been no other choice. Eahlswith had come to visit her the day she had lost her baby, and found her bleeding on the pallet. After she'd helped her deal with the awful mess, she had listened to her story, never judging once, never asking why she had not left her home yet, never made her feel bad for not being able to stand up to her tormentor. This acceptance had been the best gift anyone had given her.

"I'll be fine," she repeated, willing it to be true.

"Come. You look in need of something to eat and drink. I was about to eat anyway, so everything is ready."

The two women settled in front of a platter laden with cheese, smoked fish, boiled eggs, and bread. Eahlswith added a handful of nuts and a few plums for good measure, and poured two cups of small ale. Cwenthryth ate gratefully, as she been too nervous to break her fast that morning.

Once their cups of ale were empty, she finally asked the question she needed to ask.

"Do you know if Godfrid is still here?"

Had he finally left? Gone back to wherever he'd come from? It had now been over a week since she had disappeared without a trace. He would have every reason to think she'd gone for good, and having no one else to torment in the house, he might well have decided to go find himself another victim. This was the reason she had dared venture into the town under the cover of darkness, just before the gates were closed.

"I know not where he is," Eahlswith answered, toying with her plum. "I didn't dare go anywhere your house, in case he started asking me questions about your whereabouts. I haven't seen him at the market but that is not saying much."

"No."

Cwenthryth knew he sometimes disappeared for days on end, visiting friends he never talked about, probably individuals that were just as disreputable as he was. His absences would have been the perfect moment to leave and give herself a few days' head start, but she'd refused to leave her father at his mercy. The old man had taken to his bed shortly after Godfrid's arrival. Weak and confused as he had been, there had been no way she could have taken him with her, and she'd refused to abandon him to the usurper.

Well, the vile man might have finally left town. There was only one way to find out if he had. Tomorrow morning she would have to go back to the house and see for herself. It was a risk, but she had to know where she stood. Her stay in the Norsemen village had not been all in vain. It had given her courage. She now knew she could be desired by worthy men, she had stood her ground against an irate Steinar, she had made herself useful, and been welcome in a wonderful community. She felt stronger, no longer the timid creature she'd been reduced to by a year of misery.

"I will go and see what I can find out tomorrow."

"Do you want me to come with you?" Eahlswith asked, ever the helpful friend.

"No, thank you. I have to do this alone."

She could not place her friend in danger if Godfrid was here. And if he wasn't here, then she didn't need her, or anyone else to witness the outpouring of anguish that would inevitably follow her return to a place where she had suffered so much.

The night was spent tossing and turning on the pallet Eahlswith had provided her. But not all the nightmarish visions had to do with Godfrid and the awful memories he invoked. Some of them were caused by Steinar. Over and over again she heard his accusations. She was a liar, a wanton, she wanted to manipulate his sons, she liked men using her mouth for their pleasure.

It was awful, piercing her heart with a thousand shards.

When she woke up, unsurprisingly, she was exhausted. Gone were the nights of good sleep she'd had in the Norsemen village.

"You look awful," Eahlswith told her when she got up, blunt as ever.

"I feel awful, that must be why."

"Do you want something to eat? I went to get fresh bread."

"No. I don't think I'll be able to eat anything until I know where I stand. Don't worry about me, I'll be back before tonight, whatever happens."

With those words, she walked out of the house. No sense in putting the inevitable off any longer. A moment later, she was in front of her door, her face hidden under the hood of a cloak Eahlswith had lent her. She asked a young boy to go knock on the door, offering him a slice of buttered bread as a reward. No answer. After waiting another moment in case Godric had simply stepped out, she went to knock herself.

Still no answer.

Cwenthryth pushed the door with a tentative hand. It opened straight away, indicating Godfrid had not put the wooden bar across. Relief caused her shoulders to relax, because she now knew for certain he was not here. He'd always been very particular about keeping the door barred at all times when he was in the house. If it was open, it meant he was not in.

She walked forward.

It was the smell that hit her first, and caused her to curl up into a ball. All at once everything came rushing back to her. Her father's passing, Godfrid's assaults, the loss of her baby. Her chest tightened unbearably, stealing all her breath. So much pain in so short a time. How was she going to recover from what she had endured in the last year? How was she to carry on without her father?

Without Steinar?

The panic flooding through her was so great that she barely registered the state of the house. When she did, she understood Godfrid had indeed left for good. It was the only way to explain the sight in front of her. Having taken all he could take from her and her father, he had moved on, but not before destroying all he could destroy in a last act of spite.

Dry-eyed, she took in the devastation.

The table in the middle of the room was the only thing left intact, presumably because it was too heavy to be broken apart. Everything else was shattered, dislocated or torn to shreds. All her childhood memories, gone. All her possessions, ruined.

Well. Godfrid had made her decision easy. She would leave and settle as she'd wanted, in a small village, close to nature, away from the place that had become her prison, and start a new life, one where she was free.

True happiness seemed unattainable at the moment but she would try her best.

Cwenthryth took in a deep breath and stood straight. She would sleep at Eahlswith's house tonight as planned and ask her if she knew of a family in need of a house. They could move into the place she no longer considered hers. They could have it all because she didn't want or need it.

In the morning she would leave, never to return again.

STEINAR STARED at the frying pan suspended by the window. The last person to use it had been Cwenthryth, to fry an egg Rothgar had gone to find especially for her. Why did the sight of such a common object affect him so? He was acting like an idiot, staring at cooking implements as if they could give him answers to questions he had not even formulated.

And where were his sons? It was not the first time they had disappeared to go and play with their friends, but he would have liked to have them in the house right now. Their presence might have helped keep unwanted thoughts at bay, given him something other than the Saxon woman who had stormed into his life to dwell on.

A knock on the door burst through his thoughts most unpleasantly. He was reminded of the morning Cwenthryth had appeared on his doorstep, taking him for Astrid's brother. Could it be her, back to say she had made a mistake in leaving?

He forced himself to calm and opened the door—only to reveal his sister Eyja. The look on her face was one of intense irritation.

"Where is Cwenthryth?" she asked without preamble. "Is it true she's gone?"

"Why do you want to know?" Steinar replied with equal bluntness. Why did she care? Why did he? Now that she was gone, he should not be constantly wondering where she was, who was with her, or what she was doing.

"Well, where is she?"

Damnation, his sister was not going to give up until he'd given her an answer. She was the most stubborn woman he knew. He often wondered how Moon put up with her.

"She left the day before yesterday." Had it been only two days? It felt like months ago.

Eyja's eyes narrowed in suspicion. "She left? Or did you throw her out?"

"I didn't throw her out." Not this time at least, this time she'd announced herself she was leaving, and he had not tried to stop her, agreeing it was for the best. Not that it was Eyja's business. "She left straight after Rowena and Thorfinn's wedding, which was only to be expected, since she had no reason to be here."

He was suddenly very aware he sounded as guilty as his six-year-old son caught doing something wrong, but he stood his ground.

"No reason to be here? You idiot!" Eyja pushed at his chest with surprising force. "Don't you remember what she told you about fleeing a man?"

Yes, he did remember. The non-existent man. Why was Eyja worrying about that? Couldn't she see he was already upset?

"Leave it, sister. It's nothing to do with—"

"Don't call me sister, not when you're being such an idiot."

"How am I being an idiot?" he growled. Except for staring longingly at frying pans, that was, but she couldn't know about that.

"If you don't go to Cwenthryth right now, you are not my brother anymore, do you hear? You should never have allowed her to leave in the first place." Eyja was now wringing her hands in anguish. "You've spent years allowing Astrid to make you miserable and transforming into a snarling beast. I didn't say anything because I understood you were trying your best to save your marriage, but this is too much. Cwenthryth is the best thing that could have happened to you. She might well be your salvation. So go get her."

"She doesn't need my—"

"Of course she does! Why did she come to the village in the first place? Because she needed protection and a safe place, and she told you as much. If you don't go right now, I will ask Moon to go. He will do it, he will save her, if it's not too late. And then when he comes back, I will ask him to beat you to a pulp."

"Let him try," Steinar scoffed. "We've been there once before, remember? And I still have all my limbs, as far as I can tell."

"That's because you attacked him at the same time as Torsten, like a coward, and *Faðir* stopped him before he could—"

"Stopped *us*, more like. Your precious Moon was already on the ground when *Faðir* arrived."

"Argh, but you really are as hard-headed as the stone you're named after, you know that!" She pushed at his chest again. Once again, he made a point of not flinching. A man had his dignity. "How do you not see? We are wasting precious time. If you don't go now, I swear I will not let you see your nieces again."

This time, he stilled, because this was a more serious threat than asking his brother-in-law to beat him up. He loved Emma, and now little Frida, almost as much as he loved his own children. "You wouldn't do that."

"Well, maybe I would, because how can I be comfortable with the idea of them being anywhere near a man who thinks it's all right to rape women?"

Everything froze within Steinar. How could his sister think such a thing from him? Didn't she know him? "I don't—"

"Listen to me. If you don't go to Cwenthryth's house now, and I mean *run*, this is exactly what is going to happen and you know it. This Godfrid is going to rape her, if not kill her. Deep down you know it, only you're letting your damned pride and resentment for what Astrid did to you stop you from doing what you know is right." She turned toward the hut. "Enough of this. I'm going to get Moon. *He*'s a good man, not a coward, he's is not going to stand idle while she—"

Steinar didn't hear the rest of the sentence. He was already out the door, running to his horse.

11

As soon as she walked out of the town gate, Cwenthryth felt a weight lift off her chest. She would never come back here, she vowed, looking at the walls one last time. It would be too painful, bring on too many memories she wanted to erase. She would miss her friend, but she would make sure to send word of her new abode, and hopefully Eahlswith would come visit once she was settled. Where the new place would be, at the moment she wasn't sure. The only thing she knew was that there would be a river not too far, where she could bathe and swim every time she wanted.

Determined not to think that the last time she had fled the town she had taken refuge with a certain Norseman, Cwenthryth started walking. It was only when she reached the lake that she realized she had unwittingly taken the direction of the Norsemen village. Well. So much for forgetting about Steinar. She had not even made it one morning.

More than a little disheartened, she stopped and sat on a rock. Why had her feet taken her here, when her mind had been set on going the other way? Apparently, it was going to be more difficult than she had imagined to erase the hard-headed man from her mind.

Well, she would just have to try twice as hard. Eventually, it would work. It had to, or else she would go mad. She would not allow herself to go mad, not now that she was finally safe and free.

As she was standing back up, already eyeing up the north road, the one pointing away from the Norsemen village, footsteps disturbed the silence of the clearing. Someone was walking toward her. Without knowing why, she tensed.

"Cwenthryth."

Everything within her froze at the sound of that voice. She had never thought to hear it again, and she had hoped she would never have to look at the man's face again. Oh hell, it seemed she had been wrong to relax her guard and believe she was safe. Godfrid had not gone. He was standing just behind her, waiting for her to acknowledge his presence.

Panicked, she looked around, and saw no one who might be able to come to her rescue. It was too late to flee. She was trapped. Something died within her at the thought.

"Well, this is a surprise. I thought you'd gone."

She had. And then, fool that she was, she had come back, because she'd thought she would be able to avoid him. Why had she done such a stupid thing? It was not as if she had been able to retrieve anything from her house, was it?

"I was not best pleased to find you had disappeared," Godfrid continued, his voice sounding nearer. He said that as if she would care, as if she would feel bad for having disappointed him. She did not.

"Why are you here?" she asked, turning to face him. She'd thought he had gone too, hoped it was over.

"I decided that since neither you nor your father were here anymore, I had no reason to stay in town."

Yes, as she had thought. And then it hit her. He'd said "your father," not "our father." Could it be that she was right, and he was not really her half-brother, as she'd suspected all along? Cwenthryth pushed the question from her mind. She could not think about this now, she had to get away before he pounced. She could see the intention of doing so in his eyes. Unfortunately, she knew that expression too well.

"Well, you were right. You have no reason to be here," she said, taking a step back. "You should leave."

"I will. I had, in fact. But I remembered yesterday that I had promised to meet with a wool merchant at the fair starting next week. So I came back." Lust glinting in his eyes, he took a step toward her. "And aren't I glad I did now… It would have been a pity for us to part without one last fuck, don't you think?"

"No." Bile rose in her throat.

"And, of course, I have to make you pay for abandoning me before I was ready to let you go," he said, as if she had agreed to his proposition. Then his voice hardened. "I say when I want to discard my lovers, not the other way around."

Lovers. Cwenthryth almost laughed at the choice of words. They had never been lovers. She had been a victim and he had been her tormentor, nothing more. And she had finally decided to put an end to her torment. Her time at the village *had* made her stronger.

"I will never lie down for you."

She had sworn Godfrid would never touch her again and she would do her best to prevent him from doing so.

"Oh, you don't have to lie down if you don't want to. I like it just as well when you bend over," he said, the light voice belying the horror of what he was saying. "But you can start by kneeling at my feet."

Before he could grab her by the throat, she ran.

It was the stupid thing to do but the only option. Though she knew she would never outrun a determined man, Cwenthryth could not help it. She could not just stand there and wait for him to rape her or kneel at his feet just because he'd ordered her to— she had to do something, show him that she didn't want it, prove to herself that she had at least tried to escape.

"Oh no, you don't."

There was a roar as Godfrid started to give chase.

THE LAKE APPEARED through the trees, which meant it would not be too long before he reached the town. Finally.

Steinar urged Fáfnir on. Thanks to his earlier visit to town, he already knew where Cwenthryth's house was so he would not waste time looking for her. He promised himself he wouldn't leave before he had convinced her to go back to the village with him. If she refused, he would stay with her until he was certain the danger "this Godfrid," as Eyja had called him, represented was gone. And if she threw him out of her house, as he expected her to, then he would sleep outside by the door, and keep guard.

Whichever way, he would not let her out of his sight until he knew she was safe.

As he got near the meadow a cry of powerless rage reached his ears. A woman? A child? A young boy? He wasn't sure. What was certain was that he had to go and see. He was in a rush, but it would not take him long to ascertain what the situation was, and anyway, he could not ignore the plea of someone who was obviously in trouble.

He entered the clearing—and took in the scene in front of him in one all-encompassing glance.

To his left, there was a woman, lying on the ground with her bodice torn open and her dress bunched to her waist. Her head was turned to face him so he immediately identified her as Cwenthryth, but he had the impression he would have identified her even if her face had been hidden. She was immobile and pale as death. His own blood drained to his feet at the sight.

And then his attention was drawn to his right, where a youth was being thrown to the ground by a tall, blond man who started to beat him to a pulp. Shock seared Steinar's skin, sending blood rushing back into his veins when he recognized the boy.

Ulf.

What the hell was his son doing here, so far away from home alone? It didn't matter. What mattered was that he was being hurt by a man three times his size. Godfrid, if Steinar had to venture a guess. Who else would have attacked Cwenthryth?

Steinar's arm was up before he could think. The axe he'd brought along with him sliced through the air, as fast as a hawk and just as deadly. Two heartbeats later it was embedded in Godfrid's back, right between the shoulder blades. Everything happened with terrible inexorability. The Saxon let go of Ulf and raised his head to the skies, as if to ask for intervention from his god. Nothing came. Slowly, he fell to his knees, and finally on his front, where he lay still as a corpse, blood pooling under him in a scarlet puddle.

Everything went silent. Steinar jumped from the saddle and called out to his son.

"Ulf!" The word was one raw cry. What if he'd been too late, what if his son was already—

"*Faðir*?" Ulf sounded hesitant, as if wary to believe it was truly over and his father had come.

"Yes, I'm here." Steinar tore through the meadow. Kicking the bastard's corpse out of the way, he reached down for his son, lifting him up in his arms and cradling him as if he were still a babe. Then he forced himself to put him down again. After what he'd done, the boy would want to be treated like a man and he deserved the honor. "Are you—?"

"I'm all right."

He was not all right. His face was bruised and bleeding, one eye was swollen shut. By the gods, Steinar should have been on the receiving end of Godfrid's blows, not a youth of barely thirteen summers. He held Ulf's frail shoulders and stared straight into his blue eyes, so like his father's—and his own, or so everyone kept telling him. He had named him Ulf, which was the Icelander's real name, and never had it suited him better. The youth was every bit as fierce and protective as his wolf of a grandfather, and would grow into a dependable and fair man.

"Son, you are twice the man I am. I am so humbled and proud to be your father. What you did was…" He shook his head. There were no words to describe the bravery of the act. "I should have been here. I should have been the one stopping the foul man."

A glance at Cwenthryth, who was still lying down, immobile, made his meaning clear. He should have stopped the man from raping her. What a terrible way to find out she had not been lying about being in danger. Who the hell was this Godfrid no one in town had heard about, and why had her brother not protected her? He would make sure to find out.

"I think she will be all right," Ulf said, his voice slightly more assured. "I arrived before he could…"

There was no need to finish the sentence. Steinar nodded. Yes, it was a good thing she had not been raped, but she still had been attacked, hurt, and frightened. All because he'd been too stupid to believe she was in real danger, because he'd placed his peace of mind above her safety, because, like his sister had said, he was an idiot.

Fortunately, his son didn't seem to realize what a despicable coward his father was, as his next comment made clear.

"You knew, then?" Ulf nodded at the axe planted in the man's back. "You came armed, ready to defend her."

Steinar rubbed a hand at the back of his neck, refusing to take credit for having come. He hadn't known, not precisely. It had taken his sister's threats to make him see that he was making the biggest mistake of his life. He would have to thank Eyja for shaking him out of his torpor when he got back to the village. The stubborn little imp had saved not just one, but two people today. Had he not ridden to town on her order, Ulf would be dead by now, and perhaps also Cwenthryth.

"I came, because your aunt made me see I had made a mistake in letting Cwenthryth go," he answered honestly. He didn't deserve any praise when his son had been the brave one. "But why did you come?"

Had he known about the danger Cwenthryth was facing? Had he overheard something he shouldn't have the day she had revealed she was fleeing a man? It had to be something like that because surely she had not told the boy the situation she was in?

Ulf shook his head, indicating he had only followed his instinct, without knowing what he would find.

"It was good to have Cwenthryth with us at the village. I didn't want her to leave so I decided to go speak to her, as I knew where she lived, see if I could convince her to stay. I'm glad I arrived before that man—before he—you know."

"Yes." It seemed that the boy had no idea who Godfrid had been, or that he and Cwenthryth had a history. A terrible history. "I'm glad as well. Wait, Rothgar is not here, is he? He didn't come with you?"

He didn't think so, but he had to be absolutely certain, as he'd seen neither of his two boys earlier that morning.

"No. I left him with Uncle Torsten, though he agreed with me that I should go. He wants her back too."

That made three of them, then.

"Yes. I bet he does. Now, look away," he instructed Ulf. He didn't want his son to see him yank the axe out of Godfrid. It would not be a pleasant sight to say the least. Understanding what he had not said, the boy nodded and turned his back to him.

Without a word, Steinar wrenched the weapon from the prone body at his feet, behaving as if it were already a corpse. Perhaps it really was. There certainly was no noise, no movement indicating the man was still alive when he wrenched the blade out of him. Good. After wiping it on the grass, he replaced the weapon at his belt.

"Let's go get Cwenthryth and take her home," he murmured, making his way to the edge of the clearing.

Cwenthryth lay on her side, hugging herself. She had mercifully come to, even if she seemed too stunned to do more than shake her head from side to side. With each step he saw a new, frightful detail. Her bottom lip was bleeding, her cheek was cut, indicating she'd been hit by someone wearing a heavy ring. There was a large bruise on her thigh, the shape of it oddly circular, as if Godfrid had bitten her tender flesh after lifting her skirts. By the gods, but these were the actions of a madman.

Steinar had never hated himself more than he did in that moment. What the hell had he done, allowing her to get back to town on her own, leaving her without protection? Well, he would have to examine his conscience later on. For now, he had to take her away from here.

As she was still indecently exposed, he bent down to put order to her clothes before scooping her up into his arms. Not wishing to embarrass her further, Ulf had tactfully retreated, going to find Fáfnir while his father was seeing to Cwenthryth.

As soon as she felt his hands on her, she started to protest.

"No, no," she whimpered, her eyes still closed, her voice slurred, her movements slow and feeble, like someone drained of all hope and strength but doing what she could to protect herself. His chest tightened. She thought he was Godfrid, come back to finish what he had started after having disposed of Ulf, and she was doing what she could to stop him. "I don't want to—"

"Hush, I know. You're safe, it's over. You're safe. It's me, Steinar."

"Steinar?" Her eyes flew open at the mention of his name. There was such emotion, such gratitude in her dark gaze that they appeared almost luminous, and his heart exploded. He wanted to see that look on her face every time she looked at him, he wanted her to know she was safe as long as she was with him.

"Yes, it's me." Now that she was no longer fighting him, it was easy to gather her into his arms. He cradled her in his lap a long moment, much like he had done after their passionate encounter in the tree house. "It's all right. I'm here. It's over now."

"Ulf?"

That her first thought was for his son's safety tugged at his heart. "He's just over there with Fáfnir. He's fine."

At the words she went limp against him and started sobbing. "It's over," she repeated three or four times, the relief, the hope audible in every breath, in every word.

Steinar held her tight, not knowing what to say, doing what he could to make her feel safe. He kissed her temple, careful of not touching the cut on her cheek. In the corner of his eye, he saw Ulf looking at them intently, as if wondering what was behind the tender gesture. He didn't mind. Let his son think he cared for Cwenthryth if he wanted, it was nothing less than the truth.

"Let's go," Cwenthryth begged after a while, wiping at her eyes. "Please. I can't stay another moment near—"

"Of course." He helped her up, marveling at how small she felt. "Will you be able to sit in the saddle?" he asked, concerned at the way she was swaying on her feet. He wished he'd brought a cart to transport her to the village, but speed had been his priority, and he had only his horse with him.

"Yes. Anything to get away from here."

"You and Ulf can sit on Fáfnir then. I will hold the reins and lead him. Don't worry about anything, just make sure you don't fall. Can you do that for me?"

She nodded.

The animal was grazing peacefully next to a clump of daisies, his chestnut coat gleaming in the sunshine. Birdsong filled the air, tree leaves fluttered in the breeze. A casual observer could have been forgiven for thinking all was well and good in the world. Until he looked at Cwenthryth and Ulf's damaged faces, that was. Then he would see that evil lurked everywhere, and no one was safe from it.

Steinar lifted his son into the saddle first, then he brought the stallion to a piece of rock so Cwenthryth could climb on in turn.

"All right?" he asked, helping her up the rock. He forced himself to hold her waist gently when he wanted to crush her into his arms, become one with her so she could never be hurt again.

"All right. Thank you."

The muscles in Cwenthryth's body protested as one when she hoisted herself into the saddle but she gritted her teeth because the pain did not matter. Nothing mattered now that the nightmare was over. If Steinar had come for her, then it was truly over. His hands around her were warm and comforting. His hold around her heart even more so.

Once settled, she closed her arms around Ulf's slender frame, careful not to hold him too tight. She had seen the traces of Godfrid's violence on his face. There was no telling how damaged his body was. It had seemed to her he was walking as he usually did, but you could never be sure and she didn't want to hurt him.

"Thank you, Ulf, for coming to my aid," she murmured in his ear once the horse started walking. "You're a brave man." After what he'd done, she could not call him a boy. He deserved much more.

He shook his head slightly. "No, I don't think I'm particularly brave. But I could not let the vile man do what he was trying to do. I'm glad *Faðir* arrived, though."

"Yes, so am I."

A sob escaped her lips. Ulf should never have had to endure the beating he had endured, but she dreaded to think what would have happened had he not interrupted Godfrid. She was certain this time he would have killed her once he'd reached his pleasure. With people thinking him gone, no one would have thought to accuse him of the crime. He'd also meant to make her pay for daring to leave. He'd been more savage than usual, insulting her while he beat her to the ground, even biting her on the inside of her thigh once he'd lifted her skirts. By the time he'd started to unlace his braies, she'd been almost senseless, incapable of defending herself. Not that she had managed to do much before that, he'd just been too strong, too determined to have her.

And then, when she'd thought she would have to feel him surge inside her, someone had thrown himself onto his back, pummeling him, yelling he had to let her go. At first Cwenthryth had not recognized Ulf. Why would she? It didn't make sense that he should be here. But the young Norseman had indeed been here, defending her. He'd thrown himself at her attacker, and forced him to release her.

Unfortunately, as could have been predicted, Godfrid, being the stronger of the two, had started to punish the boy for interrupting him. It was then that Cwenthryth had fainted, overcome by the horror of it all.

Dear God.

What if Steinar had not arrived when he had? Godfrid would have killed Ulf, she was certain of it. Just like with her murder, there would have been little risk of being punished for this crime, since he was moving on anyway. He would not have allowed anyone, especially such a fragile youth, to stand between him and his pleasure.

"Well, thank you," she repeated, more grateful than she had ever been. Next, she would have to thank Steinar as well. He'd come for her, and ultimately, he was the one who had stopped Godfrid.

They reached the Norsemen village a little before dusk. As soon as she spotted the cluster of thatched roofs nestled in the hollow by the river, Cwenthryth's whole body relaxed. Never had a sight been more welcome.

Stopping in front of the hut, Steinar lifted his son off the saddle and then turned to get her. Cwenthryth leaned in to him. Ever so gently, he helped her down to the ground. Once he'd steadied her, she lifted her head to him. Gone was the usual scowling. There was an expression on his face she had never seen before, one that caused something like hope to swell in her chest. She had the impression he was about to tell her something deeply significant.

"We're home," he said simply.

12

———————

Steinar walked back to his hut under a sky strewn with stars. He had entrusted Ulf and Rothgar to his parents for the night, as he needed privacy for an explanation with Cwenthryth. In truth, he needed much more than that. He needed to make sure she was all right. He needed to make amends for the way he'd acted. He needed to beg for her forgiveness, if that was what she wanted.

When he entered the hut, he found her sitting on the pallet, her back against the wall, her arms around her bent knees, her eyes closed. The cut on her cheek had been cleaned, but he knew it would most likely leave a scar, a constant reminder of what she had gone through. Not that she would ever forget what she had endured at the man's hands, unfortunately, even without a scar.

Feeling strangely intimidated, he poured her a cup of ale and knelt down by the pallet, waiting for her to acknowledge his presence. She opened her eyes and gave a tentative smile when she saw him. That smile reached straight to his heart. So brave…

"Are you hungry?" he asked, handing her the cup.

"I-I don't know."

Clenching his jaw against the despair this answer betrayed,

Steinar stood back up to get a few strips of dried meat and the bowl of berries he had gathered in the morning. He placed everything by Cwenthryth's side, then sat back down. "Here. Just in case you are."

"Thank you." She took a sip of ale and reached out for a berry.

"Please tell me everything. Who is the bastard?"

Was the bastard, he should perhaps say. He didn't see how the man could still be alive after getting an axe in the back. But he didn't think it useful to remind Cwenthryth of the gruesome sight. Or… Had she even seen it? When he had scooped her up into his arms, she had been only half conscious, and she had hidden her face in the crook of his neck as if to block out the outside world. It was possible she had not realized quite what had happened to her tormentor. He could only hope so, even if he would have to tell her what he had done at some point. She had the right to know she had nothing to fear now.

"His name is Godfrid. He claims to be my half-brother."

What the hell? Steinar recoiled. The man forcing himself on her had been her own *brother*? Or as near as? He barely contained a growl. It could not be. But wasn't it what the old man in town had told him?

She lives with her brother.

At the time, he had taken it to mean that she'd lied about living with a tormentor, when in fact the brother and her tormentor had been one and the same. Eyja had been right. He really was an idiot. How had he not thought of that possibility?

"You said he claims to be your brother," he said as calmly as he could. Now was not the time to frighten her with the intensity of an anger which was not directed at her. "So you doubt it?"

Was it because, like him, she thought it inconceivable that a man who shared blood with her could want to possess her? Or did she have other, more objective reasons to be suspicious? She shook her head, as if she'd expressed her doubts many times, only to have them dismissed or ignored, and could not bear to hear him do the same. But he needed to know.

"Tell me," he repeated.

"Well… He looks nothing like my father did, for one," she started. "I know that isn't proof of anything, as I don't either. Still, my father was darker than most, and Godric is very fair to have been fathered by such a swarthy man."

"Mm, yes." The man had been almost as blond as a Norseman. Steinar agreed it was no proof of anything, but it was a start. If the two men had been the spitting image of one another, any doubts she had would have been harder to dismiss. "What else?"

"No one I know has ever heard of the woman he claims was his mother. If his story is to be believed, he was born some thirty years ago, in other words before my father met my mother, from a woman who'd been living in Essex at the time. Perhaps it is so," Cwenthryth conceded with a shrug. "But my father was not an adventurous man. He rarely left town, and in my lifetime, he never ventured farther than the coast. I cannot imagine what would have made him undertake such a long journey, even as a young man. The woman could have come to him, and left without telling him she was with child, I suppose, but then how come no one remembers her? I know it is not conclusive proof again, but it is all very odd to me, who knew my father's temperament and life story. He'd always led me to believe my mother was the first woman he'd been interested in."

"Didn't you ask him for more details about this conquest of his when the mysterious stranger came to your door? See if what he told you tallied with what Godfrid was saying?" Such a claim would have necessitated some investigation at the very least, and he was surprised she had not thought of it.

There was a silence, then Cwenthryth sighed.

"This brings me to the most suspicious thing of all. Godfrid arrived at a time when my father was ill, and not quite himself. His mind had started to go for months. It seemed to be a form of insanity brought on by old age. He was confused most of the time, barely remembered who I was, or what he had done that same day. In the state he was, anyone could have claimed to be his child unchallenged. I cannot help but feel it was all too convenient, as if Godfrid had been observing us, and decided on the best way to exploit my father's weakness."

"Yes," Steinar agreed. Again, this was no conclusive proof, but he trusted Cwenthryth. If her instinct told her something was wrong, then it most certainly was.

In any case, real half-brother or not, Godfrid didn't have to take advantage of the old man's illness or use his daughter to slake his lust. Who his mother had been didn't matter, he should never have touched an unwilling woman. Well, Steinar was fairly certain the man would never touch anyone ever again. It was some consolation.

"And of course," Cwenthryth added, her voice reduced to a whisper, "there was the way he treated me. Again, it's not conclusive proof, but surely if we were related, he would never have… he would not have dared…"

She shivered and hugged her knees tighter, as if trying to make herself as small as possible. Steinar understood all too well what she had not said. A man, vile as he was, aroused as he was, would normally balk at the idea of bedding his own sister. But then again, anything was possible. It had been clear that Godfrid did not have an honorable bone in his body. He'd been prepared to kill a child in order to rape a woman. If that didn't show he was past all decency, then nothing did.

"When did he attack you?"

Another silence. He fought hard the urge to scoop her up and place her on his lap again, sensing she would rather he saw her as a strong woman able to hold on to her control.

"At first, he left me alone, and behaved as a brother should. I think he was biding his time, waiting for the moment I would be on my own, with no one to care about what happened about me." She swallowed. "The first time he raped me was the day after my father took to his bed permanently."

The first time? Steinar inhaled sharply. He'd not expected such a shocking answer. "When was that?"

"About a year ago, a couple of months after his arrival."

Steinar recoiled. A year. She had been at the man's mercy for a whole year? Why had he assumed the man had only attacked her once? Because he was a fool, that was why. Hadn't he seen the bruise on her temple the day she'd arrived at the village? Hadn't she told him she was fleeing a tormentor? She wouldn't have borne such a trace, she wouldn't have made such a claim if she had been raped only once, months ago.

Cwenthryth lifted her huge, dark eyes to him, looking on the verge of tears—and ashamed of herself. It twisted at his guts.

"I know what you're thinking. Why didn't I flee after that first time? Why did I stay with a man who thought he could hurt me and use me for his pleasure?"

"No. I don't think that," he said softly. He was horrified that she would think herself at fault. He'd heard enough stories of women being abused to know that it was never as simple as simply walking away. Men were not only stronger physically and able to subdue them when the urge took them, but could also be devious and manipulate women into thinking they weren't able to escape the hold they had on them. "I know it is easier said than done."

"With my father ill and depending on me for everything, I couldn't do what I wanted to do." Cwenthryth tried to justify herself nonetheless, as if loath to have him think ill of her. "I could not leave without him, and I could not take him away from his home, when he was too weak and bewildered to leave even his bed. It would have killed him. So I stayed and, stupid me, I kept hoping Godfrid would tire of me and leave. He didn't."

"You're not stupid," Steinar said, as firmly as he dared. He knew it might take time for her to accept that she had done the best she could, but he hoped she would eventually see it. "Where is your father now? Did he die?"

He already knew he was dead, the kindly old man in town had told him as much the other day, but he wanted to keep the conversation going.

"Yes. He died a few weeks ago, in his sleep. At least he didn't suffer." Her voice wobbled, but she carried on bravely. "Once he was gone, I had no reason to stay. I was finally free, so I started to prepare my escape. Only it didn't go according to plan."

No. That was the least you could say.

She had thought to find refuge with Astrid's brother, a man who would be grateful for her help and offer her a safe shelter while she sorted her life out. Instead, she'd had to deal with Astrid's widower, a brute who had made it clear she was not welcome despite her doing everything right. Steinar clenched his jaw. Had anyone felt worse than he felt right now?

"I'm sorry."

"Don't be," Cwenthryth said in an unusually flat voice. "It's not your fault. Anyway, it's over now and these monstrous couplings will have no consequences. It is all that matters."

All the blood left Steinar's veins when she placed a hand over her stomach in a familiar gesture. Things had not gone according to plan, she'd said. Well, perhaps he knew why she'd been prevented from leaving as soon as her father had died. Perhaps she had suffered a traumatic loss, a loss he wished no woman had to go through. He should know, he who had seen firsthand what it did to her soul, not to mention to her body.

"You mean… Godfrid made you with child?" he asked in a whisper, hoping to be wrong. Not only had the bastard abused her body for a whole year, but he had also planted his seed in her womb?

"Yes. It was inevitable, I suppose." She closed her eyes, as if trying to block the painful images assaulting her mind. "May God forgive me, but I was relieved when I lost it. Do you hear? I was relieved never to have to meet my baby. It is awful of me, I know, but I could not bear to… to…"

Despite his earlier resolution not to hold her, Steinar drew her into his arms when tears started to fall down her cheeks. So much pain, so much suffering. He could not have watched her struggle without offering his support, inadequate as it was.

"It is not awful. On the contrary, it is perfectly understandable," he whispered in her ear. "No one should have to go through something like that." Though he had a horrible suspicion he already knew the answer, he had to ask the question, and make sure. "When did you miscarry the babe?"

"Just after the death of my father, a few days before I arrived in your village."

As he'd suspected. Now everything made sense. The shadows under her eyes when she'd appeared on his doorstep, the fainting spell when she'd tried to walk away. Her weakness, her despair at finding that the refuge she had thought to find was to be denied to her, her behavior toward Rothgar. How had he not seen the signs? Never had Steinar been more ashamed of himself. Lost to his bitterness and grief, he had taken his anger out on an innocent woman, wilfully ignoring the fact that it would have taken her an awful lot of courage to go to a complete stranger for help. Instead of trying to understand, he had barked at her.

Her, the purest, most honest soul he had ever met. Who welcomed grieving children into her bed and made them little pets with what she could find, who didn't shy away from the desire she felt for hulking Norsemen talking to her crudely, who helped women give birth despite her own grief, and rejoiced in couples' happiness when she'd known only abuse?

How had he ever thought this woman a schemer, a liar, a manipulator? She had been a victim, trapped in a horrid situation and yet brave enough to flee her tormentor. Now he understood why she had jumped at the opportunity she thought Astrid had given her. Where else would she have gone after losing her babe? The Norsemen village would have been the perfect place to hide from a Saxon.

"Would you like to tell me about your loss?"

Had she had the opportunity to talk about her trauma to anyone, to try and deal with it? If she had lost the child after losing her father, she wouldn't have had anyone to confide in. Later on, if she had only worried about finding a way out of her house and a new home, she might not have taken the time to absorb the enormity of what had happened to her.

She'd told him she was relieved not to have had to give birth to her tormentor's child, and he understood why that might be, but she had still gone through an ordeal, both physical and emotional, one of the worst a woman could endure. She had lost a baby that was half hers, and almost lost her life in the process. It might help her to talk about it.

Of course, after the way he had treated her, he might be the last person she wanted to confide in.

To his relief, however, she didn't seem offended at his suggestion. After a while, she started hesitantly. "I don't know if it's…"

"You don't have to talk about it if you don't want to. I'll understand," he said to ease her discomfort.

Was she ill at ease, or was there another reason for her hesitancy? Had she heard through Eyja that he, too, had lost a babe, and she was wary of reawakening the pain of his loss? It was possible that, while she was giving birth by the tree, his frightened sister would have told her she didn't want to lose her child like Astrid had.

"It is rather a gruesome story," she murmured. "I don't want it to haunt you."

There she was again, thinking of others first. But alas, he knew all too well how gruesome the loss of a child was, and he already had nightmares about it.

"Don't worry about me. Just do what you need to do. Either way, I'll be here for you." If she had gone through the ordeal without falling apart, he could certainly bear to hear about it.

She stayed silent a long time. Then she started talking.

"I woke up one morning thinking something was wrong, but I didn't immediately understand what it might be. I'd known for about a month that I'd fallen with child. I was scared." She took in a shaky breath, reliving the dreadful moment when she'd understood that her rapist's seed had taken root inside her. Yes, she would have been scared, horrified, and everything in between. "Perhaps I should have noticed it before, but I refused to think… I refused to accept he had—"

"Yes," he said gently. She would have refused to accept she was carrying the child of a man who had forced himself upon her body for months and was possibly her half-brother. The thought would have been horrifying.

"In any case, I started to feel cramps in my lower belly and soon I felt blood seeping between my thighs. It was…"

"Yes," he repeated, not knowing what else to say. Instead, he tightened his hold around her. Sometimes actions spoke louder than words.

"My friend Eahlswith arrived at that point. We'd agreed to go to the market together that morning, and it was still early, so when I didn't open the door, she walked in. She found me on the pallet. And she helped me with… with the…"

"Yes," Steinar said again. Her friend had helped her to stem the blood and dispose of what would never grow up to be a child.

By the gods, she'd been right. This *was* a nightmarish story. Would that he could kill the bastard a dozen times over for what he had made her endure, and not with a neat blow to the back. It had been too quick, too easy a death. He should have suffered, have had time to repent ten times over.

"Where was Godfrid at this point?" Would it have been good for him to be there and see the result of his actions? Would it have made him feel any guilt? It was doubtful.

Cwenthryth buried her face in the crook of his neck.

"The day after my father's funeral he'd gone to see a friend in the next town, warning me he might be gone a few days. That was why, even if I had decided to flee by then, I was in no hurry. I knew I had some time to get organized. But in the end, I spent that time recovering from the loss of blood. For days I was too weak, too stunned to do anything other than lie on my pallet. I was on my own, and could not think what to do."

"Did he know about the babe?" Steinar asked gently. Had she told him? Or had she thought to wait until it was absolutely impossible to hide her condition to let him know?

He felt her shake her head. "He never knew. It's better that way, I think. I dread to think what he would have said." She paused. "I slowly got better. Then one evening, Godfrid came back. As soon as I saw him, something snapped inside me. I knew I could not bear the situation any longer. I should have taken that decision ages ago, but I—"

"Don't berate yourself," he repeated. "The bastard was in your home—of course you wouldn't have wanted to leave. And as we agreed, you had your father to consider. In any case, you did find the courage to escape in the end. You can be proud of yourself."

She stayed silent, as if unconvinced. "I remembered what Astrid had told me about her brother on her last visit. Her supposed brother, I should say. I thought if his wife had really left him, there would be a chance he would give me shelter, at least for a few days."

Steinar gritted his teeth. She had put all her hopes in him, and he had woefully let her down. She had found the courage to do the hard part and he, who'd only had to welcome her in, had turned her away, and sent her straight back to a man who had pounced on her at the first opportunity. He had accused her of lying, of manipulating his sons, when she was only trying to find protection from a monster.

Would she ever forgive him? Would he ever forgive himself?

"I'm sorry. I have no excuse for the way I behaved."

"But you do," Cwenthryth answered, looking straight at him. "You had just lost your wife, you didn't know me, and you had your sons to worry about."

"Yes, I had lost my wife. That I was grieving doesn't mean other people were not in trouble as well. As to my sons, they already knew you and trusted you, I should have listened to them. And you were perfect with them, patient and loving. I should have given you a chance. I didn't. I did everything wrong. I…"

He had used her body most shamefully in the tree house, threatening her, telling her he would not worry about her pleasure. How could he bear the idea, now that he knew what Godfrid had done?

"You have nothing to blame yourself for. I was the one who burst in on you at the worst possible moment," she insisted.

"No. Don't make this your fault when it is not," he growled. She was berating herself for having interrupted his life, when her presence had actually given him a sense of purpose, helped Roth-gar, and prevented him from drowning in self-pity. It was unbearable, and he could not let her do it.

"I'm not saying I did anything wrong. But I understand that you reacted to my arrival in the only way you could. It was the wrong time for you." Her voice started to waver. "And yet you came back for me. You came without knowing I was in danger, and you arrived in time. I'm more grateful than I can express."

Steinar winced. She made it sound as if he'd gone to her because he felt guilty about having sent her away. He had not. To his shame, it had taken someone else to make him see sense. Well, at least he would not make the same mistakes again. He nodded, and asked the question that had been bothering him since she'd made her confession.

"Were you a virgin before Godfrid raped you?"

He hoped she had at least had one lover of her choice before the assaults began, so that she knew what lovemaking was supposed to be. His hopes were crushed as soon as she opened her mouth.

"Yes. Looking after my ailing father didn't leave me much opportunity to get out, and men didn't seem interested in a woman who had no time for them and no experience whatsoever."

He should not be surprised. The man at the market hall had said that she lived a chaste life, despite being a sweet girl. Steinar saw how it was now. Cwenthryth had sacrificed her youth for her father. And then Godfrid had taken advantage of her devotion to the old man, destroyed her innocence. By the gods, but he deserved to die ten times over for what he'd done. Steinar hoped the man was even now burning in his Saxon hell.

"I'm sorry. It shouldn't have happened like that. You should have been able to see that lying with a man is supposed to give you pleasure."

"I knew that. My friend Eahlswith had told me about it and I had been kissed a few times. It was… nice." She flushed, as if embarrassed to admit as much. "In any case, thanks to you, I now know what pleasure is."

His shaft went hard as stone in the blink of an eye. Placed

where she was, Cwenthryth would probably be able to feel it but he didn't move. He needed to have her against him. Besides, he trusted her to know he would not hurt her. No matter what his body felt, he would never make her ill at ease.

"Lie down," he said after a while, forcing himself to reason. If he didn't let her go, his erection might never go down.

"Why?"

"I want to lie next to you. If I may," he added, realizing he had no right to request such a thing from her, after the way he'd behaved. Would she refuse him?

Her answer was the most wonderful thing he'd ever heard.

"Yes, please. I want you to lie next to me."

"ARE YOU ASLEEP?"

Cwenthryth kept her voice low and tentative in case Steinar had indeed fallen asleep. He had been silent for a very long time, from the moment he had stretched his long limbs next to her on the pallet, and it was very late.

"No. I don't see how I could possibly sleep when all I can think about is that I am a bastard." His voice was soft in the darkness, but there was no mistaking the self-loathing.

Cwenthryth turned his head to look at him, shocked by the bitterness in his tone as well as the use of the word. Steinar was staring at the ceiling, his hands folded over his chest, as still as a stone carving.

"I'm sorry?" She didn't think for a moment he wasn't Wolf's natural son, so he had to mean he thought he was a bad man.

"The day you came to the village, to my hut, hoping to find help and security, I barked at you like a rabid dog, causing you to faint in terror."

"It's not quite what—"

He cut her off before she could point out that terror had not been responsible for the fainting, but rather exhaustion and the recent loss of blood.

"Then I threw you out for doing nothing more than being the most selfless, loving, and helpful person I've ever met, and giving my sons a bit of the peace they had lost at the death of their mother. When I discovered you in the tree house where the boys had had the generosity to offer, instead of being ashamed at my lack of compassion, I used you in the most—"

He stopped, evidently thinking that he had been unforgivably selfish and violent with her, using her like Godfrid once had. But it had been nothing like that. He had seen to her pleasure—twice —and he had not even entered her. He'd been gentle, even cradling her afterward.

"You didn't—" Once again she tried to protest, once again he spoke before she could.

"Then I accused you of being the most shameful wanton for doing nothing more than speaking to Haakon and I allowed you to leave unescorted the following morning without even asking where you were headed. How you didn't send me to hell after all that I will never know."

Hell. Again. If he mentioned it, then order was restored. A smile tugged at Cwenthryth's lips. Really his obsession with the place was most endearing. "I already told you. I would never send someone to hell."

"No. Not when you know too well what it's like." His voice was as rough as it had ever been. Her attempt at levity had failed. He was silent another long moment. When he spoke, his question surprised her. "Can I stay here, sleep next to you tonight?"

This time the smile teasing her lips broke through. "You sound just like Rothgar, you know."

A growl answered her. Dear, oh dear, he did behave just like a wolf when he wanted to. And she loved it.

"Do I?" he whispered turning to his side to look at her. "Do I really sound like an innocent little child, Cwenthryth?"

Well, no. Put like that, he did not. More like a virile beast of a man, one capable of making her shiver with desire. A true wolf. "You don't," she murmured, barely resisting the urge to nestle herself into his warmth and pet him like she would the furry animals if they could be trusted not to hurt humans in search of comfort.

"So, will you deny me what you allow my son to do?"

"No."

With those words, she turned her back to him, indicating he was welcome to wrap himself around her.

Accepting the unspoken invitation, he settled himself behind her, just like his son liked to do. Except that having his big arms enfold her and his broad chest walling her in safety was nothing like having a frail boy holding on to her. Cwenthryth took in a deep breath, feeling safe for the first time since.... Well, if she'd had to be honest, she had never felt that safe in her life.

"All right?"

"More than all right."

She closed her eyes. At last, she had found the refuge she'd hoped to find in the Norsemen village.

13

———————

A solid chest was caging her in. A thick arm was draped around her waist. A hot rod was pressed against the small of her back.

Cwenthryth stilled as sensations assailed her body one by one, the conclusion inevitable. She was lying in a man's embrace. It was the only explanation. Was it a dream? No, she could tell it was all too real. Should she bolt, try to flee while she could? No, because this was not Godfrid, or anyone else intent on hurting her. She had recognized who was holding her so tight. The chest was hard and broad, the arm strong and protective, the rod—

Heat crept to her cheeks as the memory of the last time this man had been cradling her against him flooded her.

"Steinar," she whispered.

The hold around her waist tightened ever so slightly, confirming her suspicion. "Mm, yes. What is it, lovely?"

Lovely.

Cwenthryth's heart stilled. Everyone knew that when someone was still in prey to sleep, they could not dissemble. For Steinar to use such a name when he was not fully awake and in control of his emotions had to mean something. As to what, she had rather not think. For now, they were in each other's arms and he had just called her lovely. It was enough.

"Thank you for sleeping with me." It had made her feel not only safe, but cherished.

The hold tightened further, making her feel even safer, even more cherished. "It was my pleasure. I was the one who asked, remember?"

"I do remember." It had been one of the most wonderful moments of her life. "And I thank you for coming to my rescue yesterday."

It only occurred to her now that she had not yet thanked him for coming to her aid, and she would hate for him to think she considered his help a due. She did not. She was deeply grateful, because she suspected he had saved her life as well as what little was left of her dignity.

There was a silence while he seemed to consider his next words. "Ulf was the one who came to your rescue. He was the one who stopped Godfrid, not me."

Yes, but then he, in turn, had stopped Godfrid from killing the boy. He had still come for her unprompted, at a moment when he couldn't have known she was being assaulted. It had to mean something, possibly the same thing calling her "lovely" meant.

"I hope Ulf is—"

"Yes. He'll be fine. I arrived just at the right time."

She nodded, relieved. Steinar would be even more anxious to ensure his son's well-being than she was. If he was reassured, then she could relax.

"Thank God."

"How do you feel now that you've slept?"

He removed a strand of hair from her brow, the gesture impossibly tender. Everything within her melted. If she had suspected just how tender and protective that fierce warrior could be on the day she'd met him, she would have ended up in all sorts of trouble.

Perhaps she already had, because now that they had unexpectedly been reunited, she didn't want to be separated again.

"I'm fine," she said, her throat tight. "What happened to Godfrid?"

There was a silence. It seemed to her that Steinar was debating whether to tell her the truth or not. Eventually, he spoke, his voice little more than a rasp.

"I used the axe I'd brought with me to strike him." Axe. Cwenthryth shivered at the word. Did she want to know what he'd done exactly? Did she need to? No.

"So he's dead?" The notion left her cold. If he was, then he had only himself to blame. No one had asked him to attack her or Ulf.

"I didn't stay to make sure but I think so. In any case, you won't have to worry about him ever again."

Her body sagged. The nightmare was really over. Now all she needed was for Steinar to call her "lovely" again and mean it.

"I—"

"Good morning!"

Without warning, Rothgar burst in through the door. Taking one glance into the hut, he ran to the pallet and threw himself into Cwenthryth's arms.

"Rothgar! Do you have to?"

While Steinar barked his displeasure to his son, Cwenthryth held the little boy and allowed the harsh sounds of the Norse language to wash over her. Why was it that it pleased her so when Steinar spoke it, even if it was not directed at her, even when he spoke it in anger? She had no idea.

"It's all right," she soothed. "I don't mind."

No, she didn't. There were worse things than to be wanted by someone. She closed her arms around the little boy who had burrowed into her softness. With a strong man warming her back and a sweet boy nestling in her embrace, Cwenthryth had never felt better.

A heartbeat later, she felt even better, because she heard exactly what she had hoped to hear.

"Sorry, lovely," Steinar purred in her ear, "but I fear there will be no getting rid of us three now."

Oh, if only.

"Where is Cwenthryth?"

Steinar turned to see Moon standing in the doorway, his thumbs hooked in the belt at his waist. Once he would have felt irritation at the notion that people came to his house asking about the Saxon, assuming that she would be here, behaving as if she were part of his life. Today he found himself smiling, as if the mere mention of her had brought peace to him.

And it did feel as if she were a part of his life.

For a dreadful moment, the day before, he'd thought she'd fallen prey to the illness that had taken Astrid. Shortly after getting up Cwenthryth had started to feel light-headed and complained of stomach cramps. Panic had seized his own guts. No, not her as well! Not now, not ever! He would not bear it if he lost her so soon after having accepted that he might indeed need her.

Then, once panic had subsided, he'd remembered that, caught up in their difficult conversation the previous evening, she had eaten none of the food he'd placed by her side. She was hungry, that had to be the explanation. Desperate to be reassured, he'd brought all the food supplies he'd found to her, forcing her to eat as much as she could. Then once she had declared herself sated, he had ordered her to spend the day resting on the pallet. After the ordeal she'd been through, physically and emotionally, she needed it and he wouldn't be gainsaid. If she thought him high-handed, too bad. She could think what she liked, her well-being was his priority. And it had worked.

By the evening, she had been restored to her usual self, and he'd been able to breathe again. She was not about to die.

"I think she's at the back, weeding the garden," he told his brother-in-law. "Why are you asking?"

"Arne came to tell me that Inga is having her baby. And Helga is already seeing to Sigrid, whose pains started at the same time. She could do with some help and she's heard that Cwenthryth delivered baby Frida. She asked us to get her." Moon clenched his jaw. Like the rest of the family, his brother-in-law had been told about what had happened the day before to her and Ulf, and he'd been outraged. "Do you think she would agree to go see Inga if she feels well enough?"

"I think she feels just fine." Her face still bore the traces of the attack, but mercifully, she had slept well and woken up in as good a mood as he'd seen her. "I'm sure she would not refuse her help to a woman in need, especially considering that this is not Inga's first babe. Between the two of them I'm sure they will manage. Let me go get her."

He found her at the back of the garden, in the part of the vegetable patch where the onions grew. She was kneeling on the ground, filling a basket with the weeds she was uprooting. And, to his utter delight, she was singing. It was a sweet song about a girl picking a rose for her beloved. Steinar's chest squeezed, and he took a moment to enjoy her voice, sweet and pure as birdsong. Despite her ordeal of the previous day, it was clear he'd been right; her spirit was intact. Only people who felt safe and carefree sang thus. It was as if she had naturally found her place here at the village, and recovered her peace of mind. He could have watched her for days.

Then he remembered that Helga was waiting and he shook himself out of his contemplation.

At his approach Cwenthryth went silent and flushed a delicious red color, embarrassed to have been caught singing. There was no need. She had not been doing anything wrong.

"Steinar," she murmured, sitting back on her heels.

"Cwenthryth. Someone needs your help." He hated interrupting her moment of peace but poor Inga needed her now.

She tilted her head. "Someone from the village?" The fact seemed to surprise her, with reason. She didn't know many people here.

"Yes."

It suddenly struck him that he'd stopped too close to her. He was now towering over her, his groin level with her head. And she was looking up at him from her kneeling position, with her mouth half parted. Blood shot to his cock at the evocative image this created in his mind and he took a hasty step backward.

He saw the moment Cwenthryth understood what he'd imagined her doing. She reddened further and lowered her gaze to the ground.

Damnation, what was wrong with him? Only the morning before she had been attacked, and she still bore the injuries to prove it. She had every reason to fear a man's lust, and he would be the last man she wanted to pleasure. Hadn't he sent her away only a few days ago? He had no right to bother her or behave so inappropriately.

"Let me help you up," he said, when she made to get to her feet. The feel of her small hand in his warmed him to the core because it betrayed her complete trust. Despite what had just happened she didn't fear him, she knew he hadn't meant anything lewd.

"Thank you. So, who is this person who needs me?" she asked, once she was up.

Me.

The word almost passed his lips of its own accord. He needed her, needed the warmth she brought to his home, the sound of her singing in the garden, the joy she brought his sons, the cakes and the rag pets she made, the heat of her body against his at night, the intimacy he had missed.

Everything.

He cleared his throat, turning his mind back to the conversation.

"Inga, the butcher's wife. She's about to give birth to her fifth child. The healer, Helga, who usually sees to these things, is already assisting Sigrid, one of Bee's friends, with her first babe. She was wondering if you could help."

Cwenthryth bit her lip, looking unsure. "I'm not a midwife, or even a healer," she said in a low voice.

"I know, but you already helped Eyja successfully, and anyway, Helga will be there too, coming in at intervals to check everything is progressing as it should and giving you advice if you need it," he reassured her. "Inga has already given birth multiple times, she knows what she's doing. I'm sure everything will be fine. It's only that she would benefit from a soothing feminine presence at this time."

"Of course she would."

Why, oh why he had been clumsy? Steinar hated himself for reminding Cwenthryth of her ordeal, when she'd had to go through the birth of her dead child on her own, afraid and unprepared, before her friend had mercifully found her and helped.

She straightened her back, every inch the brave woman she was.

"Take me to Inga."

THE MOON PIERCED the purple horizon line just as Cwenthryth was exiting from the butcher's hut. The day was over, and a new life had just dawned.

Taking a deep inhale, she stared at the sky overhead and felt peace descend inside her body. The afternoon she'd just spent with Inga had been a revelation, and she was filled with a new sense of purpose. The anguish, the self-doubt, the gory mess, everything had been forgotten the moment she had handed the beaming mother her new baby. It had been so beautiful that something had opened inside her. Finally, she knew her vocation. From now on, helping others would be what she would do. The best, most rewarding way to do that was to assist women giving birth.

Helga had been very impressed with her level-headedness and had confided that, with the village population expanding fast, she'd been looking for someone to pass her knowledge on to. Cwenthryth could be that person if she wanted to. And she did.

Celebrating with new mothers and their healthy babies, or being there to assist the ones who had to go through the trauma of being told their child would never take a breath, might be the very thing needed to help her get over her own loss. Since her discussion with Steinar the evening before, when he had coaxed her into talking about what she had gone through, she felt better, or at least different, willing to acknowledge that she had endured something traumatic, and she had survived.

And besides, helping Helga would give her a legitimate reason to stay in the village. She would have a place to be, a role to play. She would no longer be an intruder. It seemed as though she would get her wish to live close to nature after all, in a place with a river.

Steinar's hut appeared before her, familiar in the dim light. She stared at the door a moment, wondering if she should knock, wondering why she should even ask herself the question. She was only a guest. This was not her home, of course she should knock.

She raised her hand.

Before she could touch the wood, the door opened, and she found herself in front of Steinar, inches away from his strong body. All the breath left her lungs.

"Cwenthryth. I thought it might be you."

How did he know she'd just arrived? Had he been looking for her through the window?

"Yes. It's me," she answered rather stupidly. But how could she think straight with such a man staring at her? He was so tall, so masculine. He was also tantalisingly close to her. Her body inched forward, as if in search of warmth and comfort, the same comfort she had felt when she had woken up this morning with his arms around her.

"Come in," he murmured. "You must be exhausted."

Was she exhausted? She didn't think so. Exhilarated, rather. But her body did feel strangely languid.

Steinar moved to let her through, then closed the door behind her. One hand on the small of her back, he led her to the only chair of the hut, the one placed at the head of the table.

"How did it go?" he asked, ladling fragrant stew into a wooden bowl. It smelled like mutton, the pungent smell softened with the sweeter scent of onions fried in butter. Cwenthryth realized she was hungry when he placed the bowl in front of her. Too busy with Inga and her babe, she had not had anything to eat all day. Her mouth started to water and she reached out for her wooden spoon. "Well, I hope?"

"It went very well, as easily as Helga had predicted." Unable to wait any longer, she took a spoonful of stew and brought it to her lips. It was as tasty as she had imagined and she barely repressed a groan of pleasure when the thick sauce coated her tongue. "Inga was delivered of a healthy girl," she said instead.

Steinar laughed. "I'm glad. I know that after four boys she and Arne were hoping for a little girl."

"Yes. She told me as much."

Cwenthryth had often wondered in the last few weeks if her baby had been a girl or a boy. She hadn't had the courage to look, or to ask Eahlswith if she'd seen anything. It had probably been too early to tell anyway.

"I've always wanted a little girl," Steinar surprised her by saying next. He'd helped himself to stew and had sat at the opposite end of the table, on a stool, making it appear as if he, not her, was the guest. "Not that I don't love my boys, of course…"

"No." That was not in question. She could tell he loved them more than life itself, but she had seen his reaction when he'd held little Frida.

He paused, spoon poised in mid-air, like a man deep in thought. "After Astrid gave birth to Ulf, I told her I would love to have a girl next. I often wonder if…"

If what? Had he been about to reveal something significant? He shook his head and reached out for the loaf of bread.

"Thank you." Cwenthryth accepted the piece of bread he was handing her, touched that he had not only cooked for her, but also waited for her to come back from Inga to start eating. He was now asking her questions about her day, surrendering his chair, serving her as if she belonged in his village. In his hut.

In his life.

The difference with the way he'd acted when she'd first arrived was staggering. And as a result, she felt at home, in a way she had not done since her father's decline.

"This is delicious, by the way," she told Steinar, pointing at the stew with her spoon. The meat was tender, falling off the bone as if it had simmered for a long while in the sauce, the vegetables were full of flavor, and the herbs added a pleasant depth to the dish. "You're a better cook than I am."

He shrugged, as if there was nothing extraordinary in a warrior being skilled in the art of making soups and stews.

"My mother always had me helping her as a child, so I've understood how to do the simplest things from a young age. Astrid was never the best with food, and she had to spend a lot of time in bed when she carried both our sons. I quickly started to experiment with ingredients and found that the results were generally pleasing." His eyes twinkled. "Besides, I might make a good stew, but the boys are adamant you make the best flat cakes."

She smiled, remembering the way they'd always devoured the ones she'd made for them in town. "Those cakes are more or less all I do, so I do make them quite well. But I'd find it difficult to make something as tasty as this."

"I'm sure I can show you how to do it some time."

The air in the hut stilled. For him to make such a promise had to mean he intended her to stay here, at least for a while. He'd already hinted at the fact that she would find it hard to rid herself of him and his sons. But as threats went, this one suited her fine. She wanted nothing more than to spend her life here, with him and the two boys.

His bowl now empty, Steinar stood up, filling the space with his massive body. A shiver rippled down Cwenthryth's spine. Just like a sword was a weapon that could both kill a villain or defend an innocent, power in a man could frighten or arouse in equal measure, as she was finding out. She felt utterly exposed in front of Steinar's virility, and the woman in her was trembling in desire.

"I would like that," she rasped. "Stews and flat cakes go well together."

"They do. It would seem we make a team, you and I."

By now all the air had left Cwenthryth's lungs. Where was the scowling, suspicious man who had opened his door to her when she'd first arrived in the village? The one who'd replaced him could well make her lose her mind as well as her heart.

"Come. You will be tired, and it's getting late," he said, his voice low.

She was tired, but loath to put an end to the intimate moment. Being with Steinar had admittedly been hard at first, but it was now a pleasure like no other. Still, she sensed it was better to agree. Otherwise, she wasn't certain where things might go. With the boys nowhere to be seen, they would be free to indulge their wildest desires. She wasn't sure it was the wisest thing to do right now.

"Yes. I'd better go to bed."

Cwenthryth stood up and stared at Steinar intently. Would he ask if he could sleep with her again like he had last night?

To her dismay, he did not.

14

———

The day had started out quite well. Nothing had led Steinar to believe he would end up spending the night bleeding on the cold floor of a gaol.

He'd left Cwenthryth in bed while he'd gone to get his sons from his parents' house. Then the four of them had broken their fasts together when she'd woken up, with the leftover mutton stew and a fresh loaf of bread his mother had given him. There had been joy, there had been laughter, there had been sunlight. It had been perfect.

It was only later that things had gone awry. In much the same way thunderclouds could suddenly obscure the most glorious day and bring about a devastating storm, events had started to follow one another with dizzying speed.

Cwenthryth had offered her help to start work on the vegetable patch he'd been planning to extend for weeks, so they had gone to the back of the hut as soon as the boys had left for Bee and Elwyn's house. As he was getting the tools out of the shed, Steinar heard an unusual noise by the well. Three men, Saxons, judging from their looks and their clothing, were descending from a cart drawn by a strong bay horse. They walked straight to him, determination etched on their faces.

"They are coming here," Cwenthryth said in a breath.

Steinar placed his shovel down. It would seem that digging would have to wait for now.

"Do you know them?" Were they members of her family, people who were worried about her whereabouts? It was doubtful but he had to ask.

"No." She lifted huge eyes to him. "And I think they're here for you, not for me."

Indeed they were. Ignoring her completely, they came to a halt straight in front of him, bristling with intent.

"Steinar, son of Wolf the Icelander?" the man in the middle asked, confirming their suspicions.

"Yes."

"You're accused of murder."

Ah. So Godfrid had died, after all.

As Steinar had been expecting such an outcome for two days, he didn't react as the Saxons no doubt expected him to. He just stared at them levelly. By his side, Cwenthryth gave a little whimper and dropped the hoe she'd been holding. Unlike him, she didn't seem to have anticipated he would end up in trouble. He threw her a reassuring glance before addressing the men, because there would be no trouble, not if he had his way. He had only defended her and his son, no one could blame him for that. He wondered how they could possibly have found out who had killed the vile Saxon, though. As far as he'd seen, they had been alone in the clearing.

"Yes, well, some things can't be helped."

The Saxons looked at one another with a frown. Clearly they had not expected him to admit to the deed so easily. But what else was he supposed to do? He had killed the man, but he had not murdered him, and what was more, he would do it again in a heartbeat. If there were men on this earth able to witness what he had witnessed and not kill the bastard responsible, then he didn't want to be one of them. He had done what needed to be done and he refused to feel guilty for it.

"You're not denying it then?"

"No, I'm not." He was starting to get annoyed. "But you need to hear the whole story. Then I don't think you'll call it murder. You'd call it protection." He'd defended Cwenthryth and saved his son from a mortal beating, which was not the same at all as killing someone in cold blood. What other choice had he had? Should he have let Godfrid carry on?

Over his dead body.

"Protection!" the smallest of the men scoffed. He barely reached to his shoulder, something that seemed to only fuel his anger further. Steinar had noticed how short men often resented his height and strength, taking it as a personal affront, as if he were doing his best to humiliate them. They always enjoyed it when they were allowed to have the upper hand over him, which admittedly, was not often. "From what? What danger could she have posed to a man like you?"

She?

Who were they talking about? A shiver of unease went down his spine. He'd been so sure the men were here because of Godfrid. Had he made a wrong assumption? The same confusion was swirling in Cwenthryth's dark eyes, quickly replaced by what looked like doubt.

His stomach fell. Like him, she was clearly wondering who this mysterious woman was. But unlike him, she couldn't be sure Godfrid was the first person he'd ever killed. What if she'd heard the story of his father's supposed crime from someone in the village and was now wondering whether he, too, had killed his wife. *She*, the Saxon had said… It could all too easily apply to Astrid, who'd recently died at a young age. What if Cwenthryth started to fear him because of these idiots' accusations? His whole body roiled in protest.

No, not now, not after all they had gone through together!

"Wait. Who am I supposed to have killed?" he growled to the men, hating them for disturbing the hard-won truce between him and Cwenthryth.

"Who do you think? Or have you killed so many people that you've lost count, hey, Norseman?" the small man smirked.

"Who?" Steinar repeated, not in the least impressed by the taunt.

"Your wife, of course."

All he heard was Cwenthryth's sharp inhale of breath. Bloody, bloody bleeding hell, now she *would* think him a wife killer, just like Astrid's parents.

"I didn't kill her, I swear," he said through gritted teeth, addressing himself to her rather that the Saxons.

"Well, where is she then?" the man in the middle asked, before nodding toward Cwenthryth with a smirk. "That's not her, at least we can agree on that."

What he meant by that was unclear but Steinar didn't waste time wondering about it. Because the situation was suddenly very different—and ten times more dangerous than before. He was no longer justifying his actions when faced with an assault, but being accused of murdering an innocent woman. Two very different things.

Still, he would not cower. He didn't mind facing justice for having killed a bastard attacking his son after raping a woman, but he wasn't going to let them take him for a crime he was innocent of. Why were they even here? Why did they think Astrid had been murdered in the first place? Who had accused him? Astrid's father, thinking to get his revenge on him at last? Her mother, intent on avenging the humiliation of his rejection? Did it matter who had sent the Saxons? Not really, not when he was innocent and more than capable of defending himself.

"My wife died last month of a bloody flux. I didn't kill her. 6Ask anyone around. They will tell you the same thing."

"Yes, they would, as they are all Norse people."

"They would because it's the truth."

Steinar had never been a patient man and if there was one thing guaranteed to make him snap it was people's stubbornness and bad faith. If the men weren't going to listen to reason, then he would have to fight. He would not spend the best part of the day trying to convince them he had done nothing wrong. There were only three men, none half as strong as he was. He would easily dispose of them, starting with the one who'd called him "Norseman" with such contempt in his voice. Then he would go into town and tell the reeve what he thought of his men's method.

He threw a glance at the axe he'd brought out to cut out new wooden posts. It was the one he had used to put an end to Godfrid's miserable life, light and deadly sharp, but it was lying against the fence, too far for him to reach. It mattered not, he still had his hands. Besides, he didn't want to kill the men, just stop them from taking him away and give himself a chance to sort this mess out.

His hand shot out, hitting the man square on the jaw. He dropped to his knees, blood pouring from his mouth. Steinar turned to the second man, who was drawing a blade out of his boot, and scoffed. He would not be stopped by something as puny as a—

"Stop now or I'll slice her throat. It's your decision."

The declaration rang in the air, stilling his movement. Steinar turned to see the third man holding Cwenthryth by the waist, his blade at her throat. A drop of blood, the color shocking against her pale skin, was sliding down her neck. The look of terror in her eyes froze the marrow in his bones. No, by the gods! They could not hurt her to get to him.

His hands were up in the air before he could blink. Nothing was worth risking the bastard nicking at Cwenthryth's skin a second time, just to prove he was serious. His attackers instantly took advantage of his surrender. A blow to the temple sent his head spinning. It was quickly followed by another one to the jaw that sent him to his knees.

"Tie him up nice and tight. Make sure he cannot move a finger, then throw him in the back of the cart." Still holding Cwenthryth, the man gave his instructions to his friends, one of whom was still bleeding profusely.

A moment later, Steinar was trussed up with his arms around his back, his legs bound together, his mouth stuffed with a gag. Indeed, the only part of him he could move was his eyelids. It had all happened too quickly, and as his hut was the one farthest out to the back of the village, no one had heard the commotion and come to his aid.

"No, Steinar, you can't…" Cwenthryth whimpered, running to him. Mercifully, the man had let her go as soon as he'd been tied up. "You cannot let them take you. You're innocent!"

Well, he was, but he could not let the man slice her throat while he argued his case, could he? Surely justice would prevail, because this had to be a misunderstanding. Astrid had not been murdered, so he could not be punished for killing her.

But it meant the world to him to hear that she didn't even think to doubt his innocence. He'd just been accused of killing his wife, and they didn't really know one another. She would have had every reason to wonder if there was any truth in the claim.

He chewed at his gag in desperation. How he wished he could

talk to her, thank her for gifting him with the trust he had denied her when she had arrived at the village.

"Let's go, before someone comes to investigate," one of the Saxons said. "I don't rate my chances against these Norsemen."

"Aye."

The last thing he saw before being carried to the cart was Cwenthryth's beautiful face distorted by fear.

15

Another kick, to the ribs this time, caused him to double over. Then a punch to the side of the head, made him see stars. Steinar closed his eyes, bracing himself against the pain ripping through his body. The beating would stop eventually, either because he passed out, or because his tormentor got tired. Either way, it was out of his control. Begging would achieve nothing. If the man was determined to make him suffer, then he would not stop because he'd been asked, quite the opposite. He would delight in his enemy's humiliation.

Steinar made sure to keep on breathing and not uttering a sound. The bastard didn't deserve the satisfaction of knowing he was inflicting him pain; he probably knew it anyway, and enjoyed the idea.

Finally, as he'd predicted, everything stopped. His gag was removed and the ropes at his wrists tightened further.

"You're a stubborn one, Norseman, I'll give you that." The man spat on the ground and cradled his right fist into his left hand. Had he hurt himself while hitting him? Was that the reason he was stopping, because he could not carry on? Steinar scoffed, hoping it was the case. If only he could have been made of real stone… Then the Saxon would have cracked his knuckles on the first blow. "But I'll make you admit you killed your poor little wife, never fear."

"I did not kill her, so you will not," Steinar said, the taste of blood bitter in his mouth. He was wasting his breath, he knew, but he could not let such an accusation pass unchallenged. He had not killed Astrid. Nothing would make him admit to it.

The man didn't seem to have heard him. "You lost no time in replacing her, did you? With a Saxon no less." He tilted his head, as if considering. "You know, now that you're in here, unable to see to her needs, I think I will go see your new woman and give her what she deserves. She's a nice piece from what I saw, and felt soft and plump writhing against my cock when I held her."

Every inch of Steinar's body started to burn. Bile rose in his throat because he feared that this was no idle threat destined to taunt him. The man had seen Cwenthryth at the hut and he knew she would be alone while he was here. Ulf and Rothgar would be no match for him if he decided to attack her, even supposing Cwenthryth allowed them to intervene. He knew her. She would likely surrender herself rather than allowing the two boys to get hurt.

But he could not let that happen, not after what she had endured already.

"Touch her and I'll rip your cock out with my bare hands," he snarled, wishing he could shred the ropes holding his wrists captive. He would still be chained to the wall by the ankle, of course, but the gaol was not so big. If he had his hands free, he would make sure the bastard was in no state to do anything to Cwenthryth or anyone else. He *would* rip his cock out, and enjoy paying him back for the beating.

The man laughed, as if reading his mind. "How will you do that? Tied as you are, you can't even throw a punch, so my cock is quite safe, I would say."

"It might be tied for now, but I will not remain here indefinitely."

And when I come out, you will regret your words.

"Oh, I imagine you'll get out eventually, but only to hang for your crime. Then the little Saxon will be shown what I can do to women." He eyed him up contemptuously. "You're a great big brute of a man, probably only able to rut like the beasts in the field, so I wager she would welcome a more civilized lover."

"Is rape your idea of civilized?" Steinar spat. Bloody hell, forget the beating he'd just received, hearing the man's intentions regarding Cwenthryth was true torture. His body had been less damaged by the blows than his soul was being at the moment.

The vile man leaned in toward him, the foul smell of his breath becoming overwhelming. "I've never raped a single woman in my life. Never needed to. Once I have shown them what I can do, they always end up begging me for more. Your woman will be no exception. She will squirm under me and she will—"

"No!" Steinar roared. And then he realized that, tied as he was, there was still a weapon at his disposal.

His head.

The noise the man's nose made when it shattered against his skull was the most satisfying Steinar had ever heard. Then it was followed by an even better one. The sound of the man whimpering like a babe, as the pain of the blow registered.

"You bastard! You broke my nose! You'll regret that when I ask the hangman to slice off your bollocks before hanging you like the dog you are," he cried out, his voice completely different.

He spat on the floor, then he kicked him in the shin. The pain radiated all the way to his eyeballs but Steinar only smiled. He'd understood by now that the man had no real power; he would never kill or even seriously maim him. The reeve had probably given orders that their prisoner should be left in reasonable condition until a verdict had been reached, which was why the beating had stopped when it had. Fear of retribution was keeping the Saxon from inflicting any lasting damage.

"I'm not a dog, *you* are. Didn't you know? I'm a wolf."

"Don't think a broken nose will stop me from making your woman pay for what you just did."

No, unfortunately Steinar did not think that. It would only make the Saxon more determined to make Cwenthryth suffer. "The men at the village will never let you get away with it," he snarled.

Of this he was certain. His father, his brothers, Moon, Rorik, Haakon even, everyone would defend Cwenthryth as if she were their own.

If they saw she was attacked, of course. The bastard would likely make sure to take her away before pouncing, in case anyone heard her cries or realized what was happening.

The tightening of the man's lips made it clear he had read his mind. "They might well try to stop me if they saw me, but I'm hardly going to announce my intentions, am I? I will get the woman out of the village and into a comfortable bed before I show her what us Saxons can do. She deserves nothing but the best, and so do I." He cupped himself crudely. "Well, methinks it's time to go. My balls are burning something fierce. If you don't see me at your next beating, you know where I'll be."

The door slammed shut, leaving only a resounding silence.

Steinar threw his head to the ceiling and howled.

A MOMENT later the door opened again, but this time, his father entered. Everything within Steinar relaxed at the sight. Not another bastard intent on beating him, not the reeve about to ask him questions about his supposed crime, not the hangman come to take him away, but the man he most dearly wished to see.

"Son."

The Icelander knelt next to him and started slicing the ropes holding him captive without another word. As soon as he was free, Steinar brought his arms in front of him, flexing his wrists, rolling his shoulders and neck to relieve the tension in them. Never had anything felt so good.

"What are you doing here?" he rasped, hoisting himself up into a more comfortable sitting position.

In truth, he was not surprised to see him gain access to the gaol. As the undisputed leader of the Norsemen village, Wolf had the respect of the Saxons, with whom he'd worked on many occasions over the years. No one, least of all a newly-elected reeve, would have dared refuse him access to a Norse prisoner, much less if that prisoner was his son. But how had he known where he was so quickly? How could he have supposed he'd been arrested for murder and taken to town?

"Cwenthryth came to find me when you were taken. She explained everything, told me what I needed to gain access to you."

Steinar let out a sigh. "Of course." The woman had acted with decision, doing what needed to be done instead of wasting time lamenting herself. He should have known he could rely on her.

"How are you?"

He snorted. "Never better, as you can see." One of his eyes was swollen shut, his lip was cut, and he could well imagine his face was crusted with blood and covered in bruises. As to his body, it was a miracle no bones had been broken. "But never mind that. It will all heal. You must know I didn't kill—"

"I do know that. That is not even in question." His father did not let him finish. "My sons do not murder innocent women."

"No." The unwavering support was welcome. "Thank you."

Wolf straightened up, determination etched over his face. "Now. As the reeve knows me, he is prepared to listen to reason. But we must find out who accused you and why."

That was what Steinar had wondered. Who had accused him of a crime that had not even been committed, and to what end? "I have no idea. All I know is that this is a nightmare." Being accused of killing a woman, a woman he had once loved, had pierced at his heart.

"Yes." Wolf's blue eyes clouded over. "And I am better placed than most to understand how you feel. I, too, was accused of murdering my wife. The difference is that Solveig, unlike Astrid, had indeed been killed."

Steinar did know that. In fact, it was why the Icelander was here in this country. More than thirty years ago, he had been sent into exile for the murder of his first wife, an Icelander like him. His innocence had been later proved, of course, but by then it had been too late for him to go back home. He'd found his second wife, Merewen, the Saxon who was the love of his life, and she'd already been carrying their first child—Steinar himself. Merewen's country had become his. There had been no talk of ever going back.

"Yes. I know you were accused of strangling her." Steinar could not begin to imagine what his father had endured at having the people in his village, some of them friends, believing him capable of such a despicable act. "It must have been awful."

"It was. Another difference with you is that our marriage had started to go sour by then, which allowed people to think I had…"

Wolf's voice trailed off when Steinar threw him a meaningful look. No one at the village knew or even suspected the tensions in his marriage, but they had definitely been there. As far as everyone was concerned, everything had been well between him and Astrid, even if, like most people, they'd faced their share of trials, the loss of their second child being the worst of them.

Suddenly, he wanted to tell his father what it had really been like. He had hidden the truth for far too long, under the pretext of protecting the people he loved, but it was suffocating him. He'd opened up to Cwenthryth the other day, and it had been a liberation. It seemed to him that he would feel better if his parents knew exactly what he'd been through and he could stop pretending.

"My marriage to Astrid had done much worse than go sour. It had rotted away."

He told him everything, the distance settling between them, the resentment building within him at the lack of intimacy, her decision to leave him before she died. The only thing he kept to himself was the existence of a lover. Things were bad enough as it was, and he didn't see how adding to his humiliation would help in any way.

Wolf nodded slowly once he'd finished. "I cannot claim to be surprised. We didn't dare to say anything, but your mother and I started to suspect all was not as it should be a while ago."

Steinar gave a small smile. Of course, he should have guessed his mother would notice something. She had always been a particularly astute woman.

The similarities between him and his father, always at the forefront of his mind, struck him anew. Everyone agreed that, out of the three brothers, his eldest was the one who resembled Wolf the most physically. Apparently, their appearance was not the only thing they had in common. Steinar had now fallen for his own Saxon woman. He could only imagine the effect a young Merewen would have had on his Icelandic father all those years ago, when he'd been a man in exile. With her auburn hair and liquid black eyes, she would have been striking woman, nothing like the fair, blue-eyed women he was used to seeing in his country. No wonder he had bought her from the slave seller she had been given to. As soon as he had seen her offered to the crowd, he had wanted to protect her, make sure no man could hurt her.

Steinar gritted his teeth. Here the difference between the two of them was a major, distressing one.

His father had taken it upon himself to save a woman who had not asked anything of him, who had not even known of his existence and had not exchanged a single word with him. He, on the other hand, had refused his aid to the woman who had come to him in search of protection and told him many times she was fleeing a dangerous man. He'd been told she was in danger, and yet had ignored her pleas and sent her away. He had treated her as if she were his to use for his pleasure, and then allowed her to leave when everyone urged him to let her stay.

Well. No more.

From now on he would do what he should have done from the start. He would protect her, he would be there for her. Starting from now on, even if he was stuck in this wretched cell.

"*Faðir,* please, go back to the village. Look after Cwenthryth. She's not safe. The men here have their eye on her." He shook his head in disgust. "The one who beat me earlier… I fear he will—"

"Sven is at the hut with her and the children, has been from the moment she came to talk to me. He's under strict instructions not leave her side until you come home. You can set your mind at rest."

Steinar nodded, reassured at last. His brawny brother was protection enough. One look at him scowling and the Saxon would soil his braies. "Thank him from me. And thank you for coming, for believing me. *Þǫkk.*"

"You don't need to thank me for that. I will always be on your side." With a nod, Wolf stood back up. "I'll be back soon, to get you out this time. Don't worry. No son of mine will hang for a crime they didn't commit."

16

"Sven, would you please—"

The words died on Cwenthryth's lips, and her foot stopped in mid-air when she turned around to kick the door closed behind her. Because the man sitting at the table was not the one she'd expected to see. His hair was too long, his shoulders too broad. No, this was not Sven, but his older brother. The man she most dearly wanted to see. The man she had missed dreadfully. The man she had feared never to see again.

"Steinar!"

She dropped the handful of wood she'd just gathered and ran up to him, only to stop dead when he turned to face her. Her hands flew to her mouth while ice flooded her veins. Dear Lord, his face was covered in cuts and bruises. If that were the case, she could barely imagine what the rest of him looked like.

"What happened to you?" she said in a sob. Of course, she had guessed he would have endured some hardship in the gaol, but this was something altogether different. He'd been badly beaten, if not tortured, and all for a crime he had not committed.

"I'm free," he said simply, walking over to her.

"Yes. Thank God, you're free."

Cwenthryth fell into his arms. It was only when she felt his moan against her lips that she realized they were kissing. It felt so natural that she had not even registered it at first. Steinar must have lowered his head to meet her halfway because she would never have been able to put her lips on his otherwise. He might also have been the one initiating the kiss because she wasn't sure she would have found the courage to do so.

In any case, it didn't matter who had done what and who had started it. They were kissing, it was all she cared about. Until she remembered that his lip was cut and his cheeks were bruised.

"No," she protested between fiery kisses, pushing at his chest. "Wait, we must not, your injuries… I don't want to hurt you."

More heated kisses followed. Steinar didn't seem worried in the least about the damage to his face. He didn't even appear to be in pain, only desperate for her. "You're not hurting me, you're healing me," he rasped, his hands landing on her buttocks. "I need you, Cwenthryth, your goodness, your forgiveness, your under-standing. I need you, don't you see?"

What was he talking about? *He* needed *her*? She rather thought it was the other way around.

Cwenthryth didn't have time to reply or ask any questions. Still kissing her, Steinar lifted her into his arms as easily as if she'd been made of straw and sat her on the table behind her. The lewd position was made even more scandalous when he came to stand between her spread legs.

"Let me."

Oh, why was he asking? Didn't he know by now that she would let him do anything? Though she had no idea what he wanted to do, she gave her agreement. "Yes."

Just when she thought he would take her mouth in another soul-devastating kiss, he buried his fingers into her hair. Throwing his head back like a man in prey to the most exquisite pleasure, he started massaging her scalp in slow, languorous gestures, cradling her in his big hands all the while.

"Ah, yes," he rasped. "Your hair is just glorious. I've wanted to do this for years."

She would have laughed if her whole body had not been covered in goose bumps. Years, really? Now who was the liar? "You can't have. We only met last month," she reminded him in a whisper, her eyes closing of their own accord.

"Mm, I know. Too late. Much too late. Would that you'd been the woman I took to my bed as a youth of sixteen summers—that way we wouldn't have lost any time."

"I would have been Rothgar's age back then, so I don't think that would have been a good idea."

Cwenthryth's eyes snapped open. What was wrong with her? Steinar was stroking her sensually, telling her the most wonderful things, and all she could do was being ridiculously matter-of-fact? Fortunately he didn't seem put out. He let out a low growl and wedged himself closer between her thighs.

"Well, you're not a child any longer but the most gorgeous woman I've ever seen, and I'm going to make sure you feel it." With that, his fingers left her hair. "Can I?"

She nodded, realizing belatedly that he was asking for permission because he didn't want to be like Godfrid and take what she was not ready to give freely. He nodded back and a heartbeat later his hands landed on her breasts, engulfing them in delicious warmth. A groan escaped his lips at the same time as she took in a sharp intake of breath. He let out a word in Norse.

"I-I don't understand…"

"Perfection," he said, which she assumed to be the translation of the word. "Let me suckle you, Cwenthryth. Please. I need it."

How could she say no when she was desperate herself? She needed his lips, his tongue, his heat on her. She needed to know that he was back, he was safe, he was with her. Having wanted him almost from the moment she had set eyes on him, she was not going to refuse him now.

"Yes."

She tore at her bodice herself, freeing her breasts for him to feast on. Baring herself to a man was the most scandalous thing she had done in her life, but it didn't seem to matter, and mercifully Steinar didn't appear shocked. Quite the contrary. He fell on her like a starving man.

His mouth on her nipple was like a branding iron, the heat of it a delicious torture, and the tongue licking it was the best way to ease the burn.

"Yes," she said again, arching her back to offer herself more fully, placing her hands either side of his face to force him even closer to her. "More."

"More, lovely," she heard him groan back, before he whipped his hand under her skirts. "Let me feel your softness. Let me pleasure you."

There were no threats today, no mention of punishment, no warning that this would be for him only. Today he wanted to pleasure her. Well, she would let him, but she would make sure to pleasure him in turn once he was finished with her. *If* she had any strength left, that was. She wasn't certain she would be able to do anything save lie on the table in a puddle of satisfaction. Well, they would have to see, because she was certainly not going to stop him now.

Slowly, he slid his palm all the way up her thigh, using his fingertips to brush her skin, stopping only when the tip of his thumb reached her—

"Brother. You're back."

Cwenthryth froze, imagining the sight she and Steinar would present. She was sitting on the table with her legs spread and her bodice open. Fingers wrapped around his head, she was holding him pressed against her breasts. His mouth was at her nipple, his hand under her skirt. There was no room for misunderstanding. She should move, try to hide, do something. She should not stay still and silent.

Before she could, the door opened wider to let through the smiling figure of Steinar's youngest brother, who'd been staying with her these last few days. It was only then that Cwenthryth remembered that, in her shock at seeing Steinar in the hut earlier, she had not closed the door properly. Too late. Sven stopped when he saw the scene in front of him.

And then, just when she thought she would die of mortification, the wretched man winked at her.

"Oh, yes, you *are* back, brother mine, and already making up for lost time, I see. Good for you." His smile widened as he looked at her again. "Good morning, Cwenthryth. You don't need me anymore, it would seem. I can see Steinar has you… er, well in hand, shall we say?"

"Sven. Go to hell," Steinar answered, his mouth now at her throat, his body shielding her exposed breasts from view. He had not turned to face his brother, as if fearing that the sight of his satisfaction would make him snap. She could feel him vibrating with irritation against her.

"Mm, I feel I should tell you first that *Faðir* wanted to see you as soon as you came back." A pause, for effect. "And now, if you'll excuse me, I will go to hell, as 'tis probably where I belong anyway."

Once the door had closed and silence descended back into the hut, Cwenthryth and Steinar stared at one another, their breathing short, their bodies still glued together.

What now? Should they carry on as if nothing had happened? Should they dissolve in confusion? Cwenthryth had no idea. She just kept staring into the sky-blue eyes in front of her, hoping for an answer.

Slowly, Steinar removed his hand from her thigh, restored

order to her bodice and took a step back. Well, at least she knew where she stood. There would be no more kissing or suckling, no stroking or rutting today. Sanity had returned—and perhaps it was for the best. For a moment she had been overcome by relief and lust, but was it wise to allow her urges to take over thus, with a man who only the week before had wished her out of his life? She wasn't sure. Things were complicated enough between them, and she should be grateful to Sven for having interrupted them. Should be. Except that, if she were honest, she wasn't.

She would have liked to see what he would have done to her this time.

"Bloody Sven," Steinar grumbled under his breath.

He sounded like a sulky child. Cwenthryth couldn't help a smile. Perhaps he was struggling with what he felt too. This was the best thing she could have seen right now, because it helped her deal with her own wayward emotions.

"Yes, bloody Sven," she said, swearing for the first time in her life.

Steinar arched a brow at her daring, then sighed. "I should at least have thanked him for staying here with you, and making sure no one got near."

The Norseman had slept in the hut the past two nights, and remained within calling distance of her and the boys during the day. How had she forgotten he would be here when she and Steinar had started kissing? The relief at seeing him alive and as well as could be had really made her forget everything.

"Yes, you should thank him. And he's right. We should go speak to your father without delay. We need to find out who accused you of killing your wife and bring him to justice." She was adamant. Even if he'd been freed, Steinar had been beaten up, and could have been killed as a result. The deed should not go unpunished. Someone had to pay for what they'd put him through. Gently, she stroked his cheekbone, where a nasty bruise attested to the severity of the beating. "They cannot get away with it."

"No." He seemed just as determined as she was to have his name cleared, which was no wonder. "So you don't believe I killed Astrid?"

Cwenthryth recoiled at the question she had not expected. "Of course not!" She had not entertained the notion, not even for a moment. How could Steinar doubt it? She trusted him, unconditionally. His wife had died from an illness. Everyone here had had told her as much, and anyway, he was incapable of hurting a woman. It was obvious from the way he touched her. "No," she repeated more firmly.

Something shifted in his eyes. Relief? Gratitude? "Thank you. I needed to hear that."

"Don't thank me. 'Tis only normal. Now. Do you have any idea who might want you dead?" Because that was the real question. Accusing someone of something meant hoping they would get punished for the deed, and murder was punishable by death. The person who had gone to the reeve had known what Steinar was risking. "Who hates you so much?"

"I…" He sounded wary of voicing his doubts out loud, so she didn't press on. But it was clear he had an idea of who that person might be. Still seated on the table, with his strong thighs keeping hers wide open, Cwenthryth waited. Eventually, he carried on. "The only people I can think of are Astrid's parents. I hate placing blame when I cannot be sure, but I can't think of anyone else who might wish me ill. They have never liked me and might want to make me pay for not looking after their daughter properly."

Not looking after her properly? She doubted this was what had happened. A husband like Steinar, thoughtful and protective, would be every woman's dream. Her arched brow conveyed her disbelief. "Surely they don't think that?"

"I think they do. When I went to announce her death, his

father didn't seem sad, as much as pleased at this proof that she should never have left the village and, more pointedly, the man he had chosen for her. The blacksmith's wife, he delighted in telling me, was still alive, unlike mine, and with child."

"You mean… He accused you of killing his daughter?" That was shocking news. But if the stupid man was convinced Steinar had killed Astrid, then he might well have written to the reeve to accuse him of the crime.

"Not in so many words, but his meaning was clear. If she'd not married me, Astrid would still be alive and well. He considers me no better than my father, who was accused of having killed his first wife in Iceland almost forty years ago. He hadn't, of course."

Of course. Wolf, a killer? She would have laughed if the notion hadn't been so ridiculous. Like his son, the man didn't have a vicious bone in his body.

"What about Astrid's mother? Does she agree with her husband? Could she have been the one sending the message?" A woman, who had been the one giving birth to her child, might feel the loss of her more keenly and want revenge.

There was a silence, ominous. Cwenthryth braced herself. It seemed as if she were going from one shocking revelation to the next and she wondered what Steinar would reveal next. Then he spoke. "Though she didn't say a word during the conversation, she came to find me afterward, to… proposition me."

Proposition him? Did he mean what she thought he meant? One look at Steinar's stony countenance made it clear that he meant exactly that.

"She didn't!" Once again, Cwenthryth didn't know whether to be incredulous or appalled. His despised mother-in-law was the last woman Steinar would have felt attraction to, and to have her making lewd advances in such a moment would have upset him.

"I know," he said, bringing his forehead to hers as if preparing to talk in confidence. "I was as shocked as you, and I sent her away none too gently. She wasn't best pleased, as you can imagine. But that still doesn't mean she accused me of anything to make herself feel better."

"No, of course not." It would have taken a lot of effort on the woman's part to go to the reeve in town, and present a case solid enough for him to take action. She would also have been aware of the possible retribution of accusing someone of murder when she knew he was innocent of any wrongdoing. Had the humiliation of Steinar's rejection been enough to push her to do such a thing?

"To justify her actions, she told me some nonsense about women wanting me as soon as they saw me," he carried on, placing a hand on the side of her neck in a soothing gesture.

"But you must know that it is not complete nonsense," Cwenthryth murmured before she could stop herself. Hadn't Steinar guessed from what had happened in the tree house and her reaction to his kisses just now that she, too, had fallen under his spell? Astrid's mother was right in this at least. Women could not help want a man like him. "I mean, I myself—"

This time he cupped her face in his hands, cutting through the fumbled explanations. "Don't."

"Don't what?" she was startled by the intensity in his gaze, in his voice, in his body. He had gone rigid with anger.

"Don't compare yourself to that viper. What the two of us have is special, what we did is special, even if I was a fool for not seeing it at the time." With those words he placed a gentle kiss over her lips. "Fortunately, you did, and you didn't shy away from your feelings."

Oh. Everything within Cwenthryth melted. She had been able to stand up to an irate Steinar, but she was at a loss in front of this new man. He was looking at her tenderly, he was touching her, kissing her, he was telling her that what they had was special. How was she supposed to resist?

"Was that the impression you got? That I didn't shy away

from my feelings?" The truth was, she had been too overwhelmed to know how to handle them. It surprised her that he thought her able to be honest with herself. "I have never felt that way about anyone. And after Godfrid, I truly thought I would not be drawn to any man. It didn't seem to matter, as I thought no one would want me anyway."

Steinar lifted her hand to his lips and kissed it softly. "Oh, lovely. I'm sorry, because my attitude toward you would only have confirmed this idea. It was unforgivable. But you see, I…" He shook his head, as if confused or disgusted by himself. "It seems silly now that I know you, but I was wary of you because of what had happened with Astrid."

"Her having a lover you mean? You didn't trust women because she betrayed you with another?" It would be understandable. After all, she'd thought she couldn't trust men because of the way Godfrid had treated her. It was easy to be wary after a trauma.

"That's not what I mean, even if it didn't help. But if you remember, at first, when you arrived, I didn't know about Astrid having a lover. To tell you the truth, I'm not even sure I believed you when you told me about it. I didn't want to believe any of it, that she had betrayed me or that you were genuinely in search for protection and a hiding place." He shook his head again.

"What was it then?"

"I was wary of you because of the feelings you provoked inside me, feelings that had gotten me into trouble once already. It had been the same with Astrid, and I had followed my instinct without thinking. But all too quickly I became disillusioned with our marriage, realized that I had married in hurry a woman who was wrong for me and would never give me what I wanted, much less what I needed. Then you came along, when I had my children to consider. Though the attraction was immediate, I didn't want to make the same mistake again, trust someone on first acquaintance."

"Especially someone who could not get her story straight and didn't even know who you were," Cwenthryth said wryly. It would have appeared suspicious. In fact, she realized now, she would have appeared exactly like Godfrid had appeared to her, like an imposter trying to worm her way inside his home under false pretences.

"I suppose so." He seemed relieved to see that she wasn't angry. She wasn't. Everything he had said made sense and she was gratified that he was willing to explain himself.

"What were the reasons you had married Astrid if, as you say, she was so unsuitable for you?"

Cwenthryth couldn't help being curious. Would he tell her? It was a very personal question, but he seemed different since he'd brought her home after Godfrid's attack, more open, more relaxed. This new Steinar might well answer.

He did.

"She lived in one of the other Norsemen villages along the coast. We met one summer here, when my father organized a meeting for all the people of Norse descent in the area. Astrid was very beautiful and forward, and well, we slept together that night. I had no idea her union to another man had been arranged at the time, I thought she was free to indulge her senses with whomever she liked, like I was, but I was mistaken."

"Wasn't she a virgin?"

"No, which only comforted me in the idea that she was used to bedding the men she desired." He shrugged. "I never thought I would see her again, but a few days later she came to see me, utterly panicked. She was worried our encounter might have made her with child, and feared her father's reaction when he found out. Not to mention that of her future husband's, a violent man who'd been promised she was still untouched. I could not let her face this alone, so I did the only thing I thought I could do. I offered for her hand. I know I was young, only twenty summers at the time, but…"

"But?"

Cwenthryth was now more curious than ever. Twenty was indeed young to think about settling down, especially with a woman who was little more than a stranger. More than one man she knew who would have ignored her plight, or at least waited until he was certain she was with child before committing to her.

"But I had the example of my parents, which gave me hope. They met in very unusual circumstances and yet they found love in their marriage, a love I envied from a young age. I thought, why could it not happen to me as well? Astrid had attracted me from the start. We had slept together, had found pleasure in each other's arms, and she needed me. There were worse starts to a marriage. It turned out that I should have been more cautious, because it wasn't long before I saw that we weren't compatible in the least. When her real, selfish nature was revealed, it was too late. We were already married and she was carrying my child. Ulf. I could not have abandoned her then."

Cwenthryth nodded, as she reassessed their first few days together in the light of what she'd just been told. She had burst into Steinar's life at the worst possible moment, demanding the same thing his late wife had demanded of him, help and protection from a man he didn't know. Except that, unlike Astrid, she'd had no previous acquaintance to draw from. No wonder Steinar would not have wanted to get involved with yet another woman who had come in search of a protector, at the risk of seeing her turn into someone else once she felt safe and had gotten what she wanted out of him. As he'd said, he'd had his children to consider.

"I'm sorry, it was—"

"No. I'm the one who is sorry. I should not have let what had happened with someone else influence what happened between us."

A stunned silence followed that declaration. Was this truly the man who had once shouted at her to get the hell out of his house? The one who had glared at her while accusing her of using his sons to get to him? Who had told her he knew she was lying about fleeing a man? The change was incredible. He was honest with her, exposing his darkest thoughts and doubts to her.

Cwenthryth took in a deep inhale. There was something she had wondered about for days, or more pointedly something that had worried her for days. Dare she mention it now? Yes.

Since they were being open with one another, there would be no better opportunity.

"Steinar, did you..."

She hesitated, poised on a very personal, very painful question. What if she was wrong? Even worse, what if she was right? Would he want to talk about it or would he send her to hell? For once she wouldn't blame him if he did. What he had told her the day she had helped Inga give birth came back to her.

I've always wanted a little girl. I often wonder if...

If the baby he'd lost before he had Rothgar had been a little girl. She thought that was what he'd meant and she needed to know for certain. Confusedly, she sensed it would bring them even closer to have gone through the same ordeal.

"Did I what?" he asked, when it became clear she might not find the courage to speak. "You can ask me anything."

"Did you lose a child too?"

There it was, plain as day.

Steinar stared at her a long moment, as if wondering whether to answer her. Perhaps he was wary of reawakening the pain of the loss, or perhaps he didn't wish to remind her of what she had gone through herself.

"Yes, I did. We did, twelve years ago. A girl or boy, we never found out, as it was too early to tell." The look in his eyes became distant, as if he was reliving the terrible moment he had been handed what could have been his baby. "Astrid fell with child quickly after Ulf's birth, perhaps too quickly, which might be the reason for the loss. I know not, nobody could explain to us what had happened. We were only told that it sometimes happened when there was a problem with the child, a problem which stopped it from developing normally."

Cwenthryth nodded. She'd heard the same thing, which had made her wonder if Godfrid had not been related to her after all. Her loss might have been nature's way of ensuring such pairings didn't produce any offspring. "I'm sorry."

"Thank you." It was his turn to nod, the gesture betraying the pain of a loss that might never fully heal. "After that, Astrid told me she didn't want to fall with child too quickly, and I agreed. I didn't want to have to go through that ever again."

Of course. They would have been understandably wary. She had on occasion wondered at the six-year difference between the two boys. Such a big gap was rather uncommon, unless the couple had consciously decided to avoid having another babe to preserve the woman's health, like Moon had done with Eyja, making her take herbs to prevent conception after a traumatic birth. But if Steinar and Astrid had lost a child after Ulf and then been careful not to have another one too soon, then the gap made sense.

His eyes still glazed, Steinar carried on with his explanation.

"For years we were careful. I withdrew whenever we made love. But of course, the method is not always reliable and she fell with child again—Rothgar. The last few months and the birth were very hard on Astrid, like they had been with Ulf. It was years before she allowed me to touch her again. And even then, I could never make love to her like I wanted. It was all a bit of a mess, really, and unsurprisingly, the physical distance between us took a toll on our already strained marriage. Had she not died, we would likely be separated now."

Yes, they would. Cwenthryth should know—she was the one who had revealed his wife's plans to leave him, presumably to be with her lover. "Yes. She would have gone to Aldred."

Steinar shook his head. "That's not what I mean. I know you told me she was planning to leave, but I had already made up my mind to ask for a divorce before the end of the summer. So you see, it was only a question of time before we went our separate ways. It would have been hard on the boys, which was the only thing preventing me from acting sooner. But I would have, because we were too miserable. In the end, though, I didn't have to do anything." His blue eyes settled back on her. "I haven't told anyone else about my intentions. Not even my parents know."

"I'm touched."

Touched that he should trust her with his story, moved and appalled by what she'd heard. She also felt guilty, because when she'd confided in him, she'd not known about the loss of his child.

"Oh, what must you think of me…" When she had told him about her own miscarriage, she had said that she was glad she didn't have to give birth to a child she didn't want. How terrible for a man who had lost a baby he did want to hear something like that. "I told you—I said…"

"What did you say, Cwenthryth?" he asked when she could not finish. Clearly he had no idea what she was referring to.

"You were heartbroken when you lost your poor baby, and I told you the other day that I'd been relieved not to have to give birth to mine. It's terrible. I'm sorry."

She hid her face in her hands, too ashamed to look at him.

Steinar gently prised her hands apart and waited until she found the strength to look at him. When she finally did, she saw no ire, no censure in his gaze, only compassion.

"Hush. You have nothing to be sorry for. You said those things because they were the truth. And I would have felt the same in your place. That poor babe had been forced on you, mine had not. That changes everything, and you know it."

With those words, he placed a kiss on her lips. It was nothing like the kiss they had shared only moments ago, before Sven had interrupted them. That one had been full of passion, hot as the summer sun, it had scorched her insides. This one was full of tenderness, soft as a spring breeze. It brought life back into her soul.

Steinar drew back and took her by the hand.

"Come. Let's go and see my father."

"THE REEVE CANNOT HELP US."

Steinar growled. "Cannot or will not, because I'm a Norseman?"

"Cannot. He's not a bad man, but whoever wrote the note made sure it could not be traced back to him. The message accusing you was delivered by a child barely able to talk. There's nothing to be gained from the poor boy, who had no idea why he was being questioned. But don't worry, we will get to the bottom of this," Wolf said with a certainty Cwenthryth couldn't help but admire.

In that moment it was hard to doubt the formidable man would get his way. By his side, his wife seemed equally determined. Cwenthryth instantly saw what Steinar had meant when he'd said his parents were made for one another. The love, the respect, the connection between the Icelander and his Saxon wife were obvious in every glance they exchanged, in every breath they took. With such an example while growing up, it was no wonder their son had wanted to believe that marriage could bring happiness.

"Someone somewhere has to know something," Merewen said.

Yes. And Cwenthryth suddenly realized that she knew someone who would.

Aldred might know details of Astrid's life the Norsemen didn't know about. How had she not thought of this before? The man would have seen another side of his lover, talked to her about different things, met different people. He lived outside the Norsemen village, and had different connections. He might have interesting information to share with them.

She turned to Steinar, hope bubbling in her chest. It might not lead anywhere, but at least they had a starting point.

"I think you need to tell your parents about…"

She stopped, unsure how to refer to the man without betraying his connection to Astrid. Wolf and Merewen didn't know their son had been about to ask for a divorce. It was therefore reasonable to assume they didn't know his wife had had a lover, and she didn't think it was her place to make the revelation.

"You need to tell them about my neighbor, Aldred," she finally said.

To her relief, Steinar immediately understood who she meant and why it might be useful.

"Yes." Though he seemed ill at ease, he agreed this was a path worth exploring.

"Why? Who is this man?"

Steinar looked at his father, and cleared his throat. "There is something you don't know. I told you things had gone awry between Astrid and me, as you and Mother suspected. But what you don't know is that she had a lover, and was planning to leave me for him. That man is Cwenthryth's neighbor. In fact, that's why she's here, because she befriended Astrid during her visits into town."

He ran a hand over the back of his neck and Cwenthryth's heart went out to him. That his wife had been about to leave him for another man would be humiliating to admit. But neither Wolf nor his wife betrayed any surprise at the revelation or asked any questions. Clearly, they believed Astrid capable of such behavior.

"We need to go and speak to him," she said as firmly as she dared. The last thing she wanted was to appear as if she was taking control of the conversation, but she was convinced they had to talk to Aldred. "He might know if Astrid was in trouble, had made some enemies in town, or… anything. She might have spoken to him about it."

Cwenthryth reddened when two pairs of identical blue eyes and a black one stared at her. Were they offended she was telling them what to do? Admittedly, she was not part of the family and had no role to play in this.

But Steinar's mother only nodded. "I agree. Considering his relationship with Astrid, he might know something we don't. It's worth a try."

"Yes," Cwenthryth whispered, relieved her suggestion had not been dismissed. She desperately wanted to help the man she loved clear his name. "But I will have to be the one questioning him. He will not open up to—"

"Out of the question." Steinar's voice brooked no refusal. Something between a sigh and a laugh escaped her lips. How had she not guessed he would object to the idea?

"It's the best way. I'm a Saxon, and he already knows me. A discussion with his neighbor will not raise his suspicions, whereas if Norsemen he's never met came out of nowhere to question him, he would be on his guard, suspecting they were from the same village as Astrid."

"I don't care. It's too dangerous."

"No." Though Cwenthryth was comforted to see this protective side to Steinar, she would not let him stop her. She had to do this, because she was their best chance at success, and they all knew it. "Aldred has no reason to suspect I have an ulterior motive for going to speak to him. He has no idea I know you, so he will not guard his tongue. Besides, I will not accuse him of anything, merely inform him of Astrid's death." The likelihood was that the man didn't even know of his lover's recent demise, for how would he have found out? Their affair had been a secret, no one from the village would have gone to him. "I will tell him that her husband has been accused of killing her. In the discussion, he might let slip a piece of information that will lead us to the culprit."

"I will not—"

"Cwenthryth's right, it is our best solution," Wolf agreed, cutting his son's protest short. "You look too much like me, and distinctively Norse. He might recognize you from what your wife told him about you—or get scared by your inability to hide your hatred toward him. I cannot go in your place either. Everyone knows me in town. Most would also know Astrid was my daughter-in-law. A Saxon he already knows come for a casual chat is the best possible chance at finding out what the man knows."

"Well, I still don't like it," Steinar grumbled.

"You don't have to like it, just to accept it is the best way."

Wolf was implacable. Stony. Well, like father like son, she supposed. Cwenthryth smiled again.

"I will be fine," she assured, putting a soothing hand over Steinar's arm. "With Godfrid dead, I have nothing to fear in town. No one cares about me."

He reached out to her, eyes ablaze. "That's not true. *I* care."

The words shot straight to her heart, warming her. Because it was not just some idle claim, destined to make her feel better. He did care, she saw it in his eyes, heard it in his voice, felt it in the way he held her. She melted against him.

In the corner of her eye Cwenthryth saw Wolf and Merewen exchange a knowing look. Heat invaded her chest. His son, Sven, now his parents… Would his whole family think there was something between them?

And what if they did? Wasn't there something, something she, at least, wanted to explore further?

She lowered her gaze to the floor.

"Very well," Wolf concluded. "We'll go to see Aldred tomorrow."

17

Every muscle in Steinar's body tensed when Cwenthryth disappeared through the door. He could not stop himself from thinking it was a mistake to send her to investigate in his stead. Neither he nor his father knew this Aldred, they had no idea if he could be trusted or not. One of them should be in that house right now, not her. What if there was trouble? How would they know to intervene? When they had agreed Cwenthryth should be the one to speak to her neighbor, he had imagined the two of them would meet at the market or in the street, somewhere where they could keep an eye on her. If he'd been told she would end up alone in a house with a man who'd fucked half the women in town he would never have agreed to the scheme.

It was too dangerous. There was no telling how he would behave.

"Calm down, son."

"Don't tell me to calm down," he snapped. "It wasn't the plan for her to disappear from view. How would you like it if Mother was the one alone with a man we don't know right now? A man who we know is not above bedding married women?"

His father's nostrils flared. Evidently, he was honest enough to admit he would have acted just like Steinar in such a situation.

"Very well. Let us go stand near the house. If anything happens, we'll be able to hear and intervene. But we need to give Cwenthryth the chance to help you. You know that's what she wants. I think it will mean a lot to her, and I think you know why."

Yes, he knew why.

Cwenthryth had feelings for him. If she did not, she would not still be in the village. If she did not, she would not have kissed him with such fire the other day. If she did not, she would not be thinking of a future together.

Could the two of them find happiness? Could he allow himself another chance at love?

Yes, perhaps with her, he could.

Steinar felt an odd tightening in his chest. Against all odds, he felt grateful to Astrid. He had once thought she might be the woman for him, only to face the fact that he had been mistaken. But by an odd twist of fate, she had sent him a woman who could give him the life he'd not had in his marriage.

"Yes. I know it means a lot to her," he told his father, his voice hoarse from emotion. "It means even more to me that she would want to try, to know that she still wants to give me a chance after the way I acted toward her."

"I know exactly how you feel." Wolf placed a hand on his shoulder and did not ask what that way might be. "Women are often more generous toward us than we deserve. In return all we can do is try to give them the life they hoped to have."

Exactly.

In that moment Steinar promised himself he would ask Cwenthryth to marry him once this was over and he was free from the suspicion of murder. He could not be sure she would accept, at least straight away, but he would not relent until she had accepted.

Some people might argue he was rushing things again, considering that Astrid had only been dead a few weeks but he knew that was not the case. Their marriage had stopped being a marriage years ago. Her death had not affected him in the way the loss of a beloved spouse would have. In his mind he was free, and he felt ready for a second chance, ready to have the intimacy he craved at last, the love he'd hoped to have with his first wife.

Yes, it would seem that by asking Cwenthryth to come to him, Astrid had given him the best parting gift.

"Cwenthryth! This is a surprise."

Cwenthryth smiled. This meeting was not a surprise to her, of course, but she was delighted by this stroke of luck. As she'd entered the street from the north end, she'd spotted Aldred walking toward her and they had met in front of his door, as if by accident. It was the best thing that could have happened. They didn't have the sort of relationship that justified her knocking at his door and he might have been suspicious if she had suddenly visited him for no apparent reason. But he would see nothing odd in a conversation he had started himself in the street. It was perfect, just what they needed.

She had promised herself only the other day that she would never again set foot within the town walls, but she had not hesitated. This was not about her, but about Steinar. She would do everything she could to help him.

"Where have you been? I haven't seen you for a while."

"I went to visit my cousin by the coast and ended up staying with her longer than I thought," she improvised.

"I didn't know you had family there?"

She didn't, but she had not been able to think of a better explanation for her prolonged absence. Any mention of the

Norsemen village was out of the question, as was her miscarriage. A non-existent cousin would do very well.

"We fell out a while ago, that's probably why. A stupid argument about who made the best flat cakes. Then I heard she'd had a child and I decided it was time we put the past behind us." Cwenthryth was surprised by the ease with which the lies passed her lips. But now that she was free of the threat Godfrid represented, she felt like a different woman, lighter, confident, happy. That woman was fearless. "Anyway, as you can see, I'm back."

Another lie, but Aldred was not to know she would never live in the house next door again.

"Well, come on in, surely you have time for a drink? I'm just back from a visit to the harbor and I'm rather thirsty."

"Thank you."

A drink—and an interrogation. Resisting the urge to glance back at Steinar, who would most certainly hate seeing her disappear from view, she stepped inside the house.

"There you are, a fresh batch of ale," Aldred said, placing two wooden cups on the table. The liquid in it was frothing invitingly. She was thirsty as well, she realized. "I opened the cask this morning."

"It smells good."

As she drank Cwenthryth looked at the man sitting at the table in front of her. How on earth had Astrid chosen to take him as a lover when she was married to a man like Steinar? With brown hair, washed-out gray eyes and a small, pointy chin, he did not begin to compare with the Norseman. Aldred was unremarkable in every way, not just physically. He lacked masculine presence, wit and even skill at conversation. Going to him when you could have bedded Steinar was like choosing to sit indoors when there was a sunset blazing outside, like buying shriveled onions at the market in town when you had the freshest, juiciest vegetables growing in your vegetable patch.

A folly.

"I hear from Osberth the woodturner that your brother has left town," he told her, placing a plate of sliced meat in front of her. She selected the smallest sliver she could find, before starting to shred it into ribbons. Not only did it look distinctively greasy, nothing like Steinar's smoked lamb, but the mention of Godfrid had put paid to what little appetite she'd had. "Is that true?"

"It is. He's gone."

Finally. Permanently.

"Any idea where he went?"

Yes, she knew exactly where he'd gone. To hell. Sent there by the man who was obsessed with it. Not that she could tell Aldred as much. She shook her head. "Godfrid and I were never really close. He was only my half-brother, as you know, and we didn't grow up together."

A swig of ale did little to ease the tightening in her throat.

"Pity he left. The two of us got on well. We often went wenching together. He was always more popular than me, but as he didn't mind sharing his conquests with his friends, I never went without."

Cwenthryth placed her cup down with more force than she had intended. Why on earth did the man think that she would want to hear that? This was more information than any woman would want to have about her brother. Besides, she had not come to discuss Godfrid, much less to hear his lusty nature being praised. Unfortunately, she already knew all there was to know about it.

Doing her best to speak in a neutral voice, she did what she had come here to do. The quicker she got out of here, the better. Steinar would be pacing the street up and down by now, waiting for her to reappear. She didn't want to worry him unduly.

"Do you know if anyone came calling for me while I was away? Eahlswith? Astrid and the boys?" she asked, deciding it was best to pretend she didn't know about the Norsewoman's death either. After all, how would she have found out, being away from town, at her cousin's? The purpose of the question was only to introduce the topic of his lover.

Aldred's brow arched. "You haven't heard then?"

"Heard what?"

"Astrid is dead."

Cwenthryth remembered the day Steinar had told her the exact same thing. It had been such a shock. Had only three weeks passed since then? It seemed so long ago.

"Dead!" she gasped, doing her best to appear as if she didn't know. Getting him to talk, expose what he knew, would be the best way to learn information. "But how? She didn't appear ill to me the last time I saw her?"

"No, she wouldn't have, considering."

"What do you mean?"

Aldred leaned in closer, like a man delighting in imparting shocking information. Incidentally, Cwenthryth noted that he did not seem devastated by her death, despite what they had shared. Poor Astrid. From what Steinar had said, her parents had not cared about her when she was alive, and her death had left them cold. Now her lover appeared unconcerned to have lost her. The only people who had wanted to love her, her husband and her children, she had chosen to forsake.

Maybe there was a lesson in there somewhere.

"She was poisoned, by all accounts. No wonder she seemed normal when we last saw her."

This time she didn't have to pretend to be shocked. Where had he gotten this information? It was surprising enough that he should have heard of her demise, being only his secret lover and living far from the Norsemen village. But he seemed to know not only that she was dead, but also the cause of death—and it was not the one everyone thought.

Could he be right? Could Astrid have been poisoned? It was not what she'd heard at all. But then again, the symptoms she'd been given could easily have been caused by poison, and Steinar had been accused of murder. They had dismissed the accusation as ridiculous, but perhaps there was more to it than mere slander. Perhaps Astrid really had been poisoned, and some people genuinely thought her husband was responsible for the crime?

But who? The all-important question remained.

"This is horrible." It wasn't hard to sound appalled when she was appalled.

"Yes. By all accounts, her husband killed her when he found out about her…well, when he found out about me and her, shall we say." Aldred had no reason to keep his affair with Astrid a secret from her. He knew she was aware of it, having been the one looking after the children while they spent their afternoons in bed. "The big brute could not bear the humiliation of being bested by a Saxon and so he killed her."

"No, it can't be…"

How was she supposed to believe that a "big brute," in his own words, a jealous husband finding out his wife had a lover, would have poisoned her instead of killing her in a fit of rage? He would have stabbed, strangled, or at very least hit her before ripping said lover to shreds. Poison was the weapon of the weak, of cowards who planned their dark deeds with cold calculation. In other words, people who were the exact opposite of Steinar. Not that she believed him capable of striking or strangling or stabbing a woman, of course, but no one who knew him would think he had poisoned his wife.

There was only one explanation for Aldred to state it so confidently.

He didn't just know Steinar had been accused. He was the one who had accused him. And Astrid hadn't contracted a mysterious disease which had killed her, she had indeed been murdered. By her lover, the man sitting in front of Cwenthryth right now, drinking ale as if he didn't have a care in the world. As to why he had killed her, she didn't know and she didn't care. All she knew was that she had to get out of here while she could, find Steinar and his father. They would know what to do.

She forced herself not to rush out of the house there and then. She had found out what she needed to know—that Aldred was a dangerous, determined man, not above killing women and accusing innocents of the murder.

A man who might hurt her if he came to suspect why she had come.

"It's horrid," she said, not knowing if she could stomach hearing another shocking revelation, not certain how to put an end to the conversation naturally.

What if Aldred started to wonder at her attitude, wonder why she was taking such an interest in Astrid? Why she had agreed to have a drink with him despite them not being what you'd call friends? Would he start asking questions about her mysterious cousin? As she now knew him for a murderer, ruthless enough to rid himself of the people he no longer wanted, she wasn't sure what to do.

He helped himself to another cup of ale, shaking his head.

"Well, horrid people will do horrid things, and that's all there is to it."

Yes. She could only agree with him.

18

"Cwenthryth!" Steinar hurried toward her as soon as she exited Aldred's house. "Are you—"

"I'm all right," she said, walking straight past him, her lips barely moving. "Let's walk."

She would have liked nothing more than to throw herself into his arms, but that would have to wait until they were out of sight. If Aldred was watching her through the window, it would be better to appear as if nothing was wrong and behave as if she and the two brawny Norsemen stationed outside the house didn't know one another. Behind her she heard Wolf tell his son something in Norse. No doubt he was explaining her way of thinking and urging him to calm.

The men followed her at a discreet distance, making sure to appear too engrossed in their conversation to worry about anyone else. Once they reached the town square, she led them under the timbered market hall and behind a sturdy pillar. Finally, when she was certain Aldred could not see them, she relaxed her shoulders and sagged against Steinar, who had appeared behind her as if by magic. Had they been alone she would have turned around and buried her face into his chest, but as his father was here, she could not presume to—

The choice was made for her when two strong arms closed around her, drawing her exactly where she wanted to be, against a strong, sweet-smelling chest. Steinar cradled her a long moment, breathing in her scent as well, or so it seemed to her. Since he didn't seem to worry about what Wolf would think she allowed herself to enjoy this embrace to the full. Against her ear she could hear the beat of his heart, faster than she'd imagined it would be. Perhaps he had been afraid for her, more than she thought, as afraid as she had been when she'd understood she was talking to Astrid's murderer.

After a while, reluctantly, she drew back and looked at him. There was such raw emotion in his blue eyes that she knew there and then her life would never be the same—and that it would include the tall Norseman holding her. Her heart fluttered in joy. This was just what she wanted.

"You've learned something," Steinar said, sounding sure of himself.

"Yes. I'm sorry, it will not make for pleasant hearing," she said, looking at him and Wolf in turn. How was she to tell them the terrible news she had learned? Her legs were still trembling from the shock of the discovery, and she was not the one who'd been married to Astrid. How would Steinar take it?

Eventually, she had no choice but to start talking. The longer she waited, the more worried he would get.

"We'll be all right," he assured her. "Just tell us."

"I believe Aldred is the one who accused you of the murder." She paused, giving the men time to absorb the news. They seemed stunned, which did not surprise her. What reason could the man have to do such a thing? That was what she had not yet discovered, but it could wait. "There is more. I'm afraid his message to the reeve wasn't a complete lie. Even though you did not kill her, Astrid was indeed murdered."

Father and son stared at her in stupefaction. "Murdered? But how?"

"Poisoned, from what he said."

At first Steinar recoiled in denial, then he frowned, as if trying to reassess his wife's last moments in view of this new, startling piece of information. It was clear from the way the gleam in his eyes slowly dimmed that he'd reached the conclusion it was not impossible, given the symptoms.

"Yes, she might well have been poisoned," he finally said, looking horrified. "But by whom?"

This was the hardest part. Cwenthryth took in a deep breath. Would they believe her? She wouldn't blame them if they didn't, as she had no proof to offer, only intuition.

"I suspect Aldred himself poisoned her," she said slowly, "though I'm not sure quite why. But how else would he know that she had been poisoned, or even that she had died? And how would he know you had been the one accused of the murder? My guess is that she had told him she wanted to leave you and come to live with him, and he didn't want to have his life disturbed so he got rid of her."

A tryst had been well and good, but he didn't want anything more serious. It was the only thing that made sense at the moment. And it did make sense. They knew Astrid had planned to leave her home, because she had tried to ensure someone would be there to look after her children—Cwenthryth herself. The timing seemed too close for it to be coincidental. She and Aldred had been seeing one another for more than a year. Why kill her now? Because she had suddenly decided she wanted more.

"I might be mistaken, as he didn't offer any explanation, instead placing the blame for the murder on you in retaliation for their affair. But I really think he was the one who sent a message to the reeve to accuse you."

Steinar was still frowning. Cwenthryth might be right, but something was amiss here.

"Why would he need or even want to accuse me of a murder no one was even aware of?" he asked her. "We all thought Astrid had died of natural causes."

Cwenthryth made a helpless gesture. "The people in your village thought there was nothing amiss because Aldred had planned it that way. But he didn't actually witness her last moments. Something could have gone wrong. He could not be sure she died in manner that seemed natural, as he wasn't there to see the effect of the poison. If she'd started to talk about her entrails burning, for example, or had been examined by a healer who'd seen this poison in action before, then you might have gotten suspicious and start investigating."

Steinar shook his head. "We did not. She did seem to suffer a lot but we never thought to suspect it was anything other than a common flux…"

By the gods, the idea of what the poor woman had gone through was enough to chill his blood. Her agony had lasted a whole day and night. He was itching to go to find this Aldred and rip him to bits for what he'd made Astrid endure. She'd died so that the bastard she'd chosen to bed could be free to fuck all the women who crossed his path. How pathetic.

Or… Did he have another reason for killing her?

Had Astrid fallen with child from their illicit encounters? Had he panicked at the idea of her demanding that he provide for the babe? She'd done what she could not to let her husband's seed take root in her womb, but perhaps her lover was less respectful of her wishes, and after a year of bedding she had discovered she had missed her courses. Steinar shook his head. Thinking like that would only cause him more pain, and change nothing. He would have to keep his suspicions to himself.

Astrid had been murdered, it was all that mattered.

"Besides," Cwenthryth carried on, "Aldred was not to know you were not aware of your wife's affair. He probably assumed you knew, or at least suspected Astrid had a lover. Perhaps he was afraid you would come after the man who'd seduced your wife, eager to take your revenge for the humiliation. He wanted to protect himself from a private revenge and possible accusation of murder. Better to strike first and save himself than spend months worrying about being killed. With you out of the way, he could relax."

This time Steinar nodded. Yes, this would make sense. Attack was always the best defense.

The day he'd come to town to see where Cwenthryth lived, Aldred had seen him across the street, looking at the house. As his father had pointed out the day before, his looks were unmistakably those of an Icelander's son. It would not have taken the Saxon long to conclude that the Norseman stationed outside his house was none other than his late lover's husband. Fearing the worst, not knowing that Steinar had actually come to see about Cwenthryth's tormentor, he would have assumed retribution was coming.

His father nodded in turn. "It makes sense. I've seen men kill for less."

"Yes." Steinar placed a hand on Cwenthryth's shoulder. "You're right. He was probably the one who killed Astrid and then sent the message to the reeve."

This seemed the obvious conclusion. The fact that Aldred knew about Astrid's death alone was suspicious. How would a man who'd never set foot in the Norsemen village have heard about her sudden and unexpected demise? She'd only been three-

and-thirty, like him, and in perfect health. There was no reason to think she would not live to an advanced age.

"But why would the reeve even bother himself with the murder of a Norsewoman?" he wondered out loud. Even if Aldred had sent him word to him, why would the man worry about it? Everyone here knows my father is in charge of the Norse community."

Once again Cwenthryth shrugged. "This, I do not know. Maybe the two of them are friends? Maybe Aldred blackmailed him? Maybe the man hates Norsemen and saw an opportunity to rid himself of one?"

Unfortunately, this was all too possible. The Norse settlers had always been well accepted around here, working with the local folk, marrying their women, helping to build a thriving community.

Since their overwhelming victory against Harald Hardrada a couple of years ago, however, and the subsequent coronation of a ruler whose Danish blood had been diluted so much as to become insignificant, the Saxons' attitude toward them had started to change. Over the last few months some of the most aggressive and short-sighted amongst them had tried to impress upon the Norse people that this had never been their home and they should leave, go back to wherever they came from. Forgetting that some of them had lived here in peace for longer than they had been alive, they were doing all they could to rid the country of their presence, by whatever means necessary. Was the reeve one of them?

"Leave it to me," Wolf said, his voice made rough by anger. "I'll get to the bottom of this. But believe me, before the day is over, the reeve will know his place, and Aldred will not be in a position to accuse or kill anyone else."

Before Steinar could ask exactly what he meant to do, his

father stormed back to his horse, leaving Cwenthryth alone with him.

"Are you sure you're all right?" he asked, taking both her hands in his. She was trembling, and so was he. He had found it hard enough to let her face Aldred when he'd thought she'd only gone to find information. Had he known how dangerous the man really was, he would have hacked his way inside the house to get her out, consequences be damned. The axe had quickly become his weapon of choice when it came to defend the little Saxon. "The man didn't suspect anything? He didn't hurt you?"

"Yes. No. And no." A small, tentative smile was playing on her lips. Did she think him ridiculous for fussing as he was? He dearly hoped not. He didn't want to appear ridiculous in her eyes. She probably already thought him high-handed, unreasonable, and distrustful. Not that he blamed her if she did. He had been all those things with her. "Don't worry about me."

"I'm not sure I'll ever be able to do that. I find I will probably always worry about you from now on. The best, the *only* way to set my fears at rest would be for you to stay where I can see you, always."

"Where would that be?" Her voice had been reduced to a breath. She sounded wary of understanding what he meant. Steinar smiled. No need to be wary. She had not misunderstood. He'd promised himself earlier that he would only ask her to marry him once he was free to do so, but he wasn't sure he would be able to wait until then. Besides, now that they knew who had accused him and why, his father would clear his name in no time. Which meant he could finally get the woman he needed.

"Stay in my house. In my arms."

Before she could do much more than widen her eyes, he drew her into his arms and started to kiss her. Tenderly at first, then with scandalous eagerness. She was so soft, so responsive that this kiss was like no other he had ever shared with anyone. Cwenthryth moaned into his mouth, and the sound sent him hard as stone. She inhaled when she felt him press against her stomach—and it became clear that the market hall was not the best place to indulge in such activities. Another moment and he would pin her to the pillar behind her and give her the ravishing he'd wanted to give her since he'd come back from the reeve's gaol. For that, he needed privacy, he needed time, he needed her full assent.

As if to help him remain cool-headed, at that moment it started to rain.

Gasping, Steinar drew back to look into dark eyes made hazy by desire. Feeling on the verge of losing control, despite the rain, despite the crowd, despite everything, he wiped at Cwenthryth's cheek, where a drop of water had had the audacity to fall on her skin. Then he licked the one that had landed on her bottom lip. He groaned.

Fuck, they had to leave. Now.

He took her by the hand. "Let's go home."

GIVEN the intensity of the kiss they had shared in town, Cwenthryth had imagined that Steinar would pounce on her as soon as he entered the hut. He'd sent her ahead to get dry while he saw to Fáfnir, promising he wouldn't be long.

She barely had time to remove her cloak and run a comb through her damp hair before he walked in through the door, shaking his own cloak off, a cloak which, she noticed with no little amount of amusement, was made of wool and trimmed with, of all things, rabbit fur. Not quite the pelt of a fearsome animal she had once imagined he'd wear…

Instead of taking her into his arms like he had on the market square and devour her, to her utter shock, he asked her to be his wife. Cwenthryth froze in disbelief. He'd hinted at the fact that he wanted her to stay with him earlier, but marriage? She knew how deeply he had been hurt with Astrid, how wary he was of giving his trust to another woman. Yet he seemed as determined to have her accept the offer as he had been to see her leave his house less than a month ago.

She could barely believe it.

But perhaps she should not be surprised. After all, it had taken her less than a month to fall in love with him.

"Cwenthryth. I love you," he said, sitting her on the table like he had the day before, bringing his face down to hers. His braided hair was still damp. It had not rained long, but long enough to turn the gold into a beautiful, deep amber color. "I need you in my life. Say you will marry me."

Not only did he want to marry her, but he loved her as well? And he was not afraid to admit it before she'd made her own declaration? Cwenthryth could barely talk for shock, could barely think. "I...I—"

The light in Steinar's eyes dimmed at what he took for hesitation, as if he thought she was about to refuse him. She was not— she was simply too bewildered.

"I know I might not be the most appealing prospect for a young woman like you, being a decade older," he said, his tone low and husky.

"I told you I preferred older men," Cwenthryth reminded him, finding her voice at last. She could not let him think such a ridiculous thing. He was the most appealing prospect she had ever seen in her life. "And I'm not that young myself." She was three-and-twenty. At her age, the majority of women were married.

"I also have two children. You might prefer to—"

"No. I love Ulf and Rothgar. It would be my honor to help you raise them if you'll let me. They might..." She swallowed, emotion overcoming her. "After what happened to me, they might be my only chance at motherhood."

"Ah, sweet." Steinar brought his forehead in contact with hers, his hands cradling her face with infinite tenderness. He'd done the same the day before and the gesture already felt familiar. "You don't know that."

"No. But you don't either. What if I could not… What if I could not give you the little girl you've always wanted, or even another son? What if I were barren?"

"Then it wouldn't matter. I would still have you, my wife, the woman I need, the woman I love. I already have children, but I don't have you. Say you will marry me, Cwenthryth," he urged, settling himself more firmly between her spread legs. "If you don't, I will only ask again, and again, until I get my way. You know how stubborn I can get."

"Yes." The word shot out of her mouth, the only one she could think of.

"Yes, you know or yes, you will marry me?"

Her decision was made in a heartbeat. There was really one answer she could give him, because she did want to marry him. How could she not? She could not refuse to marry the man she loved, at the risk of being miserable all her life, at the risk of seeing him marry another woman. It would be pure madness.

"Yes, I will marry you because I do know how stubborn you can get. And because I love you, too."

This time he lifted her into his arms, making her wrap her legs around his waist in support. The position was shocking, perfect.

"*Ast min, kyss mik.*"

Cwenthryth's heart missed a beat. She'd always loved to hear him speak his language, but she would have liked to understand what he was saying. It sounded so heartfelt. "One of these days you'll have to teach me Norse, you know," she said, placing a hand on his cheek and giving a stroke.

"Of course. I'll have my whole life to do it." Steinar's lips stretched into a smile. "In the meantime, kiss me, my love."

She'd thought the kiss at the market scandalous enough. She now saw that it had been nothing. *This* kiss was carnality itself. Steinar worshipped her mouth with as much thoroughness as he had licked her intimate folds the other day. Of course thinking about that only added to the wickedness of the moment, and she tightened her hold around his neck for fear she would collapse to the floor.

"Don't worry, I've got you," Steinar breathed, his lips against hers. He must have felt her sag against him. "And this time, we won't be interrupted. The children are with my mother, I've locked the door and warned my brothers, or rather Sven, not to come within twenty yards of the hut on pain of death."

"Death?" she breathed back, torn between amusement and shock—and desperate desire.

"Death," he confirmed roughly, his hands kneading her bottom in the most suggestive manner. "I will not go to sleep until I've had you."

"Yes."

"Naked."

"Yes."

"Preferably more than once."

"Yes."

"In every conceivable—"

"Yes, naked, over and over again, in every position you can think of." She kissed him again, unable to contain her own desire. "Steinar, stop talking."

They fell on the pallet in a tangle of limbs. True to his promise, he shed his clothes in the blink of an eye, allowing her to at last see his body in all its splendor. Oh Lord, it was glorious, pure perfection, a model of virile strength. Adding to the effect was the silver bracelet he was wearing around his left bicep. She had never seen anything of the sort and the sight inexplicably sent her insides to mush. It was bold and unashamedly masculine.

"What's this?" she asked, brushing a light finger over the shiny metal band. It was exquisite work, decorated with intricate patterns snaking along the length of it, with a wolf's head at the center, its profile delicately chiseled.

"My arm ring. Most of us Norsemen wear one. Ironically though, this one was made by a Saxon. Caedmon. Rowena's father, the goldsmith? You might have seen him around the village." She nodded. There weren't many Saxon men around and she had indeed spotted one the day before. "Anyway, the arm ring was presented to me on my sixteenth summer by my father."

Ah, this explained the wolf's head. Cwenthryth smiled. She guessed all three sons had a similar one echoing their ancestry.

"It's beautiful," she said honestly. Never had any piece of metal stirred stronger emotions within her. Could women also wear one, she wondered? And if so, could she ask this Caedmon to make one for her? Would Steinar like the surprise? It could mark the start of the second part of her life, the one as the wife of a Norseman.

"Thank you," he growled, his mind clearly no longer on the arm ring. "And now it's my turn to see something beautiful."

"I'm not wearing anything half as precious." Or at all, she reflected, suddenly feeling inadequate. She'd never possessed any piece of jewelry. Her ears were not even pierced, something she'd long wanted to remedy.

"Who said anything about *wearing* anything?" Steinar purred, tugging at the laces of her bodice. "From what I've already had the privilege to see, you don't need any adornment whatsoever. Your body is perfection itself."

His eyes caught on fire when her breasts were revealed, proving he was not lying. He did not think she needed any adornment. Cwenthryth relaxed. This man… How did he always know what to say to make her at ease? How could he make her feel beautiful with just a look, reassure her in a few words?

In contrast to what he'd done with himself, he took his time undressing her, lingering over the task with relish, stopping every few heartbeats to kiss the part of her body he was unveiling. By the time she was naked, every inch of her had been worshipped in one way or another. And she was desperate for a more complete possession. This time his tongue and fingers, wicked as they were, would not be enough.

"Steinar, please." Here she was, begging already, and he had barely started.

"Yes, lovely."

Instead of spreading her thighs, like she had expected, he started kissing and nipping at her throat. She sighed, torn between delight at the sensation and disappointment. She was naked, under him, and all he could worry about was her neck? Surely there were more enticing places to kiss? Her mouth, her breasts, her—

"I can't wait any longer, my love. How do you need me?"

Cwenthryth's chest squeezed in gratitude. She understood what Steinar was asking, and why. He knew that after what she had endured at Godfrid's hands, she was afraid of being used. He would also remember that in the tree house she had begged him not to be rough. But she was not worried, she would never be worried with him ever again.

"I trust you, I know you will never hurt me."

"No, never that." He gave her cheek a soft stroke, proving that despite his powerful physique, he was all about tenderness. "If you don't want me to come inside your body just yet, we can do like we did the other—"

"No, I want you inside me," she rasped, knowing she would expire from need if he didn't fill her this time. "I want to feel you becoming a part of me, I want to know what it should be like between a man and a woman. Please, I need to—"

He stopped her with a kiss. "Yes, I will show you all you want to know. I will give you what you need. I will love you. I will become yours."

Become yours, not "make you mine." *Love you*, not "take you." This would be nothing like what had happened to her before, with the man she hadn't wanted.

Fully reassured, she reached out to him. Her hand landed on the column of flesh rising from between his legs. The hardness she felt under her palm took her breath away by its sheer size. She was certain he was bigger than Godfrid had been, despite his boasts that he had "everything a woman could want," and yet the idea didn't frighten her. It aroused her, because feminine instinct told her it would bring her untold delights.

"My, you really are made of stone, are you not?" she breathed, feeling bolder than she had ever been.

"Any man would be with you in their arms, my love." In her grip, his shaft gave a jolt. Her core instantly reacted, rippling in feminine invitation, calling out to this part of him that would make her complete.

"You gave me what I needed last time in the tree house," Cwenthryth murmured, bringing her mouth to his ear, "tenderness and indescribable pleasure. This time I want you to get what you need."

"Don't you worry about me. I already got what I needed." Steinar nuzzled at her throat, causing every inch of her to shiver in anticipation. "Despite my unforgivable behavior that day, you gave me exactly what I craved, the feeling of intimacy I had lost in my marriage, the satisfaction of knowing I was holding a woman who wanted to be in my arms."

"I did want you. I still do." She gave his shaft a squeeze. "And I want you inside me this time, deep inside me. I want to know how it is when we are joined as one, I want to look at you when you fill me up."

Anything less would not be enough.

"I want to look at you when I fill you up too."

"Then do."

She spread her legs, signifying she was ready for him.

It seemed that this was an invitation Steinar could not resist. Keeping his gaze locked with hers, he slid inside her, slow but sure. There was no pain, no resistance, only the most delicious feeling of completion. Cwenthryth arched her back and sighed. Yes, this was exactly what she wanted. Perfection.

He started to move, keeping up a slow, torturous rhythm and it wasn't long before, despite the delight of being finally hers, she needed more. That day in the tree house he had warned her she would beg for more, beg him to go faster, harder. It had been a threat destined to make her see that she could not handle him in all his urgency, and in truth, she had not quite believed him at the time. She hadn't seen how any woman would beg for harder, faster, when it brought so much pain.

Now she understood what he meant. Harder and faster could also bring more friction, more pleasure. The words were straining to get out. Why was she fighting to keep them in? This was Steinar, the man she loved and trusted above all others, who was looking at her with so much love in his eyes, who would not mock her or think the worse of her for saying out loud what she needed.

"Please. I need more. I need it… faster…" This simple command sounded so lewd she wasn't sure she could be more explicit, tell him she also needed it deeper, harder, fiercer.

Mercifully, he understood. "No need to beg, sweeting. I will always give you what you need."

With those words he took hold of her right leg and placed it over his shoulder. Oh. This was definitely different, opening her up wide, exposing her, allowing him easier access, placing her at his mercy. In other words, exactly where she wanted to be.

"Like this?" he asked, as he thrust in deep and hard, just as deep and hard as she wanted.

"Yes."

"And this?" His left hand landed on her hip, before giving it a squeeze.

"Yes! More."

Cwenthryth was discovering that, with the right man, she relished a bit of assertiveness. Because despite his assertiveness, Steinar was not rough. He was just himself. Honest. Raw.

Muscles straining, weight poised above her, he was moving in and out of her with increasing urgency. Heat was boiling in her veins, love was flooding her brain. It would not be long before she was overcome.

"You need to come for me now, my love," he ordered through gritted teeth. It was obvious he was fighting his own release to ensure hers came first. "I will not have you unsatisfied and I can't —Come. Now."

With that order, he changed his movements, grinding his pelvis against her, against the part of her that seemed to contain all the pleasure she was capable of containing. Cwenthryth cried out when her whole body seized around the part of Steinar that was buried deep inside her.

A roar answered her, and just as her spasms started to ebb, she felt heat scorch her soul.

"Yes!" she said, as a slow pulsing began somewhere deep in her belly, the aftermath of her release, she imagined, a second, gentler wave of pleasure that felt just as delicious.

How long did she remain on the pallet, floating in a cloud of love-scented air? Cwenthryth didn't know—or care. She was where she wanted to be, feeling utterly empty and complete at the same time.

It started to rain again, the gentle trickling over the thatched roof bringing her back to the present. Steinar was lying by her side, still panting hard, indicating that she could not have been lying on the edge of consciousness for as long as she'd thought. Smiling, she gathered the last of her strength to come nestle against his flank. Mm, so warm… Incredibly, given what had just happened, her body started to heat up in response.

"Are you all right, my love?" she whispered, lifting her head to him.

"More than all right." He gave a long sigh and moved a strand of hair from her brow. "But this was like nothing else I'd ever experienced, and almost too intense to be allowed."

Cwenthryth chuckled. What should she say if this had been too intense for him? She was no warrior made of stone. And yet, somehow, she had survived the assault, and was even ready for more.

"I seem to remember being promised more before the sun went down," she teased, pressing her breasts tighter against him.

He groaned and gave a supple jerk of the hips. In the blink of an eye, she found herself lying under him, her back on soft furs, her front pressed against a hard masculine body.

"Don't think I have forgotten what I told you, *ast min*. And you will get more. But you will have to give me a moment—I'm only a man." He kissed her stomach, then her navel, and she whimpered when she understood where he was headed. "Fortunately, there are things we can do while we wait for me to turn to stone again."

Cwenthryth woke up with her breasts plastered against Steinar's back and her arm draped over his waist.

His chest was rising and falling slowly, his even breathing betrayed the fact that he was still asleep. Little wonder, given how he had exerted himself to fulfil his promise to take her over and over again, in every possible position, before they fell asleep. Foregoing the original plan, he had carried on well into the night, despite her half-hearted protests.

Smiling to herself, she started stroking his naked skin, as smooth as finely tanned leather. How did he get to be so soft when he was the most masculine man she'd ever met? It wasn't fair. By rights he should feel as rough as tree bark.

She rounded his muscular shoulder, descended slowly along his spine, splayed her fingers over the taut buttocks that probably still bore the trace of her nails. The night had truly been wild, and she had needed more than once to hold him tight, for fear she would break apart if she didn't.

Taking her hand over to the other side of his body, she followed the trail of downy hairs gracing his lower abdomen. Mm, so soft. So perfect. Then her finger met something that was anything but soft, if admittedly just as perfect. Time for an even more intimate exploration. Amazed at her own daring, Cwenthryth wrapped her hand around the shaft that had given her so much pleasure the night before, but stopped herself before she could give a squeeze and wake him up.

A low rumble made his chest vibrate, which she felt against her whole body.

"Don't feel you have to stop here, lovely."

Oh, the wretched man! "How long have you been awake?" she asked, bringing her mouth to his ear.

He clasped his fingers over hers before answering, giving himself the squeeze she had shied away from giving him. He groaned, then brought the roaming hand to his mouth to kiss her thumb. "Long enough to enjoy the most decadent moment of my life."

Cwenthryth couldn't help a laugh at this answer. "After all we did last night, *this* was the most decadent moment of your life?" It had been very tame in comparison. All she had done was stroke him. True, she had left no place untouched, but still…

"Yes. Because I cannot remember ever feeling so close to a woman. I know that most men are only interested in fucking, but I've always been different in that regard. I told you, I've always wanted more. And you just gave me exactly what I've always been looking for, all this without me asking or even hinting at it." He turned to face her, eyes ablaze. "If this doesn't prove that you are the woman for me, I don't know what does."

Oh. As declarations went, this one was pretty perfect.

"And you're the man for me. Do you know the moment I understood I was destined to fall in love with you?" she asked, rubbing a hand on the soft chest she loved to pet.

"I don't. Though I suspect it was not when I asked if you wanted Haakon to ram his— Well, I'm sure you don't need me to repeat what I said that night," he growled.

"No. I remember it very well."

Heat flooded Cwenthryth's cheeks. Not at the memory of what he'd told her the day of Rowena's wedding, but of what she had done the previous night. Lost in a haze of pleasure, freed of all her doubts and inhibitions, she had wanted to see how it would feel to suckle a man she had chosen and taken him into her mouth. It had been a revelation and she knew that Steinar had liked it as well.

She brought her mouth to his ear, ready for a scandalous confession. "But you were right, after all. If it's with the right man, I do like having a cock down my throat."

"Bloody hell, Cwenthryth, give a man a chance. Tell me the moment you fell in love with me," Steinar rasped, sounding on the edge of his control. "Now. Before I lose my mind and beg you to take me in your mouth again."

All in good time, she thought wickedly. First, she would answer him.

"It was when I saw you with little Frida in your arms." She remembered thinking then that he looked born to have babies. "I wondered if I could one day know the happiness of having a man look at a child of mine in that way."

A big, warm hand landed on her stomach. "You will, and I hope to be that man."

She chuckled again. "Me too, since we are going to marry. Or have you already forgotten about that?"

"Hardly. As you know, I've always wanted a little girl." He brought his nose in contact with hers as he spoke. "And I hope you'll give me one very soon."

"I would like nothing more."

He was still cradling her stomach. Cwenthryth placed her hand over his and closed her eyes. Outside, rain was still hammering down on the straw roof. She didn't care. She didn't have anywhere else to go. She could stay in Steinar's arms all day, if she wanted, giving both of them what they needed.

So that was what she did.

EPILOGUE

"I want Mother."

Steinar smiled as he placed a kiss on the top of his son's head. "I bet you do, and I think I know why. Are you hungry, by any chance? Is that why you want to find her?"

The little boy didn't even pretend to look abashed. "Yes."

"Well, you'll have to wait a moment. She's outside, feeding your sister."

"Oh! Yes, Sanna! I want to see Sanna!"

Before Steinar could stop him, Rothgar shot out of the door, his favorite rabbit-shaped rag held tight in his hand.

"There you are!" he called out when he spotted Cwenthryth on the bench at the back of the hut, sitting in a spot of sunshine.

She smiled when the little boy threw himself at her. "Good morning, Rothgar."

"Good morning. I—" He stopped when he saw that the babe in her arms was already feeding. Clearly he didn't want to disturb either woman.

"Let me guess. Are you hungry?" Cwenthryth asked, brushing his cheek tenderly.

Steinar let out an amused sigh. His son was always ravenous

when he woke up, and his wife knew it. He guessed she would have something ready for him. She always did.

"Don't worry, I made some cakes earlier this morning. You'll find them on the table, in the basket, with the honey your *Faðir* found yesterday."

"Thank you!" He made to rush back inside the hut, then at the last moment turned to kiss her hand and give his newborn sister a stroke on the cheek. Steinar's heart melted at the sight of his family. What had he done to deserve such happiness? A year after Astrid's death and their first unpromising meeting, Cwenthryth had gifted him with the loveliest little girl he had ever seen, with eyes as dark as a moonless night and hair to match, a perfect replica of her mother.

The birth had been a deeply emotional moment for both of them. Cwenthryth had cried when Helga had handed her the kicking Sanna, and he'd known she'd been thinking of the baby she had lost the previous summer, and his own babe. There had been nothing to do but hold her and murmur soothing words in her ear.

"*Ast min.*" Steinar kissed his wife then placed a gentle hand on his daughter's head. "How are you this morning?"

"Never better. Now that Sanna sleeps through the night, I feel like I've been given a new life."

"Yes." So did he. The last two months had been hard on the new parents. Fortunately, they had been able to rely on their family for help. It now seemed that the worst was behind them. "Here, I guess you'll be thirsty," he said, handing her a cup of ale.

"Thank you."

She took a grateful sip before putting Sanna on her other breast and finishing the cup. Steinar looked at his two women, a contented smile floating on his lips. He would never get tired of that perfect sight. Feeling like the most blessed man in the world, he sat next to his wife and let the heat of the rising sun warm him up.

"You know, Aife came to visit earlier," Cwenthryth informed him, when she handed him the babe, who had finished feeding. Steinar started pacing up and down in front of the bench, waiting for Sanna to burp.

"Is she all right?" Something in the way she'd said those words had him frowning. Was something amiss with Moon's sister?

"Yes, don't worry. But I think… I think she fancies herself in love with your brother."

Still rubbing his daughter's back, Steinar slowed down. "Which one?"

"Sven."

He winced, because this was precisely what he'd been afraid of. "Oh. This should be interesting."

"Interesting? Why?"

Steinar resumed his rhythmic pacing, hoping to coax the baby into releasing the air she needed to expel. A moment later, she did.

"When Moon started to see Eyja four years ago, we three brothers, er…didn't take it quite well, shall we say. We thought he might be merely amusing himself with her before moving on to his next conquest. They had been friends all their lives and we didn't think he would take the imp seriously. Of course we were quickly proved wrong, and it now seems odd to think that we doubted his feelings for her but…"

Cwenthryth chuckled as she restored order to her clothes. Using the brooch he had given her at the birth of their daughter, she closed her bodice. It had not escaped his notice that she hadn't had any jewelry to call her own and he had made sure to rectify the situation. The finely chiseled band he had placed around her finger the day he had made her his wife had been the first of many gifts he had bestowed on her. She was even wearing a thin arm ring around her left bicep, just like he was. The request for one had surprised him, but he'd seen no reason to refuse her. Saxon or not, she was part of their community now.

"I see," she said, smoothing down the folds of her gown. "Now you're worried Moon's going to think the same thing of Sven and make him suffer for debauching his little sister, just like you did."

"Exactly. And he would be right to worry. Sven is not ready to settle, I don't think, might never be." Steinar tightened his hold on his daughter's back. The little girl had started to go limp against him, indicating she was falling asleep. "Torsten is serious and reliable but Sven still behaves like a youth of sixteen summers, as I'm sure you've noticed."

Another chuckle. "I have. It would be hard not to. Well, we'll have to see, won't we? It is not for us to decide who can or cannot catch her attention. Though I can't say I blame her for falling under the spell of one of Wolf's sons. They are the most compelling men."

He grunted at the heated look she threw him. "All of them?"

"All of them. But I have a particular fondness for the eldest one, the one made of stone, at least on the outside." She stood up. "On the inside, I think he's made of the softest, most delicious honey."

"Honey?" Really? Bloody hell, he hoped Sven never got to hear this. He would never let him forget it.

"Yes. Honey. I should know," she purred. "I've tasted him often enough. It is the taste I like most in the world. I can't wait to taste him again. Maybe tonight?"

Oh, was she trying to kill him? They had not made love for months, as the last few weeks before Sanna's birth had been rather rough on her and obviously her body had needed time to recover from the birth. But if she thought she was finally ready…

"Well, I'm afraid that Wolf's eldest son is going to hold you to that promise," he warned his voice dark with desire.

Cwenthryth planted herself in front of him, her dark eyes aglow with happiness and lifted her mouth to him. "I certainly hope he will."

They spoke at the same time.

"*Kyss mik.*"

Coming next

Torsten's Gamble.

ALSO BY VIRGINIE MARCONATO

Sons of the Wolf

Steinar's Gift

Torsten's Gamble

The Welsh Rebels

A Husband for Esyllt

A Savior for Branwen

A Second Chance for Carys

A Rogue for Siân

A Lover for Lady Jane

A Scot for Bethan

The Noble Norsemen

Taming the Wolf

Soothing the Beast

Wooing the Devil

Baiting the Bear

Tempting the Saxon

Seducing the Warrior

Loving the Blacksmith

ABOUT THE AUTHOR

As far back as I remember, I have been attracted to the Middle Ages, to knights in shining armour and their ladies in spectacular dresses. Now I get to write about them, I feel like the luckiest woman in the world. Being French and married to a Brit makes each book I write extra special, as our countries share a long and sometimes painful past. But in the end, in life as well as in fiction, love conquers all!

I have published several medieval romances under my own name, including series, and also have a pen name, Judith Falcon, for spicier projects, still in historical romance.

Join my newsletter and check out my other books on virginiemarconato.com.

A small press bound by the belief that every voice matters.

Sign up for our newsletter to learn about new releases and more.
https://oliver-heberbooks.com/subscribe/

Follow us on social media:

facebook.com/oliverheberbooks

instagram.com/oliverheberbooks

amazon.com/oliverheberbooks

youtube.com/@OliverHeberBooksPublisher